THE DEAD RING No. 166

Also available from Titan Books

The Blacklist: The Beekeeper No. 159

THE BLACKLIST™

THE DEAD RING No. 166

JON McGORAN

TITAN BOOKS

The Blacklist: The Dead Ring No. 166
Print edition ISBN: 9781783298068
E-book edition ISBN: 9781783298181

Published by Titan Books
A division of Titan Publishing Group Ltd
144 Southwark Street, London SE1 0UP

First edition: March 2017
1 3 5 7 9 10 8 6 4 2

Did you enjoy this book? We love to hear from our readers.
Please email us at readerfeedback@titanemail.com or write to us at
Reader Feedback at the above address.

To receive advance information, news, competitions, and exclusive offers
online, please sign up for the Titan newsletter on our website:
www.titanbooks.com

THE DEAD RING No. 166

Chapter 1

The bridge was packed, two lanes of tired commuters in dusty, beat-up cars, motorcycles, and pickup trucks. Some were headed east after hard days at oil fields, factories, and farms, others headed west from big box stores like the Walmart up the road, or even the mall, twenty miles past it.

They were tired—too tired to notice the polished silver tanker truck or the shiny black SUV behind it, no matter how much they stuck out. They didn't notice the black and gray RV with the retractable satellite uplink dish a quarter of a mile back, either. They barely even noticed the motley crowd gathered on the side of the road just before the bridge—fifty men and half a dozen women, mostly tall, all muscular, with an air of lethality and a distinct buzz of anticipation, intently watching the SUV and the truck cross the bridge, and looking just as out of place.

The tanker reached the end of the bridge and stopped. The SUV pulled out next to it, into the oncoming lane, so they were blocking both lanes of traffic.

The commuters noticed them now.

Within seconds a few stray honks became a chorus,

like a flock of geese that just wanted to get home and have a beer.

Cameras mounted at regular intervals along the bridge swiveled, taking in the entire length of it.

The honking paused for a moment as the driver of the SUV got out. He was dressed in black, with dark shades and a black cap despite the heat. He was carrying a gun.

He opened the back door of the vehicle, revealing a wire rack that ran across the width of it. Each slot held a small manila envelope, forty of them. The driver swung himself up onto the roof of the SUV, looked across the bridge and fired the gun once into the air.

Instantly, the small crowd gathered at the other end of the bridge began sprinting across it. Like a pack of animals, they moved quickly, fluidly, and inexorably around, between, and over the cars, swarming from one end of the bridge to the other. The honking resumed, increasing in volume as each car overtaken by the runners joined in.

The man with the gun hopped down and walked away, leaving the SUV in place. The driver of the tanker truck got out and followed him. Neither looked back.

The lead runner was a huge man, heavily muscled, with a blond buzz cut, wearing camo pants and a vest. He charged straight up the lane of oncoming traffic, avoiding one car and causing the next to swerve into the side rail. The car behind it crunched into its back bumper, wedging it further into the guardrail.

The second runner was a beautiful young woman with shiny black hair. She pulled ahead of the pack by flinging herself across the tops of the cars, cartwheeling and springing from one to the next, covering distance with remarkable speed. She glanced back at one of the other runners, a handsome young man with tousled blond hair and the muscles of a gymnast, who was nonetheless struggling to keep up with her. They exchanged a furtive smile, but kept on running. As she approached a gap between the cars, her heel crunched the hood of a thirty-year-old Datsun before she vaulted herself onto the asphalt and flat out ran.

The driver got out and shouted after her, voicing his anger and frustration in a spit-flecked stream of curses. But yet another runner, an olive-skinned tree of a man in a black T-shirt, crumpled him with a savage elbow to the ear as he ran past without slowing down.

The first runner reached the SUV and grabbed an envelope from the rack. Instantly, an explosion erupted at the other end of the bridge. A motorcycle and its rider flipped into the air, both spinning raggedly over the side of the bridge and onto the rocks lining the dry creek bed thirty feet below.

Drivers screamed and honked and as the runner with the envelope disappeared past the SUV, the cars surged forward in a rush to escape the mayhem. The gaps between them shrank or disappeared altogether. The sound of metal crunching against metal was followed by a handful of screams, louder than the others, as runners were crushed between cars grinding into each other as they tried to escape the madness.

The black-haired woman reached the SUV next and grabbed another envelope. A second explosion, this one in the middle of the bridge, lifted a rusted pickup truck five feet off the ground, and sent two runners shattered and twisting through the air. The truck hit the pavement with a groaning thud, followed by a throaty *whoomf*, as it erupted into flames. The blond man joined the black-haired woman and grabbed a third envelope. They ran off together as another explosion punched into the air.

In rapid succession, a dozen other runners reached the SUV and grabbed their envelopes, triggering a dozen detonations that fully transformed the bridge into a hellscape of explosions and fire.

When there was only one envelope left, two runners reached it at almost the same moment—a stout, ruddy-faced Irishman with a diagonal scar across his face and a dark-skinned Somali in fatigues and a red beret. The Irishman reached out for the envelope, but his hand closed on air as the Somali grabbed him by the belt and flung him back into the crowd of approaching runners, knocking them over like he had just bowled a strike.

Then the Somali plucked the last envelope out of its slot.

Instead of an explosion, there was a moment of quiet, marred only by the receding footsteps of thirty-nine runners clutching their envelopes. The Somali took off after them. The remaining runners froze, some standing, some still on the ground, all looking on in horror as the back of the tanker truck opened on hydraulics, releasing a torrent of straw-colored liquid.

The dozen or so empty-handed runners still on their feet turned and ran back the other way. The ones on the ground pushed themselves away on their heels, frantically trying to stay ahead of the wave of liquid.

The air shimmered with rising fumes as the choking smell of gasoline spread out rapidly before it.

The Irishman's knees and heels and hands slipped in the stuff as he tried to clamber to his feet.

A low moaning hum arose from the horrified motorists, just for an instant. Before it could resolve into a chorus of terrified screams, the fumes connected with a spark.

A curtain of fire traveled back to the open tanker truck, which exploded, flipping into the air and shooting a smoky orange ball of fire back across the bridge. The fireball traversed the length of the bridge, causing a series of smaller explosions in its wake as each remaining gas tank detonated, transforming the bridge, and everything on it, into a flaming twisted ruin.

Chapter 2

The light from the video screens blazed and flickered with angry oranges and reds, washing over the handful of people present in the dimly lit confines of the mobile control room. The technicians at their workstations and the armed guards flanking them watched with dull attention, their eyes betraying no reaction at all. They were professionals, and what they were watching was nothing new, not really.

Behind them stood the Cowboy, a soft slip of a man, unscarred and uncalloused. The false bravado he had brought with him to this endeavor had quickly fallen away as things had moved along. Now he was openly awed by the spectacle playing out in front of him. He was frightened, rattled to his core, maybe even horrified at what he had wrought, but he was definitely impressed. He would get what he paid for, even if he didn't ultimately get what he wanted.

Sitting in the shadows at the back of the room, the Ringleader tapped at his keypad and the soft buzz of precision machinery rose around him. No one in the room turned to look.

It was all enough to make one smile, if one were

capable of such things. The Ringleader was not. But he could enjoy the wash of endorphins or serotonin or whatever it was that other people confused with pleasure or happiness or love. The images on the screens provoked it with an intensity that seemed from a bygone era. It was like a religious experience. Only this was real.

It had been a long time coming. But now it was back.

The warm glow of it faded along with the glow from the video screens. But that was okay. Things were finally underway. It wouldn't be long until next time. And the best was definitely yet to come.

Chapter 3

When Keen received Red's call, she had wished, like she did every time lately, that she had some kind of excuse not to come and meet him. Or at least not right away.

But she didn't.

There had been a time when her life was so full it got in the way of work. Now, her life was even fuller, but all it was filled with was work.

Probably just as well.

She looked around at the décor: an odd mix of stylish and cheesy—conical grass hats and bright red and green Asian prints on the wall, but sophisticated blown-glass lights and elegantly set tables. She was sitting in a Laotian restaurant, because... well, because Red, of course.

She didn't have time for a sit-down lunch, but the meal and the pause would both do her good. And of course, whenever she and Red met like this, it meant something big was headed her way, something he'd be handing off to her, and that she would be bringing to the task force. That's how it worked.

It had only been a few of years since Red, once

one of the FBI's most-wanted, had turned himself in to the bureau with an offer to help them lock up his long Blacklist of international criminals, with the mysterious stipulation that Keen serve as his liaison to the task force that would investigate each case.

She drank some more water, trying to wash away the memory of the taste.

The woman behind the counter, presumably the proprietor, watched her suspiciously.

Keen tapped her phone to check the time. They had agreed to meet at three. As the display changed from 2:59 to 3:00, the door to the place opened and Red walked in wearing his black overcoat and signature black fedora.

The proprietor's suspicious face split into an eye-crinkling grin at the sight of him. He smiled back at her, his face twisted in his own weird version of a beaming grin.

Keen shook her head, feeling a smile of her own tugging at her mouth despite herself.

"Lahela," Red said affectionately.

"Reddington," the proprietor replied, grabbing Red by the elbows and looking up at him with the fondness of an aunt about to suggest he had grown since the last time she'd seen him. They exchanged a few words in some tonal Asian language, and then the old woman turned and looked at Keen with a shrug, as if maybe she had misjudged her.

The old woman followed Red over, and he sat across from Keen, taking a newspaper out from under his arm and putting it on the table. He pointed to the menu and held up two fingers.

Lahela nodded proudly, approving of his choice.

As she hurried off to the kitchen, Red looked at Keen

over the menu. "This place has the best red curried snakehead this side of the Mekong River."

"Snakehead?" She let out an exasperated sigh. "Are you kidding me?"

"Fresh-caught, too," he said, laying his napkin on his lap, then leaning forward. "People complain they're an exotic invasive in these parts, but I say if they're going to be this delicious, bring on the invasion!"

He laughed at his own joke, maybe a little too much, then stopped abruptly and slid the newspaper across the table. "Have you read the papers?"

Keen read the banner at the top of the page, upside down, without picking it up and looked up at him. "The *Fort Stockton Pioneer*? No, I haven't gotten to it yet. Still reading the *Brownsville Herald*. Why?"

He smiled but didn't put much into it. "There was an event on a bridge in Perdeen, Texas yesterday."

"That fire… Yes, it was terrible. Thirty-seven people died, right?"

"And seventeen more in the hospital not expected to make it."

"The reports said it was an accident involving a gasoline truck, right? The fire started after it somehow released its load."

"It did involve a gasoline truck, but it was no accident."

"What are you saying?"

"It was actually a preliminary round in something called 'The Dead Ring.'"

"The Dead Ring?"

"Do you remember last year a warehouse fire in Turkey killed seventy people?"

"Of course, it was a terrible tragedy."

"It capped off a week of tragedies that included

nineteen dead in a runaway train crash and a mosque swallowed by a sinkhole, all within twenty miles of each other."

"Okay."

"The year before last, a mine collapse in South Africa took fifty-five lives, ending a similarly tragic week."

"So, what do they have in common?"

"None of them were accidents. All of them were part of a sick, deadly, and highly lucrative game."

She didn't see that coming. "A *game*?"

"The Dead Ring. A cross between a reality TV show, a gladiator contest, and a snuff film. The players compete for a jackpot rumored to be in the millions."

"How come I've never heard of it?"

"None of it has ever been proven. It's the stuff of rumors and tall tales told by soldiers and mercenaries. But I believe it's true. It is highly secret, streamed on the Dark Web, strictly for the viewing and betting pleasure of a super-rich international circle of those with a taste for such things."

"Jesus," she whispered, thinking about it.

They remained quiet for a moment as Lahela brought their food. Snakehead or not, it looked delicious. But Keen had lost her appetite.

"Wait, how do these tragedies fit into a game?"

"I don't know, exactly. Presumably they represent the field of play on which the contestants compete. I don't know the nature of the games." He flashed a sad smile that seemed to be trying to mask some deep pain and sorrow. She couldn't tell if it was just from the magnitude of the evil, of the tragedy inflicted on humanity, or if it was something more direct. More personal. "The huge numbers of collateral casualties generated as the game's players compete to accomplish some task are part of the spectacle."

"And the losers never say anything about it?"

"Dead men tell no tales. There are no survivors. Only the winner."

She shook her head. "Wait, who would agree to that?"

"There's no shortage out there of aging mercenaries, former child soldiers so damaged by what's been done to them, other pathetic wretches who see this as their last chance to escape their miserable lives—one way or another. All hoping to win a fortune, and all but one of them destined to die instead."

Keen felt numb, and she was glad of it, because even through the numbness she felt a wave of revulsion that otherwise would have sickened her. She looked up at Red. "Do we know anything about the organizers?"

"We know he is referred to as the Ringleader. That's about it."

"And you're saying the fire on that bridge was part of this?"

"I believe so, yes."

"So the worst of it is yet to come."

"That's right. And the game takes about a week, so it's coming soon."

"My god."

He sat back with a grim but determined smile. "The good news, though, is that if this year's Dead Ring is taking place in the United States, we have a rare opportunity to take down the people responsible and shut down the Dead Ring for good."

Chapter 4

The task force was silent as always as Keen launched into her briefing. But the quality of the silence deepened as she relayed the specific suspicions about the nature of the Dead Ring, and the extent of the death and suffering that had been caused by it.

Ressler's eyes burned as he absorbed the horrible cruelty and injustice of it. Aram looked down as he listened. Navabi sat impassively, her face blank, as if the horrors she had already seen made these that much more believable and had prepared her in a way. As if maybe she knew that the only way to get by in a world where such things were possible was to not let it get to you at all.

"And why are they moving it to the US?" Cooper asked when she was finished.

"The location of the game is different each time," Keen replied. "The game's wealthiest bettors bid millions of dollars for the privilege of hosting it, for bragging rights, contacts, maybe. To prove they can do it." She paused for a moment. "And I guess for the sick pleasure of watching it up close and in person."

"But, we have no proof any of this is true, Agent

Keen. Isn't that right?" Cooper asked.

She cleared her throat. "That's right, sir. I expect the first item on our task list would be to confirm that it is."

Aram started quietly typing on his laptop.

"Do we have anything on the bridge tragedy?" Cooper asked.

"Not much. There were a few cars that drove across the bridge moments before it happened. They reported typical rush hour traffic, and a vehicle broke down. Then a fireball in their rearview mirrors."

"How about any of the previous tragedy sites? Turkey? Indonesia? South Africa?"

"I'm looking into it. There might be some clues at the Turkish locations but the others are all cold. Mostly bulldozed or rebuilt, or at the bottom of the ocean. I'm also looking into similar clusters of events in previous years. Reddington mentioned those three, but he suspected this had been going on for at least five years, maybe more."

"I have a friend in Turkish intelligence. Ahmet Aslan," said Navabi. "He owes me a favor."

"Hey, I've got something here," Aram cut in, looking up from his computer. "Someone posted a video."

He tapped at a couple of keys and the screen at the front of the room came to life.

The screen showed a rectangular view looking along a bridge from inside a car. Outside, car horns were blaring. The driver turned the camera around to show her face: she was an attractive young woman in her mid-twenties with a mischievous smile and a blonde ponytail. She rolled her eyes and said, "Traffic. Can you believe it?"

The tinny pop of a small-caliber gun went off somewhere outside the car, "What the...?" Then she gasped as a big guy in camo and a buzz cut ran past the car.

Laughing awkwardly she turned the camera out the back window. The road was jammed with cars, and between them, people ran, around the cars, between the cars. One woman ran over the closest car, black hair flowing behind her. "This is crazy," the driver said, tentatively, not quite sure how to react. She let the camera slowly drop.

Distorted sounds overwhelmed the microphone as there were simultaneous explosions followed by a scream.

And the recording stopped.

"This went out as a live feed over social media," Aram said quietly. "The girl's name was Anna Deritter. She died in the fire."

The room went quiet for a brief moment. Keen knew the others were experiencing the same thing she was, that puncturing of your hardened professional shell when the terrible but impersonal tragedy of many deaths becomes the personal tragedy of one face.

She cleared her throat. "If Reddington is right, if the Dead Ring is real and it's taking place on American soil, that means American lives are at stake, and many have already been lost. It also means we have a unique opportunity to not only identify the Ringleader and put a stop to this terrible game, but maybe even to identify and arrest the people betting on it—many of whom are surely wanted for other crimes as well."

Cooper thought for a moment then nodded. "Okay, let's get started then. Agents Keen and Ressler, I want you to visit the bridge scene, see if you can confirm that this is more than just an accident. Agent Navabi, reach out to your connections in Turkish intelligence and see if you can find out anything about the events there last year, especially the warehouse fire. Aram, I want you to analyze that video, frame by frame. See if it reveals any other clues. Anything else, Agent Keen?"

"The Dead Ring seems to last about a week from start to finish. If that's what this is, whatever's next is coming soon."

"Then we better act quickly."

Chapter 5

Traveling the globe had its definite upsides, even as a wanted fugitive. Lahela's curried giant snakehead might've been the best this side of the Mekong River, but it couldn't compare to the snakehead Red had eaten on the Mekong Delta itself. He thought back to the delicacy, and the delicate young woman who had served it to him, and he smiled.

But there were upsides to being stateside again. And not the least of them was Maryland crab, dusted with a ridiculous amount of Bay Seasoning and steamed to perfection. There was something exquisite about the hot crabs burning your fingertips and the sting of the spices finding the dozens of cuts left by the razor-sharp shell, and then the incredible morsels of delicate white meat pulled from the carnage. And there was nowhere better to experience all that than Fred's Shed.

The place made no pretense at being anything other than what it was, but it achieved what it set out to do with glorious indifference to anything else. The walls were unfinished wood, the floors peeling linoleum, the décor nonexistent except for a few decades-old beer signs.

But when Dominic Corrello walked in, he still somehow managed to cheapen the whole thing. He looked around at the place and sneered, with the reflexive disdain of the small-minded out of their comfort zone.

It was hard to believe that Corrello was among the most well-connected purveyors of sensitive information. If Red hadn't personally done business with him on four different continents, he'd have pegged him as the type to spend his entire life within five miles of the neighborhood where he had grown up.

Corrello exchanged nods with Dembe, and dropped into a seat across from them. Red slid one of his crabs across the paper covering the table, followed by a mallet and a nutcracker.

Corrello shook his head. "Can't believe you eat them bugs."

Red slid his butter knife into the crab's body and removed a pristine white lump. He managed to keep his hands so clean throughout the process, he had to dredge the meat in seasoning before putting it into his mouth. He savored the flavor for one moment before sliding the carcass off to the side, away from Dembe.

"Crustacea, Corrello. But I've eaten bugs, too, on many occasions. Chapulines are my favorite. Roasted crickets with chili and lime. Some say it tastes like bacon, but I think that doesn't do it justice. You should try them. You don't know what you're missing."

"Disgusting is what it is."

Red squeezed a wedge of lemon into his hand, updating the mental map of cuts in his skin as he rubbed his hands together and wiped them off with a paper towel. "What have you got for me?"

Corrello put a thumb drive onto the corner of the

table, away from the detritus of Red's lunch.

"Not much. Not even sure what it is. No one I talked to knows if this Dead Ring thing is for real. But I gotcha something, a piece of video that a guy told me was part of it—a warehouse fire in Turkey."

Red cocked an eyebrow and a smile flickered across his lips.

Corrello leaned forward. "It's crazy stuff on that video. And the guy I got it from, he said the guy who recorded it got himself killed for doing it. Ain't nobody supposed to record this stuff, and the people who set it up, they found out and killed him. The guy I got it from, he was seriously scared when he gave it to me."

Red reached out and palmed the thumb drive. "What about you, Corrello. Are you scared, too?"

Corrello grinned. "Not as long as you keep paying me for the stuff I turn up."

"Well then, as long as you keep turning things up for me, you've got nothing to fear at all."

Red paused outside Fred's Shed, enjoying the sunlight for a moment before he and Dembe got in the car.

"You really must give them a try, Dembe," Red said as he sank into his seat. "Some of the best eating around."

Sitting in the driver's seat, Dembe looked at the dilapidated exterior of the restaurant, then at Red in the rearview. They'd had hundreds of similar exchanges over the years, about similar venues and similar cuisines. He nodded noncommittally.

Red shook his head. The phone buzzed and Dembe answered it, then handed it to Red, who looked at the display and said, "Hello, Lizzie."

"We're on the case," she said.

"Good," Red replied as the car pulled back into traffic. "Have you turned up anything?"

"Maybe. Aram found a video from the bridge. One of the victims posted it live, just before the fire."

"I'd like to see that."

"Okay," she said. "You'll have to come here to look at it though. Until we have an idea how sensitive all this is, he wants to keep it inside."

"Very prudent. I won't be coming empty handed."

Chapter 6

They were standing in a darkened room in the converted post office that served as the headquarters of the task force, waiting as Aram tapped at his computer.

The screen at the front of the room came to life, showing a large warehouse building, three stories tall, with crude concrete walls, a corrugated metal roof, and the words TÜZEL ANTREPO emblazoned across the front. A dusty road ran alongside it. The darkened windows flickered and for several seconds the muffled sounds of screams and gunfire could be heard from within.

A cluster of women appeared at one of the third-floor windows, panicking and trying to open the window, to escape. A line of machine gun fire mowed them down from behind, the bullets tearing through them, shattering the glass and spattering it with blood. A large man in battle gear appeared where the women had stood, but then he was cut down as well.

A moment later, an explosion punched a hole in the second-floor wall, sending chunks of debris tumbling toward the camera. The screams and gunfire grew louder, coming through the opening in the wall. A man appeared, running toward the opening, a dark silhouette against the flames inside. Just as he was about to jump through the hole, a tight grouping of bullets tore through his midsection and he stumbled and fell, landing with his arms and torso hanging through the opening.

One by one, the windows were shot out from within, and with each broken window the cacophony grew louder. Smoke poured from each broken window, rising up into the dark sky. Women started climbing from the third-floor window to escape the flames within. The first one climbed down to the second-floor windows, but the next two simply dropped, crumpling onto the street below.

As the first woman reached the street and started to run away, the front door exploded open and she faltered in a hail of shrapnel.

Another man emerged from the hole where the door had been, wearing camo and boots, and blood. His left leg was in shreds and he dragged it behind him, down the front path, directly toward the camera. Halfway there, he stumbled and fell, but he kept pulling himself across the ground. Another man, similarly dressed, appeared behind him, eyes gleaming through a face streaked with gore, but apparently unharmed. He strode toward the camera and without pause lifted the injured man's head and slit his throat. As the man on the ground gurgled and sputtered, his killer walked past the camera and out of sight.

As the gunfire inside the building slowed to a trickle, several figures appeared at the windows, watching whatever was happening behind the camera.

For a moment, nothing happened, then a dozen tiny staccato detonations reverberated through the building and it was instantly engulfed in flames.

The black silhouette of a man appeared in one of the windows, then the fire swallowed him up.

The screen went dark. Aram hit a button bringing up the lights.

For a moment no one made a sound.

"So that's what we're trying to stop," Keen said quietly. "Red emphasized that if this is the Dead Ring, the next round will be within a day or two."

Cooper nodded. "Agent Navabi, anything from your friends in Turkey?"

"My contact put me in touch with an Agent Sadek with police intelligence. I spoke with him briefly and he confirmed that he thought what happened at Tüzel Antrepo was a part of this Dead Ring. He sounded willing to cooperate, even to share, but uncomfortable speaking on the phone. My sense was that he didn't trust that no one else was listening in, and perhaps someone high up may have been involved somehow."

Cooper grunted. "Okay. We need to get moving on this. Keen and Ressler, when are you leaving for Texas to examine the bridge scene?"

"Our plane's in ninety minutes," Keen said.

"Good. Aram, can you analyze that video for any clues at all, any identifying tags or embedded codes, anything?"

"Absolutely."

He turned to Navabi. "I'd like you to go to Turkey, talk to this Sadek, see what he knows, and what he suspects. See if you can visit the scenes of these events and find out whatever you can."

She nodded. "Of course."

"Okay," he said. "Let's do it."

As they began to leave, Keen approached Cooper. "A word, sir?"

"What is it, Keen?"

"Reddington has asked to see the video from that bridge."

Cooper thought for a brief moment, then nodded. "Okay. You can show him in here. Aram, you can set that up, right?"

He nodded.

"Good," Cooper replied. "Let's get moving, people."

Chapter 7

Keen had seen the footage before, and it paled compared to the carnage of the Turkish warehouse. But Anna Deritter, the young woman in the video, was so vibrant and full of life, it brought home the tragedy of her death, and all the others, once again.

Red watched impassively.

"I've been through both videos several times," said Aram. "I've already picked up a few interesting things I want to show you."

The video started once more, just like before. Red watched from where he was at first, a black figure silhouetted by the light streaming in from the hallway. He showed no reaction at first, but as the view shifted to look out the back windshield he stepped forward closer to the screen.

A few seconds in, Aram paused the video. "Here," he said, getting up from his computer to point at a fuzzy black shape mounted on the bridge's guardrail. "I'm pretty sure this is a video camera. They seem to be mounted at regular intervals along the bridge. And when I analyzed the Turkish video, I pulled out some very unusual codecs. It seemed to be part of a multichannel feed, not your standard YouTube fare. If I can reverse the—"

"Fascinating," Red said impatiently, taking another step closer to the screen. "Continue the video, please."

Aram looked at Keen, taken aback, like maybe he expected a little more in the way of praise.

Keen gave him an encouraging smile and nodded.

Aram returned to his computer and resumed play. He leaned forward and squinted at the screen, as if trying to see whatever Red was looking for.

The camera shifted out the rear window again, at the runners coming up behind the car, at the woman with the black hair coming over the next car back.

"Freeze it," Red barked, startling Aram but spurring him to action.

The woman's face was mostly covered by her long black hair.

"Advance one frame," Red said.

Aram did.

"Again."

He did.

They advanced three more frames until the face on the screen was perfectly visible and angled right at the camera.

Red stepped even closer, his face two feet from the screen. He raised his hand as if to touch it, then he turned on his heel and left the room.

"Red!" Keen called out, following him. "What did you see?"

"I'll tell you when I know."

Chapter 8

Keen and Ressler had gotten on the next plane from Dulles to El Paso, but the drive from the airport to the bridge took longer than the flight itself, in no small part due to the traffic clogging the tiny rural roads, trying to find alternate routes to the bridge, which was closed indefinitely.

"I guess that would be it," Ressler said, nodding over the steering wheel at the mess that appeared in front of them as they rounded a bend in the road.

Keen let out a sigh. "Yeah. I guess so."

The bridge was a charred ruin: bits of concrete and rebar hanging from the bottom, blackened metal hulks all burned and twisted clogging the top. The streambed that ran underneath it was littered with pieces of bridge and vehicles blackened from the burning fuel that had spilled.

Yellow tent cards showed where the bodies had been found, scattered under the bridge and carpeting the tarmac itself. Keen thought of dandelions taking over a neglected lawn.

The scene was surrounded by local cops from several jurisdictions, clustered by their different uniforms and mostly just watching as the state officials worked the scene.

A news van from a local network affiliate was still parked alongside the road leading up to the bridge. It was probably the biggest local story in the last twenty years. She hoped the coming days wouldn't bring any bigger ones.

Ressler parked just past the news vans and just before the long line of patrol cars. As they walked up to the bridge, one of the local cops turned around with his hands up in front of him and an exasperated look on his face. Keen got the sense he'd probably been turning away gawkers for the past two days.

But Keen and Ressler held up their badges before he could even tell them there was nothing to see.

"FBI," Ressler said, drawing looks from the other cops milling around.

Keen could hear the buzz of conversation double in volume and intensity.

The cop who had been waving them off stepped closer and asked, "Do they think this is a terrorist attack?"

"No," Keen said firmly. "We just wanted to take a look."

"Oh," the cop said. Disappointed, he waved them through and rejoined the cluster of cops in the uniforms that matched his.

The scene was under the control of the Texas state forensics team. Half a dozen techs in bright yellow protective overalls were combing through the wreckage.

A trio of agents in shirts and ties stood at the end of the bridge looking on. "Who's in charge of the scene?" Ressler asked as they approached.

They turned around and one of them said, "Who's asking?"

Keen held up her badge. "FBI. Agents Keen and Ressler."

"Deputy Barker. You guys asserting jurisdiction?" He seemed almost hopeful.

Keen felt bad for him. She shook her head. "No, we're looking into a case that could be related. We're hoping to get some info, maybe take a look around."

Barker let out a sigh. Instead of shrinking, his workload would be growing. "Yeah, all right."

"What does it look like?"

He let out a tired laugh. "It looks like a goddamned mess. Looks like the tanker truck malfunctioned and released its load. They shouldn't have been transporting gasoline in that truck, anyway. We're thinking the load may have been stolen. The truck, too, for that matter. Whatever it was, the back opened up, released a couple thousand gallons of gasoline, and the whole thing went up. Burned so hot it's hard to determine what else went on, if anything."

He handed them booties to put on over their shoes and masks to wear over their faces. "I'd say don't mess up my crime scene, but I can't imagine it any more messed up than it already is. Just watch your step and mind the spots where the decking melted through. We're all out of body bags."

Keen and Ressler booted up and walked out onto the bridge. The smell was overwhelming: gasoline, burnt plastic and other materials, and the lingering smell of charred flesh.

Visually, it was even more overwhelming. The bodies had been removed, but the bridge was still packed with the twisted, blackened hulks in which so many of them had died. The place was haunted.

Keen and Ressler slowly weaved their way between

burned-out vehicles, the techs collecting evidence, and the gaping holes where bits of bridge had collapsed.

Keen spotted something on the railing and Ressler followed her over to it.

"Is that one of those cameras Aram was pointing out when we watched the video?" she asked.

"Yeah, maybe."

She called over one of the evidence techs and asked him to collect it and bag it for her. He took a few pictures of it, then gently pried it off the railing with a screwdriver. He put it in a bag and logged it in, then held it out for Keen to look at.

"It looks like a camera, all right," she said, turning it over in her hands. "And it looks like it was clamped on with a plastic clip, not permanently attached." She pointed at the melted and charred clip on the bottom of it.

"It's got a battery pack, too," Ressler added, looking over her shoulder. "No cables at all."

"So it had a wireless connection."

Ressler looked around. "Makes you wonder what it was wirelessly connected to."

Chapter 9

Red had watched the video a dozen more times. Each time he felt more certain he was right. But not a hundred percent certain. That's why he and Dembe were on his plane headed to Paris. If it had been anyone other than Marianne LeCroix—Le Chat— there would have been people he could have called, things he could have done. Ways he could have confirmed her identity without leaving the country.

But that wasn't possible with Le Chat. The woman was a cipher. A ghost. Red was one of a small handful of people who had seen her in the flesh. And one of a much smaller handful who had touched that flesh. He closed his eyes at the memory of the taut, supple strength in her slender body.

As the plane began to descend, Reddington closed his eyes and pictured LeCroix—not the LeCroix from the video, but the one he remembered from so long ago.

It made no sense that Le Chat would be involved with anything like the Dead Ring. But there she was.

And if it was indeed her, that was a lead.

* * *

Louis Jarette was a tiny troll of a man whose outsized charm more than made up for his physical shortcomings. He was a lover of life and the better things in it, and Red had long considered him a kindred spirit in many ways. As Dembe drove him expertly across Paris, Red smiled at the thought of seeing the little man.

It was Jarette who had introduced Reddington to Marianne LeCroix years earlier.

Red had put together a complex and potentially quite lucrative deal that hinged upon a letter of credit from the president of a large, multinational bank; a man whose financial acumen was matched only by his carelessness in regards to his ingeniously original sexual peccadillos.

As so often is the case, there were photos. The bank president was being blackmailed.

Red needed the blackmail to end, which meant he needed the photos, which meant he was looking for the best second-story man out there, who, as it turned out, was a woman.

Red insisted on meeting her before agreeing to terms, and it was early enough in her career that she agreed. He had expected someone dangerous and seductive and highly secretive, an elite international cat burglar with the unique brand of effortless elegance that only the French possess.

To his surprise, she was American, although of French descent, and now living in the City of Light. Everything else was exactly as he had pictured.

They discussed the job, exchanged some banter along the way. Two days later, she returned with the photos of the bank president, as well as several of the blackmailer himself, souvenirs of a sort that were incriminating enough they could put the blackmailer under Red's thumb if it ever came to that.

It was the kind of bold move that caused Red to look at LeCroix in a new light—and he had already been looking at her with a certain radiance.

It was a Friday. Red concluded his business with the bank president that afternoon. He had dinner with LeCroix at his hotel that night. Dinner turned into a weekend.

They both knew the whole time it wouldn't be more than that. It couldn't. But they lived every minute of it as if they would last forever.

At dawn on Monday, she left. Red was awake, but he didn't let on. She wanted to slip out, so he let her. Why let the memory of a glorious weekend be sullied by an awkward and pointless conversation on a Monday morning?

He never saw her again. Almost no one did. He nearly hired her several years later, again through Jarette. By then she was using the *nom de crime*, Le Chat. Jarette told him sadly there would be no face-to-face. Jarette seemed unaware of the contact they'd shared that went considerably beyond face-to-face.

Red had wondered briefly if their tryst was somehow the cause, but he knew it probably had nothing to do with him. Just good business sense. He ended up not hiring her again after all. He told himself that was just good business sense as well.

Chapter 10

Jarette held court in a watchmaker's shop in Paris. He actually did fine work on antique watches, but it was just a hobby and a front. His job was go-between for an assortment of high-end providers of criminal services. For a time, he had tried to get people to call him The Watchmaker, but it didn't catch on. Red had referred to him that way once or twice, to be a good sport, but no one ever knew who he was talking about. He was Jarette, and that was enough.

"Monsieur Reddington!" Jarette said with a broad crooked smile when Red walked into the shop. The place looked exactly the same, muted golden light, rich upholstery, and ancient polished wood. Red knew it concealed the latest in monitoring security, and very possibly automated defense technology, as well.

Jarette had been sitting on a stool at his counter. He stood when he saw Red, and gained an inch of height at most as he did. He crossed the room and they embraced, Red leaning forward for the customary French air kisses.

Dembe remained in the car. Jarette did business strictly one on one.

"Good God, man, it's been years," Jarette exclaimed. "I thought maybe I'd seen the last of you. So nice to be proven wrong. Cognac?"

"Why not?"

Jarette produced a bottle and two tulip glasses from under his counter. He poured an inch into each, then handed one to Red.

They swirled their glasses with identical motions, coating the inside of the glasses with the brown liquid and warming it with their hands, then simultaneously raised them.

Red closed his eyes, letting the fumes rise into his nose and sipping at the same time, rolling it over his tongue and letting it take over his senses.

It was a fine cognac, delivering a moment of concentrated bliss that was as intense as it was brief. Which reminded him of LeCroix, and the reason for his visit.

Red opened his eyes to see Jarette lowering his glass, returning, perhaps from a similarly transportive experience. He smiled awkwardly, as if embarrassed at the unguarded moment.

"It's very good," Jarette said, apologizing for his reaction more than bragging about the quality of the cognac.

"It is indeed."

Jarette resumed his swirling, at a slower rate. "What brings you here, my friend?"

"I'm looking for an old acquaintance."

Jarette raised an eyebrow then sipped his cognac. This time his eyes remained open and pinned on Red.

"Not all old friends want to be found."

Their eyes locked for a moment, then Jarette looked away.

"Do you know where she is?"

He put down his glass. "I don't. I wouldn't tell you if I did, but I do not. She is gone, I can tell you that."

"What do you mean?"

"She's in trouble. Greater trouble than even all her precautions could protect her from, than I could protect her from."

"What happened?"

"She took a job. Just a regular job: jewels and artwork." He shrugged and picked up his glass, draining it in a gulp. *"Tout s'est passé sans anicroche.* Without a hitch, no?"

Red sipped his cognac and waited for him to continue.

"She robbed Claude Corbeaux. Do you know him?"

The cognac soured as it went down. Corbeaux was the powerful and vindictive head of *La Compagnie*, a brutal European crime syndicate.

Red nodded. "I do. He is not a man to be trifled with."

Jarette laughed sadly. "Indeed, he is not. Now Corbeaux's men are after her, and they always will be. He has a reputation for that."

"I know."

"Le Chat was desperate and scared. She told me she was disappearing. She asked me to liquidate what assets of hers I was holding, which I did. She said she was doing one last job, and then she was going to disappear forever."

"One last big score?" Red shook his head. "Good lord, has she never read a crime novel?"

Jarette smiled. "She made it sound like this would be something very different. I cannot imagine what."

Red's mind immediately went to the Dead Ring, but it was still so unlikely, still such a stretch. "I need to speak with her."

He shook his head. "She is gone."

"Did she leave anything? Any clues?"

"You know I wouldn't give them to you if she did, but no."

Red's eyes hardened as he tried to determine if Jarette was telling the truth, or if he was simply trying to protect Le Chat. If so Red was going to have to be more persuasive. He raised an eyebrow, conveying this to Jarette, who seemed to accurately perceive the situation.

Jarette held up one finger, then stood and retreated to the back room of the shop.

It was a delicate moment. Red wanted information that Jarette wanted to withhold. If the impasse could not be resolved, they both knew the next step might involve more than polite conversation. But Red was confident that Jarette knew better than to come at him with force.

Jarette knew the consequences, he knew he would fail, and that just wasn't his way. Dembe, waiting in the car, would be there at the slightest hint of trouble. But Red knew he could easily handle anything Jarette was capable of throwing at him.

He returned a moment later and held two keys on a ring. "Marianne's apartment. Everything she left behind is still there. You can search it for clues if you wish, but I doubt you will find anything."

Red smiled, relieved that he wouldn't have to harm his friend. As his fingers closed on the keys, he said, "Thank you."

Chapter 11

LeCroix's home was actually two conjoined apartments located in adjacent buildings: identical gray structures, solid and heavy but with the slightest Gallic slouch, honestly acquired over many, many years. One faced south, the other east, with a door installed between them.

Red and Dembe approached quietly from the east. The door was locked but opened easily and silently with the key.

Dembe waited at the door and Red entered, his gun drawn and equipped with a silencer. The interior was a mess. Magazines, clothes, and books were strewn across the floor. No matter the haste with which LeCroix had left, she would not have left it like that. As Red entered further, he could see it had indeed been ransacked. The sofa and chair had been slit and the stuffing pulled out of them.

The place had been so thoroughly searched, Red knew the slim chance of finding a clue about LeCroix's whereabouts had been reduced to none.

Luckily, a clue found him.

It emerged from the closet, leveling a gun at Red's

face, and said, "*Qui es-tu?*"

He had a bulk around his chest and shoulders that his cheap sport coat couldn't conceal. His face was hard and his eyes were the kind of dead that looked like they might liven up for violence.

Red smiled and wiggled his gun, making sure it hadn't gone unnoticed. "Well, that depends. Who are you?"

"You are American?" he said with a heavy accent.

"Citizen of the world, I like to think. But American enough."

"What are you doing here?"

"I'm looking for Le Chat."

"Why?"

Red laughed. "Same as you, I imagine. To kill her."

The other man relaxed, just a bit. "You work for Corbeaux?"

"I work for whoever pays my fee. This time, yes, it is Corbeaux."

The man spit a string of French curses.

"You thought you were the only one."

The gun came back up.

Red shrugged, unfazed. "Looks like you did a pretty thorough job searching the place. Any clues about where she has gone?"

He shook his head, quickly, vigorously, and with the enthusiastic certainty possessed only by liars. "How about you? Any ideas?"

"Actually, yes," Red said, leaning closer.

As the other man leaned closer, too, Red shot him under the ribs and took his gun. He stepped out of the way, letting the man fall unimpeded. It had been clear from the first moment that only one of them would leave the apartment alive.

Dembe rushed in, but Red held up his hands to let

him know everything was under control. He knelt down next to the man, whose groans were already fading.

"Why don't you tell me what you know about where she is, so I can get you some help," Red told him.

He looked up at Red. There was blood on his lips. "Screw... you."

One hand clutched his wound. The other was out to his side.

Red stepped on his wrist and put the silencer against the man's palm. His eyes widened. Red pulled the trigger.

He let out a sound that was a cross between a snort and a moan, as if he would have screamed if he had enough life in him.

Red tapped the fresh wound and the moan rose in pitch. "Where is she? Tell me and I'll help you."

"I... I don't know. I found nothing. Please... help me. I have a picture, that's all."

"A picture?"

"In my jacket." He coughed, a minor eruption of blood that made his eyes go round as he choked on it.

Red reached inside his jacket and pulled out a three-by-five photo. As he looked at it, he felt a hitch in his breath. It looked more like the woman in the video than the one from his memories. Clearly, though, it was both.

"Please," gasped the man on the floor. "You said you'd help me."

Red smiled and put a bullet in the man's head. "There's help and there's help."

Chapter 12

It was early the next morning when Navabi arrived in Turkey. She was used to travel. It was second nature to her. But a redeye to Istanbul followed by a two-hour drive combined with a seven-hour time difference left her feeling less than her best when she sat down for a meeting first thing in the morning with her contact at Turkish Police. She had splashed some water on her face at the airport, but you could only do so much. Now she was sitting in a slightly run-down office in the local police station, feeling pretty run down herself.

Sadek walked in with a nervous smile and closed the door to his office. "Good morning, Agent Navabi."

"Good morning, Agent Sadek," she said, even though it still felt very late at night.

His eyes moved up and down her, and he smiled again, differently. She was not unused to that, and she didn't even hold it against him, if that was as far as it went. But she felt like she'd been run over by a truck, and she was pretty sure she looked that way as well. She wondered in the back of her mind if she could trust the man's judgment.

She gave him a cold look that took the smile off his face.

"How was your trip?" he asked, avoiding her eyes.

"Long," she said. "I am hoping it will be worth it."

"As do I." He cleared his throat and sat back in his chair. "Ahmet speaks highly of you."

"He's a good man."

He lowered his voice. "He told me about Chechnya."

She paused. That was a highly classified operation. She knew he was feeling her out, and at the same time demonstrating Ahmet's trust in him. "We've worked together on a number of operations."

"But on that one, you saved his life," he said.

She exhaled slowly, determined not to speak about that operation. "Ahmet says I can trust you."

"He says the same about you." He pursed his lips for a moment, then opened a drawer and took out a small stack of file folders. "This is what we have on the warehouse fire at Tüzel Antrepo." He slid them toward her. "It is not much."

She felt a swell of anger that she knew was premature, but she'd come a long way. "You said you agreed that the fire had something to do with the Dead Ring."

His eyes flicked to the door and back. "I said *I* agreed. The official report says nothing about it."

"Why do you think that?"

"I should show you the warehouse. But you have come very far. Would you like to rest first?"

She closed her eyes for a moment and thought about it. "Maybe afterward," she said with a sigh.

"As you wish."

The day was heating up by the time they got outside, but once they left the station, Sadek seemed more relaxed. When they got in the car and turned on the air conditioning, he became more voluble, too.

"If you like, I can have translations made of the files I showed you."

"Thank you."

"I doubt you'll discover anything of value in them. I didn't. They find that the fire was caused by a hydraulic fluid leak, and quickly spread due to the plastic machine parts being molded there. A tragic accident that killed everyone inside. That is all."

"You don't agree?"

He looked at her. "I saw bullet holes, explosive residue. I know the machinery. In the right conditions some of the plastics can be explosively flammable. But that is not what I saw."

They had zigzagged down the narrow streets of an industrial area, but the buildings had quickly thinned out and now they were leaving the town.

"So you think someone is hiding the true cause."

He shook his head, sadly. "It would not be unusual for such things to be hidden, even if it was as they say: workers killed in a factory owned by a local big shot. But things I have seen with my own eyes, things I reported to my superiors, were left out of the report and never investigated. This is bigger than that."

Chapter 13

They drove in silence for a moment. The landscape alternated between parched, dusty earth and dense but dry greenery. On a hill to the left, sheep grazed on brown grass.

"Do you know anything about a train crash several days before the fire?"

He looked at her sideways as he drove. "Why do you ask?"

"We suspect it may be related."

"I suspect it as well. There were indications of sabotage, but nothing conclusive. There was another tragedy several days earlier, as well."

"The sinkhole."

"Yes! An entire mosque in Tokay Province swallowed up along with twenty-seven people."

"You think they are all related?"

He shrugged. "I don't know what to think. But I am suspicious. The mosque sat above a limestone deposit. A satellite scan had said it was vulnerable to a sinkhole, but someone in a nearby village said they heard a small explosion right before the sinkhole appeared. And there were markings on the edge of the sinkhole, as if people had climbed out of it using climbing gear."

"You think someone caused the sinkhole intentionally?"

He looked away. "What do you know of this Dead Ring?"

"I know it's supposed to be some sort of deadly game. It's supposedly shown online, on the Dark Web, so rich psychopaths can bet on it. But I don't even know if it's real."

He kept his eyes looking straight ahead. "I'm convinced it's real. I've been digging. Researching. Looking into all this."

"What have you learned?"

"The Dead Ring takes place once a year, a different place each year. There are several rounds within the space of a week or so. There seem to be one or two preliminary rounds. Like qualifying heats. The contestants must survive them in order to compete for the prize. The rounds themselves seem to be challenges set in real-life situations. Climbing out of the sinkhole, maybe, or escaping a flaming warehouse. The innocent lives—the collateral damage—that seems to be part of the entertainment factor. Part of the show."

Halfway up a small hill, they came to a pile of bricks and rubble. Sadek coasted almost to a stop, but then he gave the car some gas and they crested the hill. Below them, a quarter mile away, was a building with blackened windows and walls breached with jagged holes. There had obviously been a terrible fire, but even from a distance, it looked like there had also been great violence.

They approached it in silence.

Sadek stopped the car directly across the dirt road from the gaping hole where the main entrance had been.

"It is supposed to be bulldozed," he said softly as they got out. "Inefficiency is the only reason it hasn't been. All evidence surrounding the mosque and the train crash has already been destroyed."

Navabi looked through the entrance. The interior was filled with the rubble of the upper floors. Sadek leaned inside and shone his flashlight up on the walls.

"It is hard to see because of the soot, but there are bullet marks, do you see? From automatic weapons." He shined the light along several rows of marks.

Navabi nodded. Even from some distance, she could identify them as such, lots of them. "What did forensics say?"

"Not much. The bullet holes were old, they said, from before the fire. That is why they are coated in soot. Even though the fire burned for a full day."

They walked along the front of the building and Sadek pointed up at the holes in the wall. "These, they said, were caused by the equipment exploding."

"Who owned the factory?" Navabi asked, as they walked around the building.

He shook his head. "A conglomerate. It was under-insured and they suffered a significant loss. I didn't find anything suspicious there."

When they came back to the car Sadek leaned against it. "Here's the thing. The mosque in Tokay Province disappeared without a trace. Twenty-seven people went missing and never turned up. But we don't know who went into that sinkhole. Fifteen bodies were taken out of the train crash, all badly burned. Six were never identified. And right here," he hooked his thumb at the burned-out factory. "This warehouse had sixty workers and four managers, all killed in the blaze. Every one of them. But there were seventy bodies removed from the rubble. Four extra people."

"You think they were part of the game? The players?"

"I do. We could only identify one of them. Oskar Bielski. A Pole. Served with distinction in the military until he got kicked out of GROM, the special forces unit, under a cloud for excessive violence against noncombatants. Became a private contractor with G78, but got kicked out of that, too."

"Huh."

"There is no reasonable explanation for why he would be in that warehouse."

"Unless it was part of the Dead Ring."

"Exactly."

They were quiet for a moment. Navabi leaned against the car as well, letting the information sink in. With it came a wave of exhaustion like she'd never felt outside a combat situation.

"You look tired," Sadek said softly.

"If it's as you say, I don't have time to be tired."

He nodded, thinking. "I wanted to show you the factory first, but there was a second site."

"What do you mean?"

"Not far from here. It is some type of control room, I believe. Unfortunately, it has already been bulldozed. We passed it on the way here. On the other side of that hill."

"The pile of rubble back there?"

He nodded. "It was bulldozed immediately after forensics processed it. They said they didn't find much. But even so, the files were ordered destroyed."

She waited for him to continue. Even out there in the middle of nowhere with no one around, he looked over his shoulder to be sure they were alone.

"I kept the files," he whispered. "I snuck them out of the office and hid them in my house."

"Why didn't you send them to me?"

He shook his head. "I can't send them. It's too risky. I will give them to you when you are leaving. But you must keep them secret." He put his hands on her upper arms, as if holding her steady so he could stare intently into her eyes. "If it is discovered that I kept these files— that I gave them to you—they will kill me."

Chapter 14

Red was standing next to his car sipping coffee when Keen emerged from her motel room for her morning run. She was ambivalent about seeing him: a little curious about what he was doing there but probably more interested by the second cup of coffee sitting on the roof of the car.

Near-identical wisps of steam rose from both cups in the morning chill. He took her cup off the roof and held it out.

"Welcome to Texas," she said as she took it.

"Yee-haw," he said dryly, sipping his own coffee. He looked tired and vaguely rumpled.

"Have you been up all night?"

"Something like that." He held out a slightly grainy-looking photo, a candid shot of a strikingly attractive woman with long dark hair. "Marianne LeCroix, also known as Le Chat. She was one of those runners on the bridge. She is one of the players in the Dead Ring."

"Who is she?"

"An old friend. An acquaintance, really. One of the best cat burglars in Europe. Apparently, she robbed the wrong people—dangerous and powerful people. A man named Claude Corbeaux. Now he and his men are after her. She told a mutual friend that she was doing one last, high-stakes, long-shot score before retiring and disappearing forever."

"That doesn't make sense. I thought the players were mostly mercenaries and other trained killers. And the odds of winning..."

He sipped his coffee. "I agree, it doesn't quite make sense, but that was definitely her." He shrugged. "LeCroix is desperate, and desperate people don't always behave logically."

Keen looked at the picture again. The woman had a wry half smile and a mischievous glint in her eye. She knew she'd never seen her before, but there was something familiar about her face.

She didn't look like a desperate killer.

"Le Chat keeps her identity as LeCroix a secret. She keeps an extremely low profile, so that is likely the only picture you will ever see of her." He stifled a yawn, something she couldn't remember ever seeing him do before. "If you can find out where LeCroix is, maybe you can find the location of the next round of the Dead Ring. And if you can talk to her, maybe you can find out more than that."

Keen nodded. "We can do a facial recognition scan, monitor global video and see if we come up with anything."

"Just be careful not to tip your hand. If she finds out we're onto her, or anyone else is, for that matter, she might just disappear. And if anyone else finds out we're onto her, we could get her killed."

Chapter 15

"Do you have a minute, sir?" Aram said, poking his head into Cooper's office. He didn't know what time Cooper had arrived, but he seemed like he was already settled in. Aram had never left the Post Office. He'd been up all night analyzing video code and the remains of the burned camera.

Cooper set aside the files he was reading and took off his reading glasses. "Of course. What have you got, Aram?"

"I've been analyzing that Turkish video file, and also the video from the bridge, studying compression and the codecs. The formatting. The Turkish video is definitely part of a multichannel video feed."

"Meaning?"

"Well, whoever was downloading it would have several other channels that they could switch back and forth from in real time. Like changing channels on TV. In the bridge video, there appear to be multiple cameras, as well, suggesting multiple channels."

"So you think they are related?"

"I believe that was part of the Dead Ring, yes. And whoever set it up put those cameras there, so viewers could watch the action from multiple angles."

Cooper picked up his glasses again and glanced at his paperwork.

Aram hurried on before Cooper could tell him to. "But here's the thing: the cameras shown on the video appear to be wireless, and the one Agent Keen sent almost certainly was. I'm sure the multichannel signal is encrypted, once it is uplinked to the satellite or the network or whatever, but it looks like the individual camera feeds, before they are combined, are not."

Cooper remained quiet but his expression plainly asked Aram what he was getting at.

Aram continued. "If we can get someone close to one of those cameras and activate a very small transmitter while the video feed is active, we could slip our own program, like a Trojan horse, into the video feed *before* it's encoded. So when it's decoded by the computers on the other end, and the video file is opened, our program will be installed on their computers."

Cooper put his glasses down again. A minor victory. "What would the Trojan horse do?"

"That depends on what we want it to do. The less we ask of it, the higher the certainty that it would work and escape detection, but at the very least we could infect every computer that's connected to the Dead Ring, around the world, and reveal its IP address and maybe its physical location. We could possibly gain access to their other files on that computer, or even on their network."

Cooper nodded. "Excellent. Good work, Aram. I've already been speaking with Interpol about coordinating arrests internationally, if it comes to that. I just spoke to Agent Navabi. Her contact in Turkey, Sadek, is convinced the events there were part of the

Dead Ring. Sadek says that there are usually one or two preliminary rounds or qualifying heats that prospective contestants must get through in order to actually compete in the Dead Ring. The bridge was presumably the first. If there is a second, perhaps we could get an agent inside, undercover." He took a deep breath and let it out slowly. "I don't know if I can sign off on an agent participating in something like this, even to stop it. I can't put someone's life at such risk. On the other hand, jeopardizing innocent lives seems to be a hallmark of these 'games.' I can't knowingly stand by and let that happen, either."

"I understand, sir, of course. But we would only need maybe five minutes of transmission to infect all those computers. After that, you could shut it down."

Cooper stared at him for a moment, thinking.

"Okay." He picked up the phone on his desk. "I guess it's time to move operations to Texas."

Chapter 16

Ressler came out of his motel room, talking into his phone.

"Yes, sir, I'll tell Agent Keen about the plan." As he lowered the phone he looked back and forth between Keen and Red's car as it drove away. Walking up behind her, he asked, "What's going on?"

"We might have a picture of one of the players." She handed him the photo after taking a picture of it with her phone, then called Aram.

"She looks kind of like you," he said, following her as she turned to go back into her motel room.

"What?"

He shrugged and held up the photo. "She looks a bit like you."

She started to protest that no she didn't, but then Aram answered.

"Aram," she said. "It's Keen. We might have IDed one of the players. I just sent you a picture. Can you search the database and monitor any closed-circuit video in the area of that bridge fire?"

"Absolutely. I don't know what the density of coverage is in that area. I'll start with a twenty-five mile radius and increase it from there if we don't get any hits."

"Okay. Let me know what you turn up."

When she got off the phone with Aram, she briefed Ressler and opened her computer. "I'm going to see what we can find on this Marianne LeCroix. You spoke to Cooper?"

Ressler nodded and told her the plan.

"They want to send you into the Dead Ring?" she said. "That's insane. You'll be killed."

He bristled a little, as if it was an affront to his masculinity. "I can take care of myself."

"There's one survivor," she said. "Out of who knows how many psychotic killers? Besides, how would you even get inside?"

"We're still working on that. But I wouldn't have to compete, not really. I would just have to activate a transmitter of some sort, and stay alive. Five minutes later, the tac team will come in and shut everything down. Greg Nichols is piloting the chopper, so you know it'll be smooth as silk."

Nichols was one of the best. A tactical pilot they had worked with many times. "I can't believe Cooper would go along with this," she said.

Ressler smiled reassuringly, and a little patronizingly. "That just proves it's not such a crazy idea."

He went back to his own room to reach out to local law enforcement and the FBI's El Paso office, and see if he could come up with a list of local crime figures capable of hosting something like this.

Meanwhile Keen dug into Marianne LeCroix. There wasn't much out there. Age thirty-four. Born in Denver to Lucianne and Pierre LeCroix. He was an importer of French antiques with a weakness for gambling. She was a real estate agent with a weakness for Frenchmen, as well as alcohol, and driving while under the influence of it.

As a teenager, Marianne LeCroix was a brilliant student, a brown belt in judo, and a bit of a handful. Arrested once as a juvenile for dislocating the elbow of a member of the football team who tried to assault her. She was suspected in a string of big-ticket burglaries, but never charged in any of them because of lack of evidence.

She won a full scholarship to Princeton and dropped out midway through the first semester, traveled to France three weeks later and vanished.

Five years later, a French police report included a mention of a mysterious cat burglar known as Le Chat. There was a smattering of similar mentions over the next five years. She was also mentioned as a suspect in a pair of unsolved homicides. Both victims were criminals with histories of sexual violence, and both were killed expertly by someone using only their bare hands. But there were no photos, no fingerprints, no arrest warrants. Nothing but suspicion and speculation.

Corbeaux's file was thick with arrests, convictions, appeals on technicalities, and a steady rise through the ranks, such that it had been a long time since he'd gotten his hands dirty. He had people for that. Lots of people.

If they were all after LeCroix, that would indeed be incentive for the old "one last job and retire" plan. But from what she understood about LeCroix, she couldn't see the Dead Ring as that last job. LeCroix seemed smart, sly, sophisticated. Capable of violence, maybe, but not prone to it.

Ressler knocked on the door and she let him in.

"Find anything?" she asked.

He rolled his shoulders. "Not really. Plenty of

organized crime around here, lots of back and forth with the Mexican cartels. But the psychos seem to all be in the lower echelons. The guys with the resources or the juice to pull off something like this, they all seem like garden variety criminal businessmen. Lots of bodies in their wake, but they all seem to be just business."

"Depending on who's watching and betting, this could be a big business." She told him what she'd found and they sat there for a moment, quiet. They didn't know when the next round was going to take place, but they knew the clock was ticking toward it. And they didn't seem to be getting any closer to figuring out where or what or when it was going to be.

Then Keen's phone buzzed. She picked it up and said, "Hey, Aram."

"Agent Keen, we got two hits not far from you," Aram said.

She cupped the phone and turned to Ressler. "Let's go."

He dashed back into his room and she started packing up as Aram continued.

"Marianne LeCroix was picked up on a traffic camera in Odessa three hours ago, and an hour ago at a convenience store in a little town called Balmorhea. She bought bottled water and some granola bars, then appeared to head across the street on foot, to a place called the Yellow Rose Hotel. She's forty minutes west of where you are right now."

Chapter 17

The Yellow Rose Hotel was part rustic and part run down. The sign and the posts holding up the overhang were made to look like rough-hewn logs. Everything else was more legitimately rough-hewn, in a charmless, utilitarian kind of way: the dusty concrete slab out front, the ratty mat outside the door, the chipped cinderblock walls. It was hard to tell what was intentional and what had been baked in by the hot desert sun.

The whole area seemed oddly quiet for the middle of the afternoon, like it was siesta time. The hotel was low, one story, and C-shaped, wrapped around a parking lot incongruously full of cars, trucks, and motorcycles, like there was a convention in town or something.

Ressler parked at the convenience store across the street, and they got out, exchanging a look as they crossed the road toward the hotel. Ressler cocked an eyebrow. He sensed it, too. Something strange.

Keen spotted a video camera mounted on top of the utility pole at the end of the block. Aram hadn't mentioned that one in his search for LeCroix.

The guy at the desk was young and nervous. "I'm

sorry. We're fully booked," he said as soon as they walked in. He sounded surprised to be saying it.

Ressler badged him and said, "We're looking for someone."

The kid blanched, but seemed somehow less surprised.

Keen showed him the photo of LeCroix. "Have you seen this woman?"

The kid looked around, then gulped and nodded. "Room nineteen," he said quietly, pointing to the hallway that led off to the right.

"What's going on here?" Ressler asked. The place was oddly quiet considering how packed the parking lot was.

The kid shook his head, convincingly mystified. "We're just full up. First time it's happened, as far as I know."

As they headed down the hallway, guns out but held low, Keen noticed a security camera mounted high on the wall, pointed away from them and down at the floor. She tapped Ressler's arm and pointed it out.

They stopped outside room nineteen, and Keen heard a faint, machine sound, like a DVD player ejecting a disk. Looking back down the hallway, she saw the video camera slowly rising up, then panning away from them, aiming down the hallway they had just come from.

As Ressler raised his fist to pound on the door, the camera started to swing back toward them. Before he could bring his knuckles down against the door, the air suddenly split with the piercing scream of a fire alarm. Emergency lights flashed on and off. Almost immediately, every door in the hallway swung open and a lone occupant charged out through each, like the gates opening at a horse race. They didn't look like they'd been unexpectedly roused from whatever they were doing, more like they'd been waiting for a signal, chomping at the bit.

The hallway was plunged into bedlam, packed with biker types, buzz-cut special ops, face-tattooed mercenaries, and a handful of women in each category, all of them seemingly battle-hardened and dangerous—clawing, hitting, and kicking each other. They all moved with great determination, but all in different directions. Some entered other rooms, some disappeared down the hallway, a couple set their legs wide and stood there, lashing out at the others, seemingly at random.

It was so bizarre, so unexpected, that Keen and Ressler were both taken aback, stunned just long enough that when the door in front of them opened, they were distracted and unprepared.

LeCroix darted out, turning her shoulders and slipping between them without slowing a step.

"Wait!" Keen called out.

"Freeze! FBI!" Ressler thundered.

But their words were swallowed up in the madness around them, and so was LeCroix, a flash of dark hair disappearing into the mayhem, lithely weaving her way through the crowd.

They went after her.

Keen almost matched LeCroix's maneuvers, and her pace. Ressler lagged behind, throwing bodies left and right as he tried to clear a path.

As LeCroix approached the corner, a young man with a blond beard came toward her. His eyes were round and open, lacking the hardness of all the others. The two paused as they passed, just for an instant, looking at each other before continuing on their way.

Then LeCroix turned the corner, and by the time Keen did too, LeCroix had vanished. Keen made her way almost to the end of the hallway, but there was no sign of her.

Ressler caught up with her. "Where'd she go?" he shouted, above the din.

Keen shook her head. "I don't know."

Then, back toward the bend in the hallway, a door opened and LeCroix stepped out, clutching something in her hand.

Keen shouted, "There she is!" and she and Ressler started fighting their way back toward her. A massive figure rose up in front of Ressler, shirtless under a leather vest, arms and eyes bulging with steroids and rage. He swung an arm at Ressler's head. Ressler ducked, pivoted, and brought the butt of his gun down behind the giant's ear, dropping him on the spot.

LeCroix stood under the camera on the wall, looking straight into it. Her hair covered half her face and as she reached up to move it away, a giant of a man with wild hair and a bushy beard rounded the corner behind her, wielding a fire extinguisher over his head. His arms were spattered with blood.

He swung the fire extinguisher like a club. It obliterated the camera on the wall on its way to crushing the skull of a skinhead with a swastika on his neck. Without pause, he brought it back the other way, and on the backswing it slammed into LeCroix's ribs with a force that smashed her against the opposite wall. Her head left a bloody mark where it hit the wall, and a smear of blood where she slid to the floor.

Without pause, the fire extinguisher swung the other way, crushing the skull of a ferret-faced biker wearing denim and gang patches.

Ressler screamed "Freeze!" and raised his gun at the man, but he was already gone, pushing his way back through the mass of people and disappearing into one of the rooms.

Keen and Ressler made their way toward LeCroix. The crowd in the hallway was starting to thin, the threadbare carpet littered with bodies—the injured, the unconscious, and the dead.

LeCroix was barely conscious, bleeding profusely from her ear and her mouth. But as they tended to her, she struggled to sit up, her eyes uneven but open wide.

"Where's David?" she said, looking around at the almost empty hallway. "We have to get out of here. Quickly!"

"You're hurt," Ressler said.

"Now!" she snapped, her voice a ragged bark.

"Why?" Keen asked. "What's going on?"

LeCroix turned frantic, trying to get up under her own power, but unable to. "There's no time. We have to get out, now!"

Keen met Ressler's eyes. Both wondered what the hell was going on, but spurred on by LeCroix's frantic voice, they each put an arm under one of her shoulders and hustled her out the fire exit.

"David," she groaned as they moved her. She did her best to keep up, her legs pumping even though she was unable to walk.

The parking lot was half empty now, and they cut across it, toward their car parked at the convenience store. In every direction, cars receded into the distance.

An old guy in a white apron was standing outside the convenience store, looking at them and past them, probably wondering what the hell was going on.

Keen opened the back door to the car, and they gently positioned LeCroix on the back seat.

She seemed to be fading from consciousness, but she shot upright at the sound of a massive explosion, looking out the back window as one end of the hotel erupted into a massive fireball, sending debris high into the sky.

LeCroix screamed, "David!" her voice serrated with anguish. "No!" she cried, trailing off into a low sob that was drowned out by two more explosions, in rapid succession, that swallowed up the rest of the hotel.

Keen and Ressler were stunned for an instant by the spectacle, but before the debris started raining down on them, they were inside the car, and speeding away.

The old man watched slack-jawed until a chunk of concrete hit the sidewalk next to him, peppering him with chips of concrete and chasing him inside.

Chapter 18

The second heat started less pyrotechnically than the first, but the anticipation of it produced the same familiar rush. The staff were unaffected as always—monitoring the transmission equipment that was in the hotel or standing at the ready in case of any unexpected interruptions—maybe because they'd seen it enough, or maybe because they were professionals.

Neither was true of the Cowboy. He did an anxious little dance throughout, hopping from one foot to the other, twisting and turning along with the violence playing out on the screens. He wasn't mimicking the thrusts and punches and jabs of those attacking. His involuntary movements betrayed his identification with the victims—squirming under an onslaught, twisting out of the way. Trying not to get hurt.

A pair of noncombatants had entered the view right before things got underway, a young couple apparently looking for their room. Odd, because the Cowboy was supposed to have booked all the rooms, but whatever, a little more collateral damage was always welcome. And in an instant, they were gone, swallowed up by the mayhem as soon as the alarm sounded and the festivities began.

It was a magnificent riot of confusion and violence. Eyes filled with terror, walls spattered with blood, muscle-bound madmen standing in the middle of it all wreaking havoc on everyone around them. There were always those go-getters who liked to jump the gun and take out the competition. They rarely made it to the final round, but they added so much in the meantime.

In the middle of it all a beautiful young woman with dark hair looked straight into one of the cameras, like she was auditioning for a movie. An instant later she suffered a crushing blow to the ribs from a monstrous hulk swinging a fire extinguisher.

The Cowboy gasped at the sight and wrapped a hand around his midsection, as if in sympathy.

Sympathy.

The Ringleader let out a snort at the thought. The Cowboy turned to look at him, but quickly turned back toward the carnage on the screen, pausing for a moment as if he couldn't decide which sight was more disturbing.

Then he turned decisively to the screen once more.

Chapter 19

"Is she alive?" Red asked as soon as he pushed through the hospital's heavy swinging doors. Dembe emerged behind him, stepping through before the doors could swing shut.

"We don't know," Ressler told him. It had been half an hour since the ER staff had rushed LeCroix through an identical pair of doors at the other end of the hallway.

"She lost consciousness on the way here," Keen said. "We haven't heard anything yet."

As she said it, the doors behind them swung open and a doctor came out. She was young, her hair pulled back in a bun that had probably started the day tight, but was now springing leaks in a dozen different places. Her scrubs were spattered with blood.

Red took a sharp breath.

"I'm Doctor Prasad—"

"How is she?" Red asked, cutting her off.

Prasad looked at him, taken aback, and turned to Keen, her eyes questioning as to whether she could speak freely in front of Red.

Keen nodded as Ressler came up beside her.

Dembe took up position beside the swinging doors.

Prasad cleared her throat. "We don't know, exactly. This is not blood," she said, extending her arms. She raised a hand, holding two plastic pouches, seemingly covered in blood. "She had on these fake blood packets. They... went off... as we were removing her clothes."

Keen and Ressler both looked at Red, but he shook his head.

"Her condition is stable for now," Prasad continued. "She's in and out of consciousness, but the prognosis isn't good. She is concussed and her brain is showing signs of some swelling. She has several cracked ribs. We're running tests to see if there is any internal bleeding. The next twelve hours will be key."

"We need to see her now," Red said, stepping closer, looming over the doctor.

Prasad frowned at Red. "She's weak. You mustn't get her excited or upset. You mustn't tire her out. You can speak to her briefly. And no more than two of you."

Red was the only one who knew LeCroix. A familiar presence would help reassure her, hopefully convince her to talk, and possibly give context to whatever was said.

The doctor looked at Red dubiously, then led them through the swinging doors and down the hall. The door to LeCroix's room was flanked by a pair of state police.

Keen badged them as the doctor explained she was allowing them to talk to LeCroix, just for a few minutes. They gave Red a hard stare, but didn't stop him.

Le Croix's head was swaddled in bandages and the swelling and bruising from her head had spread to her face.

Her eyes opened as they walked in and she turned her head slightly to look over at them. She squinted, as if trying to get her eyes to focus, then almost sat up. "Reddington?" she said, bewildered.

Red smiled. "Hello, Marianne," he said softly.

"What are you doing here?" she said, easing back down onto the bed, clearly exhausted. "What am *I* doing here? I need to get out of here."

Red took a chair from against the wall and set it next to the bed.

"What were you doing there, Marianne?"

She looked at him, appraisingly, then over his shoulder at Keen. "Who's she?"

Keen held up her badge. "Agent Keen. FBI."

LeCroix made a faint snorting sound. "Then I want a lawyer."

Red shook his head. "This isn't about you, Marianne. They're not after you, and there's no time for lawyers. This is about the Dead Ring."

Her eyes opened wider at that. They looked clearer.

Red shook his head. "That's a mad man's game, Marianne," he said. "That's not for you."

She closed her eyes for a moment, and when she opened them, a tear rolled down her cheek.

"It was the only way out," she said. Then, looking at Keen, "And she ruined it."

"Ruined what?" Keen asked, stepping closer.

"Someone is after us," she said quietly, her eyes closing again.

"Corbeaux?" Red asked.

Her eyes opened, a new level of fear in them at the mention of Corbeaux's name. She nodded, not asking how he knew. "I did a job. I didn't know it was him. I would never have robbed him if I had known. I tried to make it right, but there is no way with him. His reputation wouldn't allow it. He wants blood. My blood. And he was never going to stop until he got it. Or someone else did first.

"His men came after me once. I barely got away. I don't know how they knew where to find me. You know how careful I am about my identity. And it is a good thing, too. He said he was going to kill me, and when I was dead, once he found out my identity, he would track down my family and kill them too. He said he would torture them."

Red showed her the photo he'd taken from the hit man. "They had this."

She looked at it and closed her eyes.

"So you entered the Dead Ring?" he said.

She looked almost condescendingly at him. "We weren't going to win. We knew that. We were going to fake my death on the cameras, and then David and I, we..." Her voice trailed off and her eyes went distant. "Wait, where's David?"

"Who's David?" Red asked.

"Where is he?" she cried out, looking around, frantic.

"She was asking for him in the car," Keen said quietly.

"Who?" Red asked. "Who's David?"

Bells and alarms started buzzing and ringing, a scattering of red lights blinked on the bank of machines attached to LeCroix.

Amid the cacophony, she looked Red in the eye and said, "He's my husband."

Chapter 20

Prasad had chased them out, but a few minutes later she came back out and said, "She insists she wants to talk to you. But her condition is weakening, so you better make it fast."

Red was now holding LeCroix's hand and she was squeezing his. Keen stood back, letting them have their moment.

"We left France," LeCroix said. "We were going to disappear, but he was never going to stop. In his mind, everyone was looking to see what he would do to someone who dared to rob him. They had to see death and suffering. We knew we needed him to see me die before he found me."

"Thus the blood packets."

"I was about to set them off when I was hit. If we could convince him I was dead, as far as the world was concerned, I would be dead. I was ready for a new life anyway."

Keen thought back to how LeCroix had stood under the camera, looking up at it, as if trying to make sure her face was seen.

"But why the Dead Ring?" Red asked. "Couldn't

you have staged that all somewhere less dangerous?"

"It had to be somewhere Corbeaux would see us, and we couldn't risk returning to France. So when we found out the Dead Ring was here in the States, it seemed the perfect solution."

"So Corbeaux is a member of the Dead Ring," Red said.

"Yes," LeCroix whispered. "We knew he would be watching, the evil, twisted bastard."

A tear rolled down her face and Red brushed it away with a finger. He gave her a moment to collect herself, then softly, he said, "You got married."

She looked at him and smiled. "Last year. We were going to walk away anyway, even before this thing with Corbeaux. David, my husband, he's not like us. He's a soldier, a good man. He adores me." She blushed, visible even through the bruising. "You have to find him. Save him. David Borova. We were supposed to be in Mexico by now. I have no way of getting in touch with him. If he can't find me, he'll go ahead and enter the Dead Ring. He'll look for me there, look for clues. But he won't survive it. And he won't survive Corbeaux if that monster finds out we were together."

Keen stepped up behind Red. "We're taking the Dead Ring down," she said.

LeCroix looked up at her, then at Red for confirmation. "You're working with the FBI now?"

He smiled. "There are times when our interests overlap."

"With your help we can put an end to the Dead Ring," Keen continued. "And arrest the monsters betting on it. If you're right, if Corbeaux is a part of it, we'll arrest him, too. Help us, and you'll be helping David."

"I have a ticket," she said.

"What do you mean?" Keen asked.

She let out a long shallow sigh. Her color seemed to fade, maybe from her injuries, or from her growing awareness of how serious those injuries were. "The first two rounds aren't technically even part of it. They are qualifying rounds. Too many people want to get in, so they have to kill some of them off. You have to get through them in order to even enter. That was the risk we were willing to take—that we were confident we'd get through. The first preliminary round was on the bridge. We had to get to the van, grab one of those envelopes, and get away before the bridge exploded. Inside each envelope was a key card for a room at the Yellow Rose Hotel, and instructions to go to that room today." She paused and tried to take a deep breath. It didn't seem easy. "Inside that room was a key card for another room, and a combination to that room's safe. Once the alarm went off, you had three minutes to get to the other room, open the safe and take out your invitation. Before the whole thing blew up."

"So wait," Keen said. "You have this invitation?"

She nodded. "It was in my pants pocket when they cut them off me." A wry, wistful smile played across her face. "I loved those pants."

Keen was about to turn away, but that smile stopped her. She smiled back. Although she'd never been terribly concerned about clothes or fashion, Keen could identify with LeCroix's concern about her pants. It was such a human moment, such a mundane concern, that she felt a momentary connection with this dying thief she had never met before. In other circumstances, they might have been friends.

She brushed LeCroix's hair away from her face, generating another smile, this one raw and desperate, grateful but filled with mortal fear. LeCroix grabbed Keen's hand, squeezed it hard.

Red seemed to pick up on the moment that passed between them. He didn't move, but he stayed quiet and his presence somehow receded, as if he was willing himself out of the way.

Keen would have stayed there with her, she would have waited with LeCroix until she recovered or died. But the clock was ticking. Lives were at stake and she had a job to do.

LeCroix seemed to sense it, too. The moment was gone. Her smile went from intimate and vulnerable to polite and reserved. She pulled back her hand and turned away, looking at nothing.

As Keen went to the closet and rooted through the bag of tattered, bloody clothes, LeCroix started coughing, a deep, wet rumbling cough that seemed too big to be coming from her.

Red asked, "Who is the Ringleader?"

"I don't know," LeCroix replied, her voice cold and clipped. "I only know there is one. I don't know any of the people involved. Just David."

"How did you get in? How did you know about it?"

"I actually found out about it while I was researching Corbeaux, trying to find out who this monster was that was trying to kill me. Then I asked around among the most unsavory people I could find. It wasn't that hard once I knew what I was looking for."

Keen found a small brown envelope, a few inches across, in the pocket of LeCroix's mangled jeans. "Is this it?"

LeCroix nodded, and held out her hand.

Keen handed it to her and she tore it open and slid out a piece of thick paper, folded in the middle, adorned in ornate calligraphy.

LeCroix read it aloud. "'Congratulations. You have won entry in The Dead Ring.' There's GPS coordinates, then it says seven P.M., and today's date. Under that it says, 'Pack light.'"

She handed it to Red, who handed it to Keen.

"So how does this work?" Keen asked, staring at the card, considering the implications.

"What do you mean?" LeCroix asked, her voice straining on the last syllable as she stifled a cough.

"Are you supposed to just show up?"

"That's how it worked before," she said. "That's all I know."

Red turned to look at her, questioningly, as if he could sense the process taking place in her head. But then LeCroix started coughing again, and Keen turned on her heel and left the room.

When she got out into the hallway, Cooper and Aram were standing with Ressler.

"Sir," she said to Cooper. "I didn't know you were here." She and Aram exchanged nods of greeting.

"We just got here," Cooper said. He tipped his head toward the door behind her. "What's the latest? What's going on in there?"

"She's not doing well. But she gave us this." Holding up the invitation.

They all stepped closer to look at it.

"What is it?"

"It's our ticket inside the Dead Ring," she said. "But I think there's going to have to be a change of plan."

"What do you mean?" Ressler asked.

"One of us is going to infiltrate the Dead Ring. But it's not going to be you, Ressler. It's going to be me."

Chapter 21

Keen explained her reasoning: her resemblance to LeCroix, how few people knew what LeCroix looked like, and how whoever was behind the Dead Ring—or watching it—would have reason to expect her to be participating.

Cooper was silent, seriously considering it. Aram was wide-eyed at the prospect.

Ressler screwed up his face, dismissing her plan. "That's ridiculous." He shook his head. "These are battle-hardened trained killers you'll be up against. You wouldn't last ten minutes."

Keen bristled, even though she had thought pretty much the same thing when Ressler told her he was going in. "Well, I'll only have to last five minutes, you said so yourself. And I don't have to try to win anything, I just have to stay alive until the cavalry comes."

Cooper let out a heavy sigh. "That actually makes sense. Okay, let's revise the plan and see what it looks like."

"Sir, you can't be serious," Ressler said, but before he could argue further, a bell started ringing in LeCroix's room, followed by another and then a loud buzzer.

Prasad ran past them and into the room, followed two seconds later by a trio of nurses pushing a crash cart packed with medical equipment.

"Oh no," Keen whispered, taking a step after them.

The nurses disappeared into the room, and an instant later, Red backed out of it, watching them work, until the door closed in front of his face.

Dembe, Cooper, Aram, and Ressler gathered around them, listening to the jumble of beeps and buzzes, urgent voices calling out orders and readings, shouts of "Clear!" followed by the percussive punch of the defibrillator. One by one, the other sounds faded away, replaced by the lone, monotone wail of the heart monitor flatlining.

Then it stopped, too.

The door opened and Prasad came out. She stopped short as if she didn't expect them to be standing there. Like she wasn't quite ready to say the words she had to.

She looked at Red, then at Keen. "I'm sorry," she said. "We did everything we could."

Keen thanked her and she slipped away.

Red nodded.

He didn't cry, of course. Keen was pretty sure he was incapable of it. But she knew he felt pain—a lot of pain—and he couldn't always hide it. His face was a mask most of the time but that didn't mean the pain wasn't there.

Ressler and the others faded back to a respectful distance, giving them the moment they needed.

"I'm sorry," she said.

He nodded, acknowledging it. His eyes stared at the closed door as if they were seeing something else entirely.

"You two were close?" she said.

"More or less." His eyebrows shrugged. "More and

less, actually. We shared a moment of great meaning and little duration. I was very fond of her."

He looked at Keen and tried to smile again, that strange, strained, inappropriate smile that would wrestle across his face when human emotion got the best of him.

"She gave us some useful information," he said, looking down. "That invitation is just what you need to get Ressler into the Dead Ring."

"He's not entering it," she said quietly, knowing he was not going to like the change. "I am."

His head whipped around, his eyes piercing. "What are you saying?"

She explained her reasoning.

"Lizzie, that's preposterous. I won't allow that."

"It's not up to you. This plan makes the most sense. You know it does. The first round starts tomorrow."

Red glared at Cooper. "Are you signing off on this plan?" he demanded.

Cooper had been standing there with his head down and his hands clasped in front of him. Now he widened his stance, his demeanor changing from respectful condolence to resolute, and maybe slightly defensive, authority. "Under the circumstances, I think it's the best plan we have. Yes. And I know it's not without risk, but we'll be taking every precaution to ensure Agent Keen's safety."

Red looked at Ressler, who shook his head ever so slightly, letting him know he did not agree with the decision.

"We won't get a better chance than this," Keen said.

But Red stormed off, pushing his way through the swinging doors without looking back.

Chapter 22

The coordinates on LeCroix's invitation matched a place called Pinella Hunting Camp. It was an abandoned campground that had been purchased with cash from a sheriff's sale six months previously. The FBI's logistics unit had set the task force up with a temporary field office fifteen miles away in an abandoned school, Cavelier Elementary, which had been run by a local minister until the nearest town lost one employer too many and withered away to almost nothing. The school had only been closed a couple years, so it wasn't in too bad a shape. The main work area was in the lobby—a high-ceilinged room with tile floors and blue cinderblock walls. Cooper was set up in the principal's office, separated from the lobby by a large window and a wooden door.

The classrooms extended off in two wings at right angles, forming an "L" shape. The upper school classrooms were set up with cots for sleeping, the lower school classrooms with the weapons locker and other supplies. They also had a couple rooms at a motel not too far away, for showers and such.

"Mr. Reddington was pretty upset, huh?" Aram

said as he spread a thin layer of glue onto the nail of Keen's big toe. They were in the nurses' office, down the hallway with the sleeping quarters.

Aram seemed nervous, even more than usual, and Keen sympathized. It was an awkward situation for her, too, and an oddly intimate moment.

"He sure seemed to be," Keen replied, watching him do it. "But he needs to learn that he's not in charge of everything," she said. "And he's certainly not in charge of me."

She hadn't meant to say that, not out loud. She didn't like to share her thoughts or feelings about Red with the rest of the team. In the two or three years since he had appeared out of the blue insisting on working only with her, she had been determined to maintain the appearance that their relationship was strictly professional, even if she knew, somehow, that it was more than that. Their relationship outside of work had consisted almost entirely of him trying to protect her from danger while at the same time constantly embroiling her in it, and maintaining a level of mystery about their past so relentless that it had become almost mundane.

Aram cleared his throat, as if her words made him even more uncomfortable than having his hands on her bare feet.

"Okay," he said, holding up a small, paper-thin device the size of a dime, or a toenail. "This is the tracker and transmitter, or TNT. As you can see, it's incredibly thin. It needs to be invisible, secure, and backed by something solid to protect it. Affixing it to your toenail is the perfect solution. So, before it's activated, it operates as a passive, line-of-sight tracking device. We will be constantly pinging it, and whenever we have a line of sight, we'll be able to track your location. The signal will go through your shoes or clothing or whatever, but it can't pass through metal. So if you're in a vehicle or a building, just try to hold it outside once in a while, so we can track you. It's lightly scored down the middle. To activate the transmitter, just bend it in half along that line until it gives slightly. When activated, it's a two-way signal booster and transmitter. You just need to locate it within ten feet of one of their wireless cameras and we're in. The battery only lasts ten minutes after that, but once the video uplink starts—and the two-way signal is sending video out and bringing bets placed by the viewers in— we only need five minutes of transmission to get our code into the video signal, and to receive confirmation that it's working."

The tactical team, or "tac team," assigned to the operation was based at an air force training facility forty miles away. They'd move to one of several closer locations when things got underway, so they could be onsite wherever Keen was, to shut things down within five minutes as soon as the Trojan horse was in place and the infected computers were all reporting back.

Aram carefully placed the TNT onto her toe, then sat back and let out a deep sigh. "Just let that dry for a few minutes," he said. "Then it will be repositionable. So you can stick it back on if need be, or use the adhesive to affix it somewhere else, like on the camera or one of the cables, maybe."

"How close to the camera does it need to be in order to work?"

He shrugged. "The closer the better. But anywhere within ten or twelve feet should work."

Keen smiled. "Should be a piece of cake."

Chapter 23

Red hadn't meant for Keen to end up as a contestant inside the Dead Ring, and he was incensed that the decision had been made without consulting him.

Sometimes she seemed determined to aggravate him, to put herself in danger for the sole purpose of defying him, and ignoring his wisdom.

The task force was going ahead with this plan despite his strong objections, but Red had ways of influencing things less directly.

That's why he was calling Dominic Corrello.

"I guess you liked what I got you," Corrello said.

Red could practically hear the smirk over the phone. He wondered if Corrello could hear him rolling his eyes. The man was useful, but he had a ridiculously inflated sense of his own value.

"With the kind of work you do, Mr. Corrello, I imagine your discretion is almost as important as the information you provide."

"If you're asking can I keep my mouth shut, the answer is yes."

Red grimaced at the choice of words. Corrello may well have been able to maintain confidence, but keeping his mouth shut seemed beyond him. He almost ended the call right then, but instead he said, "Otherwise, I guess, your clients would come back and kill you, right?"

Corrello paused. "My clients got nothing to worry about."

"Good. Then I guess we can continue to do business and I will never have to worry about tracking you down and killing you."

"I guess so."

"The Dead Ring is real. And it is taking place as we speak, in west Texas. I need to know who is hosting it. If you can find that out for me, I will compensate you generously."

"Who am I looking for? What kind of guy?"

"I don't know, Mr. Corrello, that would be what I'm paying you for. Among its enthusiasts, I would imagine hosting the Dead Ring is somewhat prestigious. Proving you have the resources and the connections to pull something like this off, especially in the United States, would be quite a feather in some people's caps. I'm fairly confident the person I am looking for is not deeply involved in local organized crime, but perhaps might be looking to become involved in international crime."

Corrello grunted, like maybe this was a bigger fish than he wanted to go after.

"Second thoughts, Mr. Corrello?"

They both knew that it was too late for that.

Corrello had encouraged Red to share sensitive information with him. If he backed out now, they both knew the fact that Red was looking for this person could become the sensitive information someone else was looking for.

So Red would have to kill him.

Like it or not, Corrello had just advanced to the big leagues. Like it or not, he would have to produce for Red or else find himself out of the game completely, or even retired in a more elemental way.

Both men remained quiet. Red was letting the man acclimate to his new reality, and the risks and rewards that went with it.

"Right," Corrello eventually said, his voice laden with new gravity. "I'll see what I can turn up." He sounded like a new man, and that was as it should be, thought Red. He was either a new man, or a dead man. "I'll get back to you in the next day or two."

"Excellent," said Red. "I knew I could count on you."

Chapter 24

Navabi woke to a soft tapping at her door. She was disoriented for a brief moment. It should have been night time, yet golden light was streaming through her curtains across simple and utterly unfamiliar furniture. In an instant, though, she had regained her bearings and was standing next to the hotel room door, one hand on the doorknob, the other hand holding her gun.

"Who is it?" she asked, her voice quiet and terse.

"Sadek," came the reply, equally hushed.

Recognizing his voice, she opened the door.

Sadek slipped inside and closed the door behind him. He seemed both worried and excited. Under his arm he had two thick manila envelopes. He dropped them onto the coffee table and sat in the chair facing it, then opened one of the envelopes and slid its contents out onto the table.

"This is the control room," he said. "There's a full forensics report, although nothing that turned up any leads before the investigation was shut down. There were several sets of fingerprints, but none of them matched anything on our database. Nothing."

He picked up a thin sheaf of photos and laid them down one-by-one on the table. They showed a simple room with roughly cut holes in the wall, and bundles of cable protruding from them. The room looked like it had been stripped, but that it had once contained lots of high-tech electronics.

Sadek pointed to the cabling. "You see why I say it looks like a control room, eh?"

She nodded. "That's a lot of bandwidth."

"Exactly. Multichannel video perhaps, or something similar."

Navabi studied the photos for another moment, then leafed through the forensics reports. She held up the sheets of fingerprints. "You said you ran these but didn't come up with anything?"

"That's right."

"Do you mind if we run them on our end?"

"I hope you do, and that you have better luck. Just make sure it doesn't come back on me. That means you don't fax it or email it, anything like that. Not from here. You take it and you go."

Navabi picked up the case summary, her eyes traveling down the page, looking for information Sadek hadn't previously told her about. When she got to the bottom, she looked up at him. "There is another case referenced here. Another case with some of the same fingerprints."

He smiled, his eyes gleaming, as he held up the other envelope.

"I was ordered to destroy this last year as well. When I went to do so, it was not in the file. I assumed someone else had already destroyed it. Just to be sure, I checked again before I came over here, and there it was."

"What is it?"

"When we ran the fingerprints from the control room, we didn't come up with any hits. Shortly after the warehouse fire, police responded to reports of a disturbance, and found four men in a room, unconscious. The room had been heavily secured, but it had been broken into and left open. It also showed the same type of high capacity computer infrastructure as the control room."

He slid out more photos that looked like they could have been from the same room as the previous case. "The four men were taken to the hospital with signs of opioid overdose. They were found to have high levels in their blood of a chemical called remifentanil, an opioid gas that is known to have been used as an incapacitating agent. The Russians used it on Chechen militants when they took over that theater a few years back. Also found at the scene was a syringe with traces of naloxone, which counters the effects of opioids, including remifentanil."

Navabi let out a soft grunt as she considered that.

"Security footage from a nearby bank showed a man being bundled into a van by two other men. Police had assumed it was an abduction, but the four men brought to the hospital said no one was missing. They said it was a robbery."

"And what was taken?"

"They were hazy about it. They said nothing."

"So what is the connection?"

"Police took their information, then they were treated and released. When police had follow-up questions, the men had vanished. Someone ran their fingerprints and they matched some of the unidentified prints at the control room."

"So what is the connection?" she said again.

He shook his head. "The fingerprints match. Both files were ordered destroyed. What is the connection? I don't know. But I know that there is one."

Chapter 25

For the first twenty miles or so, Keen was shocked every time she looked into the rearview mirror. Her hair was darker and her eye make-up totally different. Each time she got over the shock of it, she was pleased to observe that her expression was different, too. Her whole demeanor had changed.

She was wearing five hundred dollar Dolce and Gabbana Chelsea boots, three hundred dollar black jeans, a black sweater identical to LeCroix's, and the garnet pendant and bracelet she'd been wearing when they brought her into the hospital. At the small of her back was a flat knife in a soft leather sheath they had also taken from LeCroix. She was also wearing what she hoped was a pretty close imitation of the cat burglar's knowing smile.

All of it helped her get into character enough that by the time she'd been on the road for fifteen minutes, it was like someone else was looking back at her in the mirror.

The GPS coordinates from the invitation led to an old abandoned tourist camp. A subsequent satellite sweep showed the place had been recently updated, with a brand new fence. A handful of pickups and SUVs were parked outside it.

As she drew nearer Keen saw a massive black and gray RV with some sort of apparatus on top, a couple of Humvees—one matte black and covered in dust, one bright red and shiny with chrome—along with a handful of jacked-up pickup trucks with monster truck suspensions, several motorcycles, and a smattering of plain old cars.

Cooper had suggested she wear an earpiece or at least have a cell phone, so she could be in touch until the very last moment. Keen had declined. She didn't want to risk tipping her hand, in case they were monitoring signals or had hacked into the local cell towers. Plus, she wanted to use the drive to get into character, to let herself become LeCroix. She had studied what little there was in the way of a file, and done her best as a profiler to get to the heart of the woman, to understand her background, her motivation, as well as her affectations and speech patterns.

Keen was glad she had met LeCroix, however briefly. She felt much more prepared than she would have otherwise.

As she approached the camp site, she felt a physical wave of pure fear wash over her. She had no idea what she was getting herself into, other than that many people would consider it a suicide mission. Her foot eased off the accelerator and the car slowed as she fought the intense urge to turn around and go back the other way.

But the feeling slowly subsided. She gritted her teeth and pushed down her foot.

Three minutes later she pulled up between one of the Humvees and a trio of Harley Davidsons and parked with the front of her car a foot from the brand new cyclone fence that surrounded the place.

She got out carrying nothing but the invitation LeCroix herself had retrieved from the hotel room and resisted the urge to look skyward at the CIRRUS high-altitude surveillance drone she knew was up there silently watching her.

As she approached the gate, it slid open on metal rollers.

With a tremendous force of will, she walked through without hesitation. Directly in front of her was a boxy, cement stucco building, with a sign over the door that said PINELLA HUNTING CAMP—CHECK-IN.

She walked straight up to it and entered.

The inside was like the lobby of a crappy motel. A small sitting area with saggy armchairs surrounded a worn bentwood and wicker coffee table. There was a registration desk, and the guy sitting behind it looked even worse than the rest of the place—his hair greasy and his clothes grimy. He smiled as she walked in, what would have been a toothy grin if he'd had more teeth. Standing behind him were a pair of almost identical-looking guards carrying assault rifles. They had the unmistakable appearance of PMCs—Private Military Contractors—and they looked crisp and clean compared to the man sitting in front of them.

The guy at the desk made it clear that his smile was about him enjoying the view and not being friendly. When he was done looking her up and down, he said, "Who the hell are you?"

Keen slapped the invitation onto the counter. "You can call me Le Chat."

He inspected her invitation then shrugged and made a note in the log book in front of him.

"I'm Yancy." He opened a metal strong box and put it on the counter. "Car keys."

She took them out of her pocket and tossed them in with the other sets of keys, which nearly filled the box.

"You got any weapons?"

She pulled out the knife from the sheath at the small of her back.

He nodded toward a large plastic bin on the floor to the side. It was already half full with firearms, switchblades, blackjacks, and trench knives.

He laughed. "Don't worry, you'll get it back if you win." Then he laughed harder. "Hell, you can have all of 'em if you win. Everyone else will be dead."

He thought that was hilarious. When he was done laughing, and tainting the air with the sour milk smell of his breath, he put an old-fashioned room key on the counter. "You're in cabin number twelve. Game starts at sunrise. When you hear reveille over the loudspeaker, report to the flagpole in the main square."

Keen swiped the key off of the desk, gave him a dead-eyed stare, then turned and left. She was relieved to see the cabins were prominently numbered. The last thing she wanted right then was to go back in and ask for directions. Number twelve was on the right, toward the end of the row.

As she walked down the thoroughfare, the door to number seven opened and a massive pillar of muscle and menace emerged onto the small stoop. He picked at his teeth with the corner of a matchbook and stared at her. She glanced at him with the same dead eyes she'd given the guy at the desk, then looked away and kept walking.

She slipped her key into the knob and the door easily opened. The rest of the place might be run down, but the locks were brand new. As soon as she closed the door, Keen wanted to curl into a ball in the corner and give herself over to the shakes that had been trying to set in since she got out of the car. But she didn't trust the place wasn't wired for video.

The interior was rustic but clean and in decent shape.

There was a small table with a single-cup coffee maker, a case of bottled water, a box of protein bars, and a dozen MREs, military field rations. In the bathroom, she found an admirably complete toiletries kit.

After she had inspected the room, she slid off her boots and lay down on the bed, closed her eyes and practiced her breathing. Lying there in the dark, she went over the plan and her profile of LeCroix in her head, again and again, and waited for sleep, and for sunrise.

Chapter 26

"She's in," Aram said, looking up from the dot on the screen that represented Keen's line-of-sight tracking device. "Looks like she's in cabin twelve."

Cooper nodded, but didn't say anything. Neither did Ressler.

As much as it made sense on paper, no one was crazy about the plan. No one liked the idea of Keen being in there on her own with a bunch of lunatic killers, much less entering into a deadly game that could only have one survivor.

Aram knew that just like him, they were telling themselves she'd only have to survive five minutes of actual game time before the tactical team shut things down and got her out safely. But the fact remained, Agent Keen was inside the Dead Ring.

He knew that's what they were all thinking about. As they were about to go back to their work, the heavy exterior door opened, and Agent Navabi walked in.

Aram shot to his feet. "You're back."

Ressler looked at his watch, a confused expression on his face. "You must have only been there a few hours."

Cooper walked in and said, "You look tired, Agent Navabi."

"You might say that, yes," she said, briefly looking around the place, then leaning against the wall. She handed him the two envelopes Sadek had given her. "These are the files Sadek's superiors wanted destroyed. He insisted I keep them on me, to make sure they couldn't be traced back to him."

Navabi told them what Sadek had told her, and they told her about LeCroix, and about Keen going into the Dead Ring undercover. She was worried like everyone else, but conceded right away that the logic behind the plan was sound.

"I need a shower and a bed," she said, yawning. "Where are we staying?"

Aram told her about the cots in the upper school wing, but gave her a slip of paper with the name and address of a nearby motel on it. She looked like she needed a real bed. "It's good to have you back, Agent Navabi," he said, smiling.

She took the piece of paper and smiled back. "Thanks."

As she turned and left, Aram watched her and considered that smile.

Director Cooper came up behind him and cleared his throat. "Aram, perhaps you could get started running those fingerprints while we're waiting for the signal from Agent Keen."

"Of course, sir," he replied, momentarily flustered.

Once he opened the file, and immersed himself in the tasks at hand, he was grateful for the distraction. It would stop him from worrying about Agent Keen, or thinking of Agent Navabi, for that matter.

Much of what Navabi had brought back consisted

of reports from the Turkish forensics lab, in Turkish. Much of that he simply forwarded to Interpol for translation. But there were some fingerprints, as well, and he got to work scanning them and entering them into the system.

One set of prints seemed like it was physically encrypted, jumbled like a jigsaw puzzle. Aram spent some time trying to make sense of it, then gave up and put it aside as he finished processing the rest of them.

When they were done, he sat back and waited for the algorithm to run them through the various databases. With an idle moment, his mind quickly turned to worrying about Agent Keen.

Twenty minutes later, he was surprised to see he'd gotten a match on one set of prints. A small wave of trepidation passed through him when he saw that he was blocked from the result. It was from the US Department of Defense database.

"Sir?" Aram called out. Cooper reappeared in an instant, Ressler following behind, in case it involved Keen. "I got a hit on one set of prints on the DOD database, but I don't have clearance to access it."

Cooper scanned the screen, then leaned forward and started typing. A moment later, the screen showed a picture and biography of a man named Simon Wall.

He had a round, open face and intelligent eyes. Aram scanned the text and summarized it. "Former cryptographer for US Army Intelligence, a handful of awards, recruited several years ago by Hoagland Services the military contractor. Stayed with them when they were bought out by another military contractor, G78. Pretty straightforward stuff—oh wow."

"What is it?" Cooper asked.

"I recognize some of his work," Aram said. "The

guy was brilliant. Until recently, his encryption was considered state of the art."

Cooper nodded and patted Aram on the shoulder. "Good work. See what else you can find on him."

Chapter 27

"Th-that's all of them?" asked the Cowboy. It was one minute after midnight, and the only movement on the screens in the last hour and a half had been at the stroke of twelve, when Yancy closed the log-in book with a yawn and the staff rolled the gate closed and locked it.

One of the technicians turned in his seat and spoke past him, making it clear that he was not answering the Cowboy's question but talking to someone else.

"Thirty contestants, sir. That matches what we tracked from the hotel."

"Is th-th-that all of them?" the Cowboy asked, this time confronting his fear and looking directly at the Ringleader.

"Yes," he replied from the shadows, his voice sounding coarse even to his own ears. He rarely spoke, but even after all these years, his voice still sounded like someone else.

The technician turned to the Cowboy now. "Forty keys were distributed on the bridge. Ten key-holders went down at the Yellow Rose. That leaves thirty."

"Okay," he said. "Thanks."

The technicians and the guards all paused at the same moment and put their hands to their earpieces, listening. One of the technicians tapped a few keys on his keyboard, then handed the Cowboy a simple remote as all four of them left the vehicle.

The large screens were now divided up into smaller screens, each one showing a view of the interior of a different cabin, angled across the bed and into the bathroom. Some of the inhabitants were exercising, some were reclining, some were eating. Some were clothed, some were not. Some were bathing, some were voiding their bladders or bowels. Some were pleasuring themselves.

The Cowboy peered into the shadows, questioningly. "Is this part of the broadcast?"

"No."

The Cowboy absentmindedly swept the remote control across the screens, and as he did, the windows enlarged and then shrank again, one by one. He swept it back, this time lingering on the one-eyed Iraqi woman, standing there naked, drying her hair.

"This is j-just for us?"

"Just for you," he rasped. "They are yours. If you want to get to know them."

The Cowboy tried to look away from the screen, but was unable. "But I don't..." he started to say, as if they hadn't done their homework on him. As if they didn't know everything about him and his particular tastes.

He sank into a deep and absorbed silence as he flicked from screen to screen, mesmerized by the figures on them.

Chapter 28

Keen awoke with a start half an hour before sunrise. It took her a moment to remember where she was and several more to convince herself of it. She used the toiletries kit to wash up and brush her teeth, gagged down an MRE for breakfast, followed by an entire bottle of water.

She gave it a few minutes to settle in, then did some stretching exercises while running through LeCroix's profile in her mind. She had Red's description, what little was known from her file and, of course, Keen's own impressions of her.

She felt like she had a grasp of the woman's personality, but she was glad LeCroix had been so secretive in life. That would help her avoid getting tripped up.

At five minutes to seven, a loudspeaker crackled to life outside: "Attention, participants. Assembly is at the flagpole in five minutes."

Keen came out of her stretch, tightening her abdominal muscles against the wave of nervous nausea that swept through her.

She told herself, LeCroix probably would have

also been nervous right now. But then again, LeCroix would also be hiding it.

At just under five minutes, Keen took a deep breath, opened the door, and stepped outside.

The sun was low, but already blinding, coming in sideways and casting long shadows of the crowd assembled around a flagpole in the square. It looked like a parade ground on a military base. There was no flag, but the rope slapped against the pole in the light breeze.

Within a minute, it seemed like everyone was out there. Thirty of them: mostly big, mean-looking men, although Keen was not the only woman. There was a beautiful Iraqi woman with an eye-patch, and a Kenyan woman whose eyes were blank, her face completely immobile.

The men were big, mostly scarred, and battle hardened. Half of them seemed completely oblivious to the women, or to each other for that matter.

The rest of them stared at the women, with expressions ranging from lascivious to homicidal. Keen seemed to be drawing more attention than the other two, or at least that's what it felt like. She tried not to acknowledge it in any way.

A huge Australian stared at her intently with smoldering eyes, as if he was going out of his way to be obvious about it. He was bald, the side of his head marked with fresh burns, but he looked vaguely and unsettlingly familiar.

There was another one staring as well. He was younger, softer, and saner-looking than the others. He watched her nervously, his eyes flickering over to her, then looking away any time she looked back at him. Several of the others were looking at him the way predators look at prey.

They stood there for a minute, although it felt much longer, then Yancy approached, wearing the same grimy clothes as before and looking decidedly unwashed himself. He was followed by a man in matching fatigues and a beret. He was in his late fifties, with short blond hair and the kind of face that might once have been boyishly charming, but was now ravaged by bitterness and hatred. A diagonal scar spanned his entire face, from just over his right eye, across his nose, and down his left cheek.

"Okay, ringers," Yancy barked. "Stand to attention."

The group formed into two lines of seven and two lines of eight. Some of them seemed determined not to line up too quickly or too cleanly, as if making a show of defiance. A couple of the men, two Russians who seemed to know each other, started pushing and shoving, until Yancy yelled, "Knock it off!" then muttered, "Save it for the games."

He cleared his throat and held up a hand in the direction of the man standing behind him. "This is Sergeant Corson. He will be running things throughout the Dead Ring. That means he is in charge of you. For most of you, he will be in charge of you for the rest of your lives. You will obey him completely. I work for Sergeant Corson. I help him keep you crazy bastards in order. You will obey me completely, as well."

Yancy stood to the side and said, "Sergeant Corson?"

The other man stepped forward to occupy the space where Yancy had stood when he spoke.

"Welcome to the Dead Ring," he said, with a dark smile. "One of you will be leaving here with a minimum of five million dollars in cash, enough to retire from whatever horrible things you've been doing for a living. The rest of you will not be leaving at all. At least not alive. Each game will have its own rules and you will be told those rules before the game begins. Other than the rules we tell you, there will be no other rules inside a game."

The two Russians started pushing again, and Yancy stilled them with a murderous stare.

Keen sensed movement behind her, and glancing back saw three PMCs with assault rifles standing behind the formation.

Corson continued, "Outside that game, however, there are many rules. No communication with the outside world is allowed during the Dead Ring, and no communication about the Dead Ring is allowed, ever. Even if you win. There is no fighting outside the game. No rough-housing. If you want to hurt someone, by all means, please do, but do it inside the game, so the cameras can show it for the entertainment of our sponsors."

The two Russians started pushing again. As Yancy moved to step toward the disruption Corson put out a hand, stopping him.

"We do not operate under military law in this camp," Corson said, earning half-hearted cheers from a handful of the players.

One of the Russians pushed the other one out of line entirely.

Without a word, Corson drew his sidearm and shot the pusher in the head. The crack of the gunshot echoed across the landscape. The hole in the Russian's forehead let out two large burps of blood, but by the time his body hit the ground, the bleeding had slowed to a trickle. His leg shook once, then stopped.

"Get back in line," Corson said, to the man who had been pushed.

He did as he was told, stepping over the body. He

kept his eyes focused straight ahead, not looking at his dead comrade.

"In here, we follow my rules," Corson continued, his voice rising. "And the penalty for failing to obey my rules is death. Does anyone have any questions?"

His gun was still out and still raised. After a moment, he shrugged and holstered it. "Good. We often lose more than one while going over the rules."

He smiled at that, as if at some fond memory.

"The game itself will start at sunrise tomorrow. Today," he gestured to a grassy field at the far end of the compound, "we do the Combine."

Chapter 29

Corson carried on with his speech as if nothing significant had happened. The remaining Russian player watched as Yancy wordlessly directed two of the other ringers to drag the corpse of his friend from the square. Keen had to resist the urge to watch them as they dumped the body off to the side and returned to their places in the formation.

Two more PMCs came out of the main building carrying video cameras on tripods. They were headed toward a wide grassy field that appeared to be set up with exercise or training equipment.

"The Combine is not part of the competition," Corson explained. "And there is no betting on it. Frankly, most of our bettors don't even watch it. You will each be put through your paces in a number of basic athletic competitions—running, jumping, climbing, obstacles—for the benefit of those viewers who choose to watch. We want to give them an idea of who you people are, so they can decide to bet on you or against you, how many rounds you will survive. Whatever they want. Keep in mind that the size of the winner's purse may be determined in part by how much is wagered, so even though this is not an official round of the Dead Ring, you will be expected to do your best."

Corson stayed where he was as Yancy led the group toward the grassy field. Most of them stepped around the blood on the ground, but the Australian seemed to make a point of planting his foot right in it.

As they walked, Keen could hear some of the other ringers muttering to each other, a low-level buzz that she did her best to block out as she considered the implications of this unexpected stage of the proceedings.

She hadn't had a clear idea of what to expect once she got inside, or of how quickly the games would get underway. But she had not expected there to be another preliminary round of any kind.

Looking ahead at the field in front of her, Keen focused on the PMCs positioning the video cameras. They were going to record the Combine, meaning there would be a multichannel video feed going out, presumably uplinked to the satellite, but there would be no betting, and no signal coming in. It dawned on her that when the video signal started, Aram would be waiting for her to activate the transmitter. But with no bets coming in, maybe no signal of any kind coming in, she had no idea if activating the transmitter would send Aram's Trojan horse out to the other computers, or if it would go nowhere. And Corson had said most of their viewers didn't even log on for this, so the majority of the subscribers wouldn't be included in the bust. Once the transmitter had been activated for five minutes the tac team would shut the whole thing down and the operation would be blown. They'd have Corson and Yancy. They could charge them for the murder of the dead Russian contestant. Maybe they could get some information out of them, but it wasn't a good bet.

Even worse, they had agreed that if Keen didn't activate the transmitter within five minutes of the beginning of the satellite feed, they would assume she was in jeopardy and the tac team would come in anyway, shut it all down and extract her.

She had to warn them off.

Her mind was racing, trying to come up with a plan, but by the time they reached the field, she had come up empty.

The field was surrounded by a track, and inside it were cones and tires to run around and across, a set of weights, a climbing wall, and some gymnastic equipment. In the middle were the two cameras on tripods, their operators panning back and forth as if they were already broadcasting.

At the far end, there was a table with several dozen metal water bottles, stacks of folded towels, and bundles of some other white material.

Keen thought it oddly reminiscent of a high school athletic tryout. She scanned the equipment and the field looking for ideas, for some way she could communicate with the task force that wouldn't give her away. She knew that incredibly high in the sky, invisible to the naked eye and too far away to hear, the CIRRUS drone was flying a slow pattern. Watching her.

She wanted to run out in the field and simply wave her arms, "*No, don't come!*"

But that wasn't an option. A crazy idea flashed through her head that maybe she could arrange the towels or the water bottles, to send a coded message without being caught.

She knew the idea was ridiculous but, while she struggled to remain cool and impassive on the outside, inside she was becoming increasingly frantic. She had mere minutes to figure it out, and if she didn't, the whole thing would come down in crashing ruin. She thought again about the towels and the water bottles. And then she had an idea.

As the rest of the ringers filed onto the field behind her, she crossed to the table with the towels and the water bottles. As she approached it, Yancy's hoarse voice called out, "Le Chat!"

She stopped and turned around, but reached out as she was doing so and grabbed one of the water bottles.

"Get over here!" he snapped, pointing to the middle of the field where everyone else was gathering.

She didn't show him she had grabbed a water bottle, but she didn't hide it either, sauntering back to the field, ignoring the stares of some of the fellow contestants: some predatory, some curious. The two women stared at her with an almost identical combination of pity and contempt.

When she reached the edge of the group, she stopped and got down on one knee, extending the foot with the transmitter in front of her. She reached down with both hands, and began rolling the water bottle back and forth over the tip of her foot.

"Le Chat," Yancy barked again. "What the hell are you doing?"

Keen winced and looked up, but didn't stop what she was doing. "Got a cramp."

Yancy snorted and shook his head. "Oh, you'll do great out there."

Chapter 30

Aram had stayed up throughout the night researching Simon Wall and tinkering around with the jigsaw fingerprint, but he'd kept one eye on the tracking signal, which hadn't moved until five minutes earlier. The CIRRUS drone video was grainy but the tracking signal was strong and clear. He had watched through bleary eyes as Keen and the other competitors assembled in the clearing at the center of the compound.

Then one of the contestants was shot and killed.

Aram had woken up quick at that point. Cooper had appeared almost instantly behind him, already dressed.

"What is it?" Cooper asked.

Ressler appeared in the doorway, his shirt unbuttoned and untucked, his face crease-marked but his eyes alert.

Aram told them both about the shooting.

Now the three of them watched as the entire group of competitors walked to a playing field set up with track equipment. As they began to stretch, a green signal light appeared in the corner of the screen. At the same time, a soft chime filled the room.

"Oh crap," Aram muttered, giving his head a vigorous shake to clear it.

"What is it?" Ressler asked.

"The video uplink. It's live." He rolled his chair to the other end of the table, and started frantically typing, recording the signal and simultaneously sending it to the FBI's distributed network for decryption.

"Are you sure?" Cooper asked, as he took out his phone to call Nichols and activate the tactical team. His voice was steely but so calm it seemed to slow Aram's own heart rate.

Aram took a breath and double checked. The signal didn't seem to be taking up as much bandwidth as he'd expected, and it was still heavily encrypted, but it was unmistakable. "Yes. Twenty seconds ago." He looked up. "Nothing from Keen yet."

Cooper initiated the call and turned away. "This is Deputy Director Cooper," he said into the phone. "We have uplink. No, there is no word from Agent Keen. Have your team ready and prepare to implement the contingency plan."

The tactical team was roughly four minutes from the campground by helicopter. It had been agreed that the team would embark after three minutes instead of the full five to reduce the response time, especially in case something went wrong.

As Aram went back to his computer, he could feel his heart rate slowly rise again.

The distributed network harnessed the available and currently unused computing power of hundreds of FBI computers, and the decryption software was state of the art. But the progress bar on the screen, which he knew was almost entirely ornamental, was also at the moment infuriatingly slow and seemingly stuck at two percent.

Once the transmitter was activated, Aram could embed the Trojan horse into the video signal so it would be encrypted along with the rest of the signal. It should work regardless. But without breaking the encryption, he wouldn't know if it was working. And even if it did work, if they did get their code onto all those computers, if they didn't know what the signal contained, they'd have a hard time making any kind of case, or enlisting foreign agencies in rounding up the bettors.

He kept waiting for the progress bar to flicker up to thirty percent, then announce it was complete. But it didn't.

He looked at the clock. "One minute," he said.

Ressler was suddenly dressed in black tactical gear, lacing up his boots. He had said earlier he was going to head out to the campground by car as soon as the signal was given. Better to get there late than never.

He and Aram shared a glance, both thinking, *That's one minute and still no signal from Keen.*

Cooper lowered his phone but didn't end the call.

"Nothing from Keen?"

Aram shook his head. He could see her on the screen. The tracking signal flickered then came back, flickered again. He felt a surge of anxiety at the thought they might lose the signal altogether.

The visual was jumbled, but Keen seemed to be taking up a larger footprint than if she was standing like the others. He wondered if she was sitting, but that didn't seem quite right either. He zoomed in, and the image grew larger but less distinct, but it also appeared to be moving somewhat, a vague back and forth motion.

"We're sure that's Keen, right?" Cooper asked, his voice losing some of its calm.

Aram resisted the urge to shrug. "I'm sure that's the tracker." He paused, thinking for a moment. "Yes, I'm pretty sure that's Agent Keen."

Cooper nodded.

Ressler checked his assault rifle, slid out the clip and checked that, too. The muscles in his temple throbbed as he immersed himself in the routine preparations for battle. The sight of Ressler's weapons was a grim reminder of how high the stakes were.

Aram checked the time. "Two minutes," he announced.

The progress bar was still at two percent. He had a sense that the plan was coming apart. Technically, they didn't need to decrypt the satellite feed in order to insert their code, but they would be doing it blind. There would be no way to tell what they were inserting it into, a level of uncertainty that was unacceptable for such a sensitive operation.

Cooper raised the phone. "Prepare to execute the contingency plan in three minutes."

Aram knew that if the tactical team went in hot and Keen wasn't ready, there was a chance she'd go down in the crossfire. The operation would go south, yes, but much more important, Keen would be in great danger.

The progress bar on the decryption wasn't budging.

Cooper checked the clock. "Two and a half minutes," he said into the phone.

Ressler let out a deep sigh and went outside. Aram wondered if Ressler was just trying to shave whatever seconds he could off his response time, or if he just couldn't watch the screen any longer.

The progress bar hit three percent. The clock hit three minutes.

Cooper gave the tac team the order.

The tracking signal was flickering again, almost

rhythmically, but sometimes quickly and sometimes slow.

Aram moved his face closer to the screen, and mumbled out loud, "What are you doing, Agent Keen?"

Her form was definitely moving, and as he looked closer, he realized it was in time with the breakages in the tracking signal. As if she was doing it intentionally. Slow and then quick. Dots and dashes. She was sending a code.

Morse code was not the kind of thing that stayed on the tip of your tongue, or in the back of your mind. But if you grew up the kind of kid Aram was, it was in there deep.

Almost without conscious thought, he started decoding the message. "... O-P... S-T-O-P... S-T-O-P..." It took only an instant to realize she was sending the word STOP over and over. "Sir!?" he called out. "I think Agent Keen is sending us a code!"

Even as he said it, the pattern changed and as Cooper rushed to his side, Aram resumed decoding, "S-T-A-N-D... D-O-W-N... She wants us to stand down. We need to call back the tactical team."

For a moment, Cooper's face seemed like it was going to shatter from the internal pressure.

"She said, 'STOP... STOP... STAND DOWN,' in Morse code. She seems to be using something to shield and unshield the TNT. She's still doing it, 'W-A-I-T... F-O-R... S-I-G-N-A-L.'"

Cooper raised his phone and said, "Abort the mission. Repeat, abort the mission. Return to base and await further instructions."

Almost simultaneously, the flickering stopped. The grainy figure of Keen got to her feet and rejoined the others.

Chapter 31

"That's enough!" Yancy barked at Keen. "If you're so delicate that you're already cramping up, the bettors deserve to know it so they don't waste any money on you."

Keen had no way of knowing if her message had gotten through, if it had even been recognized as a message. As she got to her feet and joined the others, followed by snickers from some of the other ringers, she resisted the urge to look to the sky and try to find the drone that she knew was up there. She knew she wouldn't have been able to see it anyway. And if the tac team came in, well, they'd all know it soon enough.

"During the games, you can wear whatever you want," Yancy announced, "but for the Combine, our bettors need to know what you're made of, and they need to be able to compare you objectively. On that table over there, next to the towels, you'll find white overalls with your names on them, or whatever stupid nickname you choose to go by." He drew a mixture of snorts and scowls with that. "So go find your new uniform and change into it. You can leave your ratty-assed gang colors or camo under the table until we're done. Now let's get moving."

Keen moved with the rest of them over to the table, determined not to be the first or the last, or to show any fear or trepidation. The outfits had been arranged in neat stacks, by size, but by the time the first wave of ringers had found theirs, the bundles were all jumbled together.

She found hers all the way to the left, with the smallest of them. She tore open the plastic and found a single white garment, more a jumpsuit than coveralls.

She turned to Yancy. "There's no shoes."

He laughed. "That's right, princess. We're doing this barefoot. If you got a problem with it, you are more than welcome to leave." He laughed again and drew his sidearm, standing there with an expectant look on his face, like he was waiting for her answer. He waited two seconds, then holstered the gun and said, "Hurry up and get changed."

The other two women were already pulling on their jumpsuits. The Kenyan was called Ebuya, apparently, and the Iraqi was called Masri. The men were in various stages of undress, including some who apparently took seriously the many meanings of commando. There were a variety of musculatures, from massive steroid bulk to taut and wiry, but all hard and strong. And they seemed to all be looking at her.

She knew the longer she put it off, the more attention would be focused on her, so she slid off her boots and socks, pulled off her black jeans and her sweater. For a moment, she stood there in her cotton bra and panties, feeling incredibly exposed with the sun and the breeze and all those eyes on her skin. Then she quickly stepped into the jumpsuit, which was a light synthetic fabric with a lot of Lycra. The front and back said LE CHAT in bold black characters. She realized how ridiculous it was, with the very real possibility that she was going to die in this mission, but she was very glad to be clothed again.

As she buttoned up the front of it, she looked down at her pedicured toes, the nails painted to conceal the transmitter.

Oh, no, she thought. The transmitter. It had never occurred to her that they'd be doing anything barefoot, for god's sake. The adhesive was strong, but it was made to be removable and repositionable. She would have to be incredibly careful not to dislodge it.

Before she could worry about it any longer, Yancy blew a whistle and announced the first event—the four hundred meters. She looked at the bare feet around her, some huge, others jagged with gnarled and broken toenails.

She'd have to stay out of the pack to avoid getting stepped on. Probably not a bad idea anyway.

Yancy directed them to line up at the starting line and pulled his gun. A real gun. No need for a starter's pistol out here. He fired it into the air and they started running.

Keen started along with everyone else, but then held back. As she expected, the rest of the ringers ran flat out and immediately condensed into a thick knot, jostling and elbowing each other. Before anyone had run a hundred meters, the Iraqi woman went sprawling, obviously shoved by someone in the pack. She went down hard but hooked out an arm and a leg, sending three other runners stumbling and careening into others.

Keen stayed well away from them. The surface of the track was spongy, almost soft, and actually quite forgiving on her bare feet.

As the pack moved past the halfway point, the elbows stayed active. One of the big guys must have gotten too aggressive with one of his counterparts, because at one point a loud grunt exploded from the middle of the pack, and a massive bear of a man stumbled sideways across the track, his nose bloody and his eyes vacant.

Keen wove around him and noticed that several of the fallen runners were catching up behind her.

Three-quarters of the way around the track, Keen moved to the outside lane, well away from anyone else, and arced around the pack. For a moment her competitive nature urged her to try to win the race, but she resisted, finishing respectably in the top third.

For the next forty-five minutes, Yancy guided them all through the rest of the challenges, most of which—long jump, climbing wall, high stepping through tires—seemed intentionally designed to remove a transmitter adhered to a toenail.

Throughout the course of the events, the ringers seemed to self select into two categories. None of them let down their guard, but half of them demonstrated willingness to share an occasional obliquely friendly head shake or eye roll at some ridiculous aspect of the situation. Chief among these were the one-eyed Iraqi woman, Masri, and a bearded Nigerian named Okoye, who at times seemed almost catatonic, but at other times quite civil, even friendly.

Keen thought of this group as the "humans."

The other half of the ringers shared almost no social contact and smiled only at someone else's pain or misfortune, especially if they themselves were the source of it. Chief among these were a Chechen named Dudayev and a massive South African named

Boden, who seemed to be the sociopathic equivalent of friends, and the bald Australian giant, whose name was apparently Titus.

Neither of those groups included the nervous young man who had been staring at her earlier. But now Keen saw the name on his jumpsuit, BOROVA, which explained why he was staring at her. He was LeCroix's husband.

Chapter 32

Reddington arrived at the temporary field office less than fifteen minutes after Cooper called him. He took a seat and placed his hat on Cooper's desk, then listened patiently and implacably as Cooper and Aram explained what had happened with the video feed and Agent Keen's coded message, the aborted launch of the tac team, and the dismaying fact that the FBI's distributed network had failed to decrypt the satellite feed.

"And it didn't just stall," Aram told him. "It simply gave up—the progress bar hung at three percent for twenty minutes, and then the system announced that the code was unbreakable."

Reddington turned to Cooper. "Always expect the unexpected. Isn't that right, Harold?"

Cooper shrugged, conceding the point.

"That's why I didn't want you sending Lizzie in there," Reddington continued. "It was a bad idea, a deeply flawed plan, and it could cost Lizzie's life."

Cooper spread his hands. "I'm not any happier about where we are now than you are, but we all know a certain amount of danger comes with the job.

Fortunately, we may have caught a break in all this."

"And what is that?"

Cooper turned to Aram and gestured for him to explain.

"When I couldn't break the video uplink's encryption system, I started digging into the little bit of analysis the system was able to complete. I realized it was some type of military intelligence encryption, one that I had never encountered, but it had some similarities to a system called RIX, developed by Army Intelligence. It's even more similar to a system called ARIX-34, which was based on RIX. ARIX-34 is a proprietary encryption technology developed by Hoagland Services to encrypt multichannel signals. There are a few advanced systems that can break it now, but up until recently, it was state of the art."

"Hoagland Services. The military contractor?"

Cooper cut in. "Hoagland was acquired by G78 in a controversial takeover several years ago and G78 ceased to exist a year later. The CIA employed both companies extensively. Pretty much everything else about the two companies has been classified in the name of national security. When I requested access to the records, I was rebuffed."

"So you called me."

Cooper shrugged. "I could have initiated an official process to get them released, which would have taken months and resulted in a thick sheaf of pages redacted beyond recognition. But I know we both want to get to the bottom of this, and to do what's best for Agent Keen. Do you know anything about them?"

Reddington looked dubious. "I knew Michael Hoagland. He founded Hoagland Services with five thousand dollars and two tons of stolen guns, and he turned it into one of the most sought-after military contractors in the world. Hoagland was brilliant and ruthless in battle and in the boardroom." He smiled and shook his head. "He'd always been a little bit crazy—a prerequisite of the job, I guess. I think it contributed to his success. His competitors often suffered curiously timed misfortunes. I remember once, Hoagland had been underbid on an oil field security job in Bahrain. The next day, someone tipped off a local warlord about the time and location of the competitor's convoy. Six IEDs took out twelve of their vehicles, leaving them unable to fulfill the contract. Hoagland became the Bahrainis' go-to security company for the next ten years. As the company grew bigger, Hoagland himself became increasingly unstable. When he started talking about moving the company's headquarters to Peru, the board started talking about ousting Hoagland from his own company. He called a meeting at the proposed new headquarters with the board and the entire senior staff. No one knows for sure what happened, but apparently rebel forces in the area caught wind of the meeting and attacked with mortars. Took out Hoagland, his entire board and most of his senior management."

"My God," Aram whispered, despite himself.

Reddington continued. "The company was in a shambles. Another military contractor, G78, one of Hoagland's rivals, came in and bought what was left of it at a fire sale price. Its founder was a man named Edward Stannis, equally brilliant and ruthless. Both companies and both men were based in Dallas. Their rivalry was sometimes personal as well as global and strategic. A lot of Hoagland's remaining people left, maybe out of loyalty—they were said to be almost cult-like in their devotion to Hoagland—or because they didn't like the change. Maybe they were traumatized by losing Hoagland and their entire command structure. Shortly afterward, Hoagland's widow, Dorothy, married Stannis. I guess she had a type. No word on how well they knew each other before Hoagland's untimely demise. Or timely, I guess, depending on how you look at it. A year later the happy couple liquidated the company and disappeared, apparently to a private island somewhere." He turned to Cooper. "But what you've told me isn't much of a break. What else do you know?"

Cooper turned to Aram and nodded.

"Last night we got a hit on a set of fingerprints Navabi sent us from the Turkish factory fire," Aram said. "Simon Wall, a former civilian DOD employee who later worked for both Hoagland Services and G78."

Reddington's eyebrows inched up. "Interesting. What else?"

Cooper nodded for Aram to continue.

"When I dug into RIX, I found that Simon Wall was one of the lead developers."

"And where is Wall now?" Reddington asked.

"We don't know," Cooper replied. "We're hoping maybe you can help us locate him, without letting him know we're onto him."

Reddington picked up his hat. "Is that everything?"

Cooper nodded, but Aram said, "Actually, there is something else. I just found a mention of Wall in an FBI file. It says that after he left G78, he helped form a group called Hackers Helping Humans, or H3."

"Hackers?" Cooper asked.

Aram nodded and read from a printed page. "H3's website describes itself as 'A secretive humanitarian group that uses hacking as a tool to fight against oppression and war and to provide aid and comfort to its victims.' There has been no sign of him since then."

"I'm familiar with H3," Reddington said. "Some less-than-savory former associates of mine have been taken down following embarrassing data dumps. The Dead Ring is about everything that H3 is supposed to be against. Perhaps he was working undercover."

Cooper frowned. "Yes, but for which side?"

Chapter 33

After two hours of athletics under the West Texas sun, Keen was hot, tired, and sweaty. The anxiety over being undercover amid several dozen psychotic killers had faded into the background, and keeping her toe out of harm's way while performing the requisite athletic tasks became second nature. Physical discomfort had risen to primary importance.

By the time Yancy announced they were done, Keen was dying to get out of her sweat-soaked jumpsuit, but she had no interest in changing again in front of her fellow ringers. Several of the men were watching her—most conspicuously Boden and Dudayev. She noticed the other women heading back toward the cabins in their jumpsuits, so she gathered up her clothes and her boots and followed them.

She had just turned down the thoroughfare and passed the first row of cabins when she was grabbed by the collar from behind and thrown to the side, into the narrow space between two of the cabins. She dropped her clothes and put out her hands, but still almost sprawled on the ground. By the time she got her legs under her and turned to face her attacker, he was on her.

It was the bald Australian with the burned ear, Titus. He clamped his hand around her throat and slammed her against one of the cabins, then thrust his face out so it was almost touching hers.

"Who the hell are you?" he hissed.

His hand was cutting off her air and her vision was starting to dim. She knew she had to act fast. He was holding her up on her tiptoes, so she had no leverage from the ground. She placed one foot against the wall behind her, trying to brace herself so she could kick him hard with the other.

"I'm Le Chat," she hissed back, her throat constricted. "Who the hell are you?"

He laughed. "If you were Le Chat, you'd know who I was. Because I'm the guy who killed her."

As soon as he said it, she recognized his eyes. When she'd seen him before, at the Yellow Rose, everything else had been hidden under his wild mane of red hair and his big, bushy beard.

The burn made sense if he'd gotten caught in the explosion. The shaved head, too.

She finally got her foot planted against the wall, and she kicked him as hard as she could in the groin.

He let out a grunt, but didn't loosen his grip. Instead, with an angry, evil smile, he tightened it.

Keen's vision was rapidly fading now. Through the rushing in her ears, she heard a strange sound, like tearing paper, but metallic. Titus loosened his grip, and she sucked in enough air that her vision cleared somewhat.

As Titus half turned around, she heard a zipping sound and saw a spray of red. Then he let go of her altogether.

She slid to the ground, coughing, and as her vision continued to clear, she saw Titus from behind, clutching at one bloody eye. He growled and stepped forward, then he stopped, fell to his knees, and tumbled onto the ground as blood spurted out of his throat.

Borova stepped toward her over Titus's body. In his hand was half a soda can, torn jagged, folded to a point, and dripping with blood.

He held it under her throat. "Who are you?" he demanded. "And if you say Le Chat, I'll kill you, too." His voice was hoarse, almost cracking.

Keen scrambled to her feet. She could hear others approaching. "My name is Keen," she said, massaging her throat. "Marianne LeCroix is dead. I'm sorry. She was fatally injured at the Yellow Rose. She told me your plan before she died. She asked me to help get you out of here."

Borova was stunned, his eyes welling up. But Keen got the impression he already knew LeCroix was dead, even if he hadn't admitted it to himself.

"We weren't supposed to be here," he said. "I just... I didn't know what to do. I hoped Marianne would show up."

Miraculously, considering how much blood was on the ground and on Titus, there was hardly any of it on either of them, just a few streaks and spatters on Borova's right hand.

"Right now, we need to hide him and get out of here," she said. "Put that down."

He dropped the jagged can and she kicked it under the cabin. Together they slid Titus's body as far underneath the cabin as they could.

The voices were getting closer.

She gathered her clothes and boots then pulled him by the elbow, down the two rows of cabins, and around the corner.

"Which cabin are you in?" she said.

"Seventeen," he said, dazed. "Was he working for Corbeaux?" he asked, nodding in the direction of the man he had just killed.

"No," she said, looking both ways and then pulling him along to the next row of cabins, until they were outside number seventeen. "It was this sick game. But I'm trying to take it down, the people who set it up, and the people who support it. Including Corbeaux."

He looked up at that, terrified but energized at the prospect of revenge.

"I'm not going to survive in here," he said, his breath fast and shallow, like it was getting away from him. "Marianne was the strong one. We weren't supposed to still be here. I only came here because I hoped somehow she might show up, too."

"Look," she said, giving his shoulders a firm but gentle shake. "We're going to shut this down as soon as it starts. You won't have to survive the game. You just have to survive the first five minutes of it. But I might need your help. So I need you to stay alive, okay?"

He nodded again.

"Good. Now get inside and wash off that blood before they find the body."

As he stumbled inside, she took off running, and she didn't stop until she was inside her own cabin.

Chapter 34

Navabi opened the door to her motel room at the second knock, looking none the worse for wear. "Welcome back," Red said with a smile, handing her a cup of coffee. "Quite a whirlwind tour you had there."

She smiled ruefully and nodded to Dembe, standing behind him. "Not the most relaxing trip, but high on the productivity scale."

"So I gathered. I spoke to Cooper and Aram."

"I know. Ressler's on his way here to pick me up. We're headed to Dallas to see if we can turn up anything on Stannis."

"Good thinking. I was hoping we could talk for a moment, before you left."

She stood back from the door. "Of course."

Dembe waited outside.

The motel room was humble but clean—bed, bath, armchair, and a wooden desk and chair. Red turned the desk chair around and sat on it, placing his hat on the desk behind him. "The operation seems to have gone a bit sideways."

"Because they're unable to decrypt the uplink?"

"Because they sent Lizzie in there at great risk, and

now they're unable to decrypt the uplink."

Navabi shrugged and sipped her coffee.

He told her how the encryption was similar to RIX and ARIX-34, and how they had IDed Simon Wall's fingerprints.

She put down her coffee. "His prints were at the control room?"

"No, at the other site, where the men were drugged."

She sat back, processing that.

"An interesting twist to Simon Wall's career is that after G78 folded, he is thought to have helped form a group called Hackers Helping Humans."

"H3? Really? That doesn't make sense if he's involved in this stuff."

Red sat forward. "So, I need to clarify a few things, Agent Navabi. There were four men found drugged at this other site, where the police thought there was a robbery or an abduction, correct? And their prints were also found at the control room site?"

"That's right."

"But where the men were drugged, there was also a fifth set of prints, belonging to Simon Wall?"

"That's what you just told me."

"And the four men were drugged with remifentanil gas, but there was a syringe found at the scene that contained naloxone, which is an antidote to remifentanil?"

Her eyes widened ever so slightly. "You think it wasn't a robbery or an abduction," she said.

"I think it was a rescue."

As she sat there considering it, Dembe knocked on and then opened the door. He gave Red a nod and held up a cell phone.

Reddington stood and grabbed his hat. "Good luck

in Dallas, Agent Navabi," he said. "I'll let you know if I find anything."

As he slipped out the door, he put the phone to his ear and said, "Hello?"

The voice on the other end sounded like a bag of wet rocks. "Is Reddington?"

"Koltov, my friend. How's the knock-off oxycontin business treating you?"

"Do not even joke," he said in a thick Siberian accent. "I heard you are looking for me."

"I am, Koltov. I am indeed. There's only a few people I know who move remifentanil, but I know it's a specialty of yours. There was an incident exactly a year ago in Turkey. Someone used remifentanil gas to incapacitate a small security crew. I want you to tell me who the seller was, and who the buyer was."

"Don't know remifentanil."

Reddington laughed as he got into the back seat of the car. "Ivan, Ivan, Ivan, there was a minute there when I thought we weren't going to do this little dance. I do so love to dance. But I prefer to lead, as I think you know. So... this is where I remind you that your boss doesn't know about the fact that you are not only stealing his stolen oxycontin and substituting it with your own bathtub concoctions, but that you are selling the real stuff to his main competitor. And then I point out to you, if you haven't figured it out, that while he doesn't know about it, I do. And then we both laugh at how hilarious it would be if I told him. Remember?"

Red listened for a moment to the silence on the other end of the phone, then let out a big, not entirely fake, laugh. "Ah, that was fun. But now let's get back to business. You were about to tell me about the remifentanil."

"You want remifentanil?"

"No, I want to know who has been buying remifentanil, and you are going to tell me, or I'm going to get in touch with Gulavitch and tell him about your hilarious pranks, remember? The ones you didn't think were that funny and that Gulavitch will think are even less funny."

Koltov sighed over the phone. "Customers pay for discretion."

"I'm giving you my discretion for free—and offering you your life at a very low price."

He let out a sigh. "I sold remifentanil. Buyer was hacker named Kevin Burton. Lives in Los Angeles."

Chapter 35

As soon as she got inside, Keen slammed the door and flattened herself against the wall, taking deep breaths and trying to slow her heart rate, to calm herself down. She was drenched in sweat, her jumpsuit soaked and clinging to her skin. She was dying to get out of it, but she knew at any moment Titus's body would be discovered. She was waiting for some kind of alarm or commotion. But the seconds ticked by, then the minutes, and there was nothing, just the conversational tones of the other ringers outside—muttering, snickering, complaining about this or that—as they returned to their cabins.

After five minutes, she started to relax a little bit. Her feet were dirty and sore and she was dying to peel off her jumpsuit and get in the shower. First, she got herself a glass of water from the tap and drank it. Then, looking down as she put her glass on the table, she gasped.

The transmitter was gone from her toe.

"Oh, no," she whispered, crouching down to examine her toe more closely, cursing as she confirmed it was indeed missing.

It had been there when she finished the Combine. It must have become dislodged when Titus attacked her. When she was kicking him. She cursed him, glad that he was dead.

She thought about changing, putting on her own clothes and some goddamn shoes, but she knew she couldn't waste a second. The transmitter was probably out there in the dust, right where she and Titus had fought. Right in front of where she and Borova had stashed his body. At any moment, someone was going to discover him, and then it would be too late.

She slipped out the door and paused, looking both ways, and then hurried around the corner of the cabin.

She smelled them before she saw them. Sweat and testosterone, stupidity and menace—all mixed with the almost musky stink of pot smoke.

Boden and Dudayev, the psychopals who had been making a show of staring at her earlier. Boden was passing the joint to Dudayev.

She tried not to think about how they had smuggled it in.

Turning the corner, she practically bumped into them, but she angled around them and kept moving. She was in a hurry.

Boden stepped out in front of her, blocking her way. "See what I mean, Dudayev?" he said, holding up the joint. "If you wish hard enough, the fates will provide."

Dudayev laughed and stepped behind her, blocking her retreat.

"Get out of my way," Keen said, with as much bravado as she could muster. She was still more concerned about the transmitter being discovered than about whatever these two had in mind.

Over Boden's shoulder, she saw Okoye

approaching, the friendly but maybe somewhat unstable Nigerian. Boden turned to look at him, and she tried to take advantage of the distraction to slip away. But Dudayev was fast and he was strong, clamping his forearm around her neck in a flash and holding her tight.

Dudayev was her main concern, but Boden would be a bigger problem soon enough. While he was still looking at Okoye she used Dudayev to brace herself and put everything she had into her right leg. With Dudayev lifting her backwards, her aim was not what it might have been, but she connected with the top of her foot to something soft, and Boden dropped without ever turning back around.

Okoye looked on, amused, still approaching. "Let the lady go," he said.

Keen struggled to get free, but Dudayev's arm was like a steel bar.

"This doesn't concern you, friend," Dudayev said. "Just keep walking."

Boden rolled over on the ground, groaning and clutching his groin.

Okoye's eye twitched violently for a moment, but he shook his head and smiled again. "Come on, man. Save it for the game."

"I said keep walking."

Okoye's arm flashed out so quickly Keen barely saw it. For a microsecond she thought he was striking her, but his arm passed over her shoulder and she heard a loud clapping noise behind her head as his hand connected with Dudayev's ear.

The Chechen immediately let go of her and howled, stamping his foot as he clamped his hand over his ear.

Keen stepped away from Dudayev and Boden.

"Thanks," she told Okoye as she stepped around him to hurry on her way.

He put his hand on her arm, leaned in close, and said, "I know you are not Le Chat."

Chapter 36

Before Keen could react, the air erupted with the screaming wail of a siren. A voice came over the loudspeaker, tersely directing all ringers to report to the main square immediately.

Ringers emerged from just about every cabin, filing down the rows toward the center of the campground, asking each other what they thought was going on. Keen and Okoye looked at each other and went along with them.

She desperately wondered what he meant—was he saying he knew her real identity was LeCroix, or did he know she wasn't Le Chat at all? Did he know she was undercover, working for the FBI? Was he threatening her with exposure? He seemed a decent enough guy, and he had come to her assistance, but that didn't necessarily count for much.

She wanted desperately to know, but she was almost grateful for the interruption so she didn't have to ask him, at least not yet. She needed to think.

As they approached the main square, she refocused her anxiety from Okoye and what he did or didn't know, to whether they had discovered Titus's body, and what would be the ramifications from that.

Enough of the ringers were military trained that they lined up as a matter of course. She got into formation and Okoye stepped up next to her. A few seconds later, Dudayev and Boden arrived, walking gingerly and staring daggers at them both.

Clearly, she and Okoye had made a couple of enemies.

Yancy and Corson had emerged from their cabins and strode toward the main square flanked by a pair of PMCs. Corson was visibly furious, his scar even redder than the rest of his face. It was hard to tell with Yancy—he always looked angry. As they approached the front of the square, one of the PMCs came up and spoke to Yancy, then the two of them walked off.

"There's been an egregious violation of the rules," Corson roared. "One of our contestants has been murdered!"

The crowd had already been buzzing at a low level, and the buzz remained absolutely unchanged, with no variation in tone, timbre, or volume. A few ringers looked around, trying to figure out who had been killed, but for the most part they didn't seem to really care.

"When we find out who is responsible, there will be severe repercussions," he said. Keen looked around and saw no sign of Borova. "You people know why you are here. If you want to kill each other, fine, but save it for the game. Goddamn it, the first round is tomorrow at daybreak, so you savages need to hold off on killing each other for twelve goddamn hours."

Yancy came back and hurried up to him, whispered in his ear and handed him something. Keen's heart sank.

Corson pushed Yancy aside and held up Keen's lost

transmitter. "We found this at the site of the murder," he said with a sly smile. "I don't know what the hell it is, but it looks important. Perhaps the rule-breaker is missing something?"

A moment later, one of the PMCs ran up and said, "Borova is not in his cabin."

"Search the grounds," Corson barked, sending them scrambling. Then he turned to Yancy. "Get the bee."

Yancy grinned. It was a terrible thing.

"Perhaps there have been two infractions, or perhaps we've found our violator," Corson said. "Either way, you will see what happens to those who break my rules."

A few minutes later, a trio of PMCs returned. "No sign of him, sir," one of them reported.

Corson smiled. Yancy returned, pushing some kind of cart with fat, rugged tires. It had a large black box on the bottom shelf, a smaller box on the middle shelf, and a monitor screen on the top. Yancy quickly pulled the boxes out and put them on the ground.

He opened the smaller box and removed a tablet computer, which he handed to Corson. Corson handed him Keen's transmitter, and Yancy put it in his shirt pocket.

The screen came to life, a flat gray rectangle.

Corson manipulated the tablet with his thumbs, and the larger box began to hum. The top opened and a quadcopter drone rose out of it, hovering in the air six feet off the ground. It was sleek but almost flimsy except for what looked like a gray brick attached to its underside and a spherical camera mounted next to that.

A picture appeared on the screen, a shaky image of the assembled ringers. As the drone slowly rotated, the picture panned around until it showed a distressing close-up of Corson's face.

Corson moved his thumbs and the drone rose high up into the sky. The camera angled down and the view on the screen showed an aerial view of the campground, rapidly shrinking.

The camera angled out a few degrees, and slowly rotated. Corson and Yancy stared intently at the screen as the horizon scrolled past, coming to a jerky stop focused on a small cloud of dust in the distance. The image zoomed in, revealing a lone figure stumbling across the desert, dragging his feet and kicking up dust.

Simultaneously, the quadcopter buzzed loudly, zipping away out of sight, and the image on the screen pulled sharply back out of the zoom, and then began to grow once more, slowly.

Everyone was silent, watching, the lone, distant figure slowly drawing closer on the screen. In less than a minute, the figure had resolved once more into the distinct figure of a man, faltering as he ran. As the drone approached, he looked up over his shoulder.

It was Borova. His face twisted in horror and he ran just a tiny bit faster.

Corson and Yancy looked at each other, then Corson slid his thumb across the tablet. The camera image centered Borova, then surged forward, so close the drone must have been almost touching him, its shadow large across his back.

Then the screen flashed and turned to static.

A few seconds later, the thin crack of a small, distant explosion echoed past them.

They had blown him up. Borova was dead.

Chapter 37

"What's g-going on?" the Cowboy asked, his voice already shrill with fear. "What is it?"

The technician turned to look into the shadows, waiting for a nod before he continued. "One of the ringers was found murdered."

On the screens, Corson had the ringers lined up in formation, reading them the riot act. He held something up in his hand.

"What's that?" the Cowboy asked.

"I don't know. Some sort of contraband," the technician replied.

Everyone in the room went quiet for a moment, listening to their earpieces—all except for the Cowboy and the figure in the back of the room, in the shadows, tapping at his keypad.

"What's g-going *on*?" the Cowboy demanded, his voice rising in pitch, indignant that he was being left out.

"I don't know, sir, but Corson doesn't seem to think it's important," the technician announced into the shadows. "Wait, one of the other ringers is missing..." He raised his voice a notch. "We have a runner."

They all went silent again, except for the *tap-tap-tap*.

"Yes, sir," the technician said in reply to some silent command.

They watched the screen in silence as Yancy wheeled over the cart and launched the bee. One of the darkened screens in the mobile control room came to life, showing the camera feed from the bee as it rose into the sky, locked onto the small figure on the horizon, and zoomed toward it.

The small room filled with palpable excitement as the figure running across the desert grew on the screen, as he looked over his shoulder in terror, and as the screen went dark.

The room went silent except for hoarse, heavy breathing coming from the back.

The technician cleared his throat, awkwardly, and announced, "The target has been taken out."

Chapter 38

"Hello, Kevin Burton. My name is Raymond Reddington."

Red was sitting in Burton's living room, as he had been for the past twenty minutes waiting for Burton to return home. Dembe was in the bedroom, out of sight but there if he was needed. Red knew he wouldn't be.

Burton shrieked and dropped the bag in his hand. It hit the wood floor with a wet smack, rupturing and releasing a spurt of what looked like pad Thai. Judging from the filth that coated the floor, it might not have been the first time that had happened.

"Who are you?" Burton demanded, his voice trembling. He was fat and soft and hairy and unkempt, wearing a T-shirt with a superhero on it whose physique made Burton's look that much worse by comparison.

Red cocked an eyebrow at him and gave him a second.

"Well, what are you doing here? What do you want?"

"Sit down, Kevin." Red moved the gun ever so slightly, just enough to draw Burton's eyes to it, to remind him of the power dynamic.

Burton sat, obediently, on the sofa across from the

armchair Red was sitting in.

"You're going to tell me where to find Simon Wall."

"I don't even know who—"

"I know you were the one who got the remifentanil."

Burton's eyes crystalized into twin orbs of panic and fear.

"Pretty ambitious, that rescue operation," Red conceded. "It's impressive that you people at H3 were able to pull it off, with your specialty being so much more focused in the virtual realm. I know you've been keeping quiet about it." He laughed. "And that's a pretty smart impulse, because the people you went up against are extremely active in the physical realm, if you know what I mean. And they do not know how to take a joke."

"What do you want?"

"It's nice of you to offer."

"I didn't—"

"I want you to tell me where to find Simon Wall."

"Simon? I don't know where he is."

"Yes you do."

"I can't tell you—"

"Yes you can."

"I don't know—"

"Kevin, please. This is going to end with you telling me where Simon Wall is. There is no other way either of us is leaving this room. I appreciate that he's your friend. I appreciate that you went to great lengths to bust him out of that room in Turkey."

Burton paled and looked around, as if he was checking to make sure there wasn't anyone else around who could have heard what Red had just said.

"But here's the thing," Red continued. "I am not going to hurt Simon Wall, and I am not going to let any harm come to him. Believe it or not, he and I are going to be working on the same side of something—something he will want to be involved with. So I am not going to muss a hair on his head." He smiled and raised the gun.

"But I'm not going to be working with you." He waggled the gun back and forth between them. "You and I are not on the same side of this fight or anything else. So I can't make you the same guarantee. You can tell me where he is now, while you're still a young man in... well, not 'good health,' but for the sake of argument let's say 'fair health.' Or you can tell me two minutes from now, between screams while you roll around on the floor clutching the bloody, shredded remains of your left kneecap. And if you're tougher than either of us really thinks you are, you can tell me in four minutes, while clutching both ruined knees, and wondering, if you make me pull the trigger a third time, will the last time you had sex end up being, well... the last time you had sex."

There was a distinct possibility that the next time Burton had sex would be the first time he had sex, but that might have even given the message some added heft.

Burton had gone white and was starting to turn green. He had a hand clamped over each kneecap and his legs were pressed together firmly enough to earn a nun's approval. A tear rolled down his cheek, and for a moment Red felt bad, but this was important, Red was in a hurry, and a few tears now would probably save Kevin Burton a lot more in the very near future.

"You promise you won't hurt him?"

"Him? Yes. You? Only if you tell me where to find him in the next thirty seconds."

Red looked at his watch for emphasis.

"Okay. Okay. He's here in LA. In Canoga Park." Red

moved the gun another fraction of an inch. "I'll write down the address."

Burton got up and found a pen and paper, scribbled the address and handed it to Red.

"Thank you," Red said, taking it. "And if you warn him I'm coming, you know I'll be back here. And there won't be anything I'll need from you other than to show you the error of your ways."

Burton nodded briskly, but once Red put away his gun, some of his color returned and he seemed momentarily emboldened.

"You know, it's not so smart to mess with hackers. We can mess up your life in ways you can't even imagine."

Red nodded, thinking about it. Then he took his gun out again and raised it. "I guess you're right. I should probably kill you now, just in case."

Burton gasped and took a step backward, clenching his eyes and holding up his arms in front of his face. "Sorry," he said. "I won't do anything, I swear it."

As he said it, Dembe stepped silently out from the bedroom so he was standing directly behind Burton.

"Luckily for you, I don't have to worry about such things," Red said. "But Burton..." He waited until Burton opened his eyes. "Don't make me come back."

Before he could reply, Dembe whispered from behind him, "Excuse me," causing Burton to shriek and jump out of the way.

"Thank you," Dembe said, following Red as he walked out the door.

Dembe closed the door behind him, and as they walked down the hallway, they heard Burton gag and what sounded like more pad Thai hitting the floor.

Red winced in distaste. "I hope he made it to the bathroom."

Chapter 39

Highland Park was an upscale area of North Dallas, half an hour from the airport. The tiny police department there still had an open file on Edward and Dorothy Stannis's disappearance.

Red had explained that Edward Stannis and his bride had cashed out and disappeared to live like royalty in some third-world paradise. Their families weren't so sure. Navabi and Ressler were meeting a detective named Tim Scheller to debrief and take a look at the case file. Then they were going to interview the family in light of recent developments.

They were halfway from the airport to the police station when Navabi got a call.

"Hello, Aram," she said, answering it.

"Hi, Agent Navabi." He sounded nervous, like he always was when speaking with her, but he also sounded down.

"Is everything okay?"

Ressler looked over while driving, trying to read the situation.

"Yes, it's fine. Agent Keen is fine and everything. Director Cooper asked me to update you, though, that David Borova is dead."

She put him on speaker and he told them what had happened.

"Jesus," Ressler said. "They've got drones?"

"Apparently," Aram replied. "Director Cooper has ordered us to pull ours back so they aren't detected by theirs."

Ressler cursed under his breath. "We should be there," he started, but Navabi held up a hand to silence him.

He had been complaining like hell about not being there to go in with the tac team in case the signal from Keen came in while they were in Dallas. Navabi wasn't crazy about not being there either, but she understood. This could be nothing, or it could be an important part of the investigation.

"Thanks for letting us know, Aram. Is there anything else?"

"No. No, that's it."

"Okay. We should be back there in a few hours."

As soon as she got off the phone, Ressler started up again, but she cut him off.

"Okay," she snapped. "I know. So let's get these interviews done, see if there's anything to uncover and get back there before we miss anything."

Scheller didn't wear a rumpled trench coat, but he was the kind of cop that would have if he'd been working anywhere north of there. He had a saggy gut, yellow teeth, and piercingly intelligent eyes.

They met in a coffee shop three blocks from his HQ. He had a muffin and a coffee and a file on the table in front of him.

They shook hands all around and he invited them to sit.

"Hope the flight was okay and the drive wasn't too bad," he said, turning the file around and sliding it across the table toward them. "This is what we have. It ain't much."

He asked if they wanted coffee and when they said yes, he motioned to the waitress while they examined the file.

Most of it consisted of bank documents: asset transfers, stock liquidations, account closures. All of it was from within three days of the last confirmed sighting of Edward and Dorothy Stannis, at a banquet at their country club, eight years earlier.

There were witness statements, too. Dorothy Stannis's sister Renee and Edward Stannis's brother Nick. Ed and Dorothy Stannis had told friends they were going to their lake house for a couple days after the banquet. Four days later, they both began missing appointments. That's when their absence was first noticed.

There were crime scene photos of the house, which did not look like a crime scene and probably wasn't. While liquidating their accounts, Edward and Dorothy had also donated the house to a local charity that Dorothy Stannis had been supporting for years.

Navabi looked at the file again then up at Ressler. He nodded that he was done, so she closed it and slid it back to Scheller.

"It's interesting, but there's not much in there," Navabi said.

Scheller shook his head. "Nope. There wasn't much out there. But it is interesting. Anyway, unfortunately, it turns out Nick Stannis died six months ago. Lung cancer. But I called Renee Selby, Dorothy Stannis's sister, and she's expecting you."

"So what do you think really happened?" Navabi asked.

Scheller sat back and scratched his neck. "With the Stannises disappearing? If I had to bet, I'd say they probably cashed out, like everybody said. They liquidated everything, transferred it all offshore. I guess they decided to enjoy their money while they were still young enough to." He shrugged. "Mrs. Stannis was a lovely woman. Sweet as can be. I don't think it had been easy being married to her first husband."

"Michael Hoagland," Ressler said.

"That's right. He was a bit of a mean cuss." Scheller looked around and put up his hands, defensively. "Don't get me wrong. He was a hero, and everything. And more power to him, building that company, and helping to support the troops and all that. But he could have been nicer to her."

"Evidence of physical abuse?" Navabi asked.

Scheller leaned forward. "I never took any calls, so I can't say for sure, but if he did, he had the kind of juice that'd make those calls go away, I imagine. Sorry to say it." He looked at his watch. "I need to get back to the station. Do you need anything else?"

"One more question, if you don't mind," Navabi said. "Did you have any thoughts about what happened to Hoagland? About Stannis buying the company and marrying the widow so soon after?"

Scheller smiled and looked at his watch again. "I'll tell you what. Give me a call after you talk to Renee Selby. Then we'll compare notes."

Chapter 40

Renee Selby's house was massive, lush, and meticulously groomed. It was not the nicest house on her block, but it was definitely one of them. And it was a nice block.

"Geez," Ressler said, as they pulled into the driveway. It was the fourth time he'd said it in the past five minutes, as the houses had gotten progressively bigger.

Selby was waiting for them as they pulled up. Early sixties, she had snow white hair, attractively styled. She seemed as meticulously groomed as her house.

"How do you do, Mrs. Selby," Navabi said as they got out. "Thanks for agreeing to see us."

"Not at all," she said with a practiced smile. "I'm glad to help. Come inside."

They followed her into the cool interior, a marble vestibule, followed by a luxurious formal living room, and then finally a comfortable sun porch, light but well air conditioned, with sturdy wicker furniture and plush cushions.

Navabi and Ressler sat on the sofa. Selby perched on the edge of the armchair, her posture perfect as she looked at them across the coffee table.

"So," she said, folding her hands on her lap. "What can I do for you?"

"Mrs. Selby, we're investigating a case that might be somehow related to Hoagland Services and G78. We wanted to ask you a few questions about when your sister and Edward Stannis disappeared."

She nodded, her face darkening slightly. "I don't know what happened to my sister, but I can tell you one thing: she would never have left without saying goodbye to me. Without keeping in touch." She shook her head. "I don't care what they say."

"What kind of a man was Edward Stannis?" Ressler asked.

She shrugged. "He was good to Dorothy. I must say, I didn't care for the business both of her husbands were in. I didn't like it at all. When her first husband died, I somewhat hoped she'd no longer be involved in all that. But... well, apart from that Edward was perfectly nice. And he adored my sister. Treated her like a princess." She laughed as she said it, as if at some faded memory. Then her laughter faded, too. "Not like her first husband, Michael."

"That's Michael Hoagland?" Navabi prompted.

"Yes. They got married quite young, you know. He came from a good family, but he went into the military and it changed him."

"Changed him how?"

"He just came back... meaner."

"And what exactly happened to Michael Hoagland?" Navabi asked. She'd heard one version of the story. She wanted to see if there was another.

She looked off into the distance. "Well, who knows, really? Those companies get up to all sorts of crazy stuff. The story, as I understood it, is that Hoagland and his top people were in a meeting in Peru, at their base of operations there. Rebels attacked the place with bombs or some such, and took out the entire leadership of the company. Stannis bought what was left of the company not long after, folded it into his own company, G78." She leaned forward again. "I don't think Edward had anything to do with what happened to Hoagland, if that's what you're getting at."

"What do you mean by that?" Navabi asked.

Selby waved her hand, dismissively. "Oh, you know, people are always spreading silly rumors."

"Rumors like what?"

She rolled her eyes. "That Edward was somehow involved in whatever happened to Michael and the others. Just because he had expressed an interest in buying Hoagland Services."

"Before the attack in Peru?" Ressler asked.

She waved her hand again, annoyed, as if trying to swat a pesky detail. "Yes, yes, but I understand those companies were always talking about trying to purchase each other. They were very competitive."

Ressler looked at Navabi.

"Mrs. Selby, how did Edward Stannis and your sister meet?"

She smiled, like she was relieved at the change in topic. "I believe they had met at several Chamber of Commerce events. But they got to know each other when they both served on the board of a local educational charity."

"When was that?"

She shrugged. "Some time ago. Maybe ten years ago?"

"Before Michael's death?"

"Oh, yes," she said. Her face darkened. "You must understand, this is a small community. We all travel in the same circles. How could they not have known each other?"

"And then Stannis bought the company and married Hoagland's widow?" Ressler asked. "But you don't think he had anything to do with the attack?"

She sighed and glared at him. "As I said, you're not the first person to mention the possibility, but it's preposterous. Impossible. Ed Stannis was a good man, and I know Dorothy would never abide with anything like that. She's a smart lady. If that's what had happened, she'd know it."

Selby looked at her watch and huffed impatiently. Navabi got the sense the interview was about to end.

"Did you have any inkling at all that they were planning on leaving the country?"

She shook her head. "No. I know Dorothy had talked to Edward about retiring, getting out of that dreadful business. Maybe she finally prevailed upon him." Her lips started trembling and her eyes welled up. "But I saw her just before she disappeared. She gave no indication whatsoever. And I knew my sister. I would have known if she was planning to leave."

Navabi could tell that Renee Selby was losing her patience with them, and a moment later Selby announced she had another engagement and she was very sorry, but that was all the time she could spend.

"Certainly, Mrs. Selby. We appreciate your time. One last question, though, if you don't mind."

Selby gave her a polite but strained smile.

"Have you heard from your sister or brother-in-law since they disappeared?"

"No," she said without hesitation. "Not a peep."

Selby saw them to the door and graciously thanked them for looking into her sister's disappearance, but it was clear she was relieved to be rid of them.

As soon as they stepped outside, Ressler took a deep breath, but Navabi discreetly held up a finger, telling him to wait until they were in the car.

"So what do you think?" he said as soon as they closed their car doors. "Stannis is the guy, right?"

"Maybe," Navabi said as she got out her phone and called Scheller.

"Maybe? Stannis had already revealed his intention to buy Hoagland out. And he already knew Dorothy Stannis, who was in an unhappy marriage with her whack job husband. Stannis takes out Hoagland, he gets the girl and he gets Hoagland Services at a great price."

"Maybe," Navabi said. Then Scheller answered his phone. "Detective Scheller," she said. "This is Agent Navabi. We just left Renee Selby and I was hoping we could compare notes, as you suggested."

"Of course. What's your take on the situation?"

"Well, it's hard to say. Looks like it was part of a well-planned and carefully executed plan."

"I agree."

"We were wondering about Hoagland's death. We hadn't realized Dorothy and Edward Stannis knew each other before Michael Hoagland's death."

"Yes, apparently they did. There are some conflicting reports about how well."

"I see. We also didn't realize Stannis had previously expressed an interest in buying Hoagland Services."

"There is some indication that he had previously reached out to several of the board members who died in the Peru attack."

"Hmm."

"What are you thinking?" Scheller asked.

Navabi looked at Ressler. "I'm thinking it's looking

like Edward Stannis was behind the attack that killed Michael Hoagland, that he wanted the man's wife and his company."

"Well look, I didn't want to steer you one way or another. Whatever happened down in Peru was not my case, and whatever happened here, with Edward and Dorothy Stannis disappearing, didn't appear to involve anything criminal. Our case file is closed, as far as that goes. But I had an interesting incident a couple of years ago. Picked up some hard case on an assault charge. Broke a guy's leg in a bar-room brawl. Turned out he was a local kid who joined the service then found work with Hoagland. He said he was in Peru, working security when the attack went down. He said he saw Edward Stannis down there an hour before the attack."

"Who was this? Can we talk to him?"

"Guy's name was Taylor Clark, and there's a bench warrant for him. He made bail and vanished."

Navabi thanked Scheller, ended the call and told Ressler what he'd said.

"Stannis was down there?"

"That's what one not necessarily reliable witness said, but yes."

"So Stannis killed Hoagland, then took his company and his wife."

"Looks like."

"So a murderous billionaire with a history of spectacular violence cashes out and disappears, goes off the grid right around the time this Dead Ring thing first appears. Are you thinking what I'm thinking?"

Navabi nodded. "Edward Stannis is the Ringleader."

Chapter 41

Simon Wall lived in a run-down shack. The yard was dirt, and pitted with holes that looked like they had been dug by a dog, presumably belonging to a previous tenant, since Wall didn't own a dog. He might want to get one after this, Red thought.

Red and Dembe had parked down the block to wait for him. They'd already been inside and had a look around. The place was a worse mess than Burton's, which was why Red had decided to wait in the car.

They'd been sitting there an hour when Dembe looked at him in the rearview mirror, making sure Red had already spotted Wall, walking up the street.

"I see him," Red said.

Wall might not have been able to take care of his place, but he seemed to be taking care of himself. He was lean and well muscled, his hair cut short. The difference between him and Burton couldn't have been more stark.

They waited until Wall was inside, then another ten minutes, to lessen the chances of making him suspicious. Then Dembe pulled the car up to the curb in front of Wall's house, and Red got out.

He walked up the path and knocked on the door, then stepped back, unthreateningly. He had his gun out and the silencer on it, but held it behind his back, hidden in the folds of his overcoat.

Wall opened the inner door, but not the screen door.

"Yeah?" he said, suspiciously.

"Simon Wall?"

"Who are you?" He looked up and down the block. He might have seen Dembe.

"We have mutual friends."

Wall slammed the door. Red used one bullet to pop the screen door latch, then two more to take out the lock. He dashed inside and caught Wall as he was unlocking one of three deadbolts on the back door.

"I'm not here to hurt you," Red said, calmly.

Wall flashed him an animal glare and threw open another deadbolt.

"Simon, stop," Red said calmly.

Wall reached out for the third deadbolt.

"Simon, stop," he said again.

Red took a step toward him and when the floor creaked, Wall whirled and sprang at him, his hands out like claws. Red stepped back again and brought the gun down across Wall's knuckles. The pain stunned him and when he paused, clutching his hand between his legs, Red swept his feet out from under him.

Wall hit the floor hard enough to knock the wind out of him.

Red knelt beside him and said, "We need to talk."

Dembe appeared in the front door, surveying the scene.

Wall started making a strange keening sound. It took Red a moment to realize he was crying. A lot. Big, whooping sobs wracked his body and he put his hands over his face. He started moaning through it, unintelligibly at first, but as he took a couple of breaths, his words took recognizable shape: "I can't go back, I can't go back, I can't go back," over and over again.

Red looked over Wall's shoulder as Dembe went into the kitchen, his eyes smoldering with rage—not at Wall, but at the people who had done this to him, who had kept him locked up for however long.

Dembe found the paper towels mounted on the side of one of the cabinets. He tore off a length and handed it to Red.

"It's okay, Simon," Red said quietly, folding the paper towels and handing them to Wall. "No one's taking you back there. No one is making you go anywhere or do anything you don't want to do."

Dembe retreated to the living room and looked on as Red sat with Wall, as the sobs quieted to weeping, and then to snuffles, and finally, after several minutes, a long sigh.

"Sorry," Wall said, quietly.

"No need to apologize," said Red. He got to his feet and grabbed some more paper towels. He handed them to Wall, who wiped his eyes and his nose.

"Who are you?" Wall said, looking up at Red.

"My name's Raymond Reddington."

"The 'Concierge of Crime'?" He laughed despite himself. "No really, who are you?"

"I'm trying to—"

"Holy crap, you're really Raymond Reddington?" Wall got to his feet, stunned out of his misery at the unlikelihood that Raymond Reddington would be standing in his kitchen.

"I am. I'm assisting the FBI. We're trying to take down the people who were holding you last year."

Wall stopped smiling, and the fear returned to his eyes.

"Someone very close to me has gone undercover, and she's in danger," Red continued. "I need your help. To save her, and to stop them from what they're doing."

"Sorry." Wall shook his head. "I can't help you. I'm done with all that. I got away from those guys once, and I'm not doing anything that could land me back there."

"Who are 'those guys'? Who was holding you?"

"I don't even know," he shook his head again. "I don't. There were two guys with names, Yancy and Corson. And there were a bunch of rent-a-psychos, private military contractor types. They didn't have names, and they never spoke."

"Who was in charge?"

"Corson was in charge of me. He made that abundantly clear. But who was in charge of him? What I was working on, all that stuff? They talked about a guy called the Ringleader. Other than that, I have no idea. They knew enough about me to know what I could do, and enough about what I could do to tell me what they wanted."

"And what were you doing for them?"

"I'm a cryptographer. I was doing encryption."

"Encrypting what?"

"I don't know. And I don't want to know. I just want to get on with my life."

"Have you ever heard of the Dead Ring?"

He paused, thinking about it. "The Dead Ring? No."

"That's what you were working on. It's a kind of a sick game, for sick people to bet on. There's only one winner, one survivor. Everyone else dies. And so do a lot of other people. When you were in Turkey last year, that's what was going on. There was a factory fire, and before that a train crash. There was also a sinkhole that swallowed up a mosque. Scores of innocent people have been killed each year, in addition to all but one of the people actually playing the game."

"Look, I don't know anything about that, man. They held me prisoner, for months. They made me work for them, and I didn't know anything about that other stuff. Didn't have anything to do with it."

"Well, this Dead Ring is happening again. In this country. Dozens of people have already died. As I said, someone very important to me is trying to stop them. And she is in danger now because we can't break their encryption." Red gently but firmly pressed his finger into Wall's chest. "Your encryption."

Wall looked down at Red's finger as the words sunk in.

"I'm hoping you'll help us because it's the right thing to do," Red continued. "To save innocent lives. But another thing to keep in mind is that I found you. It wasn't that hard. Do you really think they won't find you again, too?"

Chapter 42

It was almost eleven P.M. when Red walked into the field office. Aram glanced up from his computer, but just for a second.

"Agent Keen looks like she's staying put for the night," he said, yawning and tapping a few more keys. "The tac team is standing down and Ressler and Navabi are on their way back from Dallas." Then he saw someone else walking in behind Red. "Who's this?"

"Aram Mojtabai," said Red, "meet Simon Wall. He's here to help with the encryption." He turned to Wall. "Simon, this is Aram. He is the man your encryption software has been so bedeviling."

Cooper appeared in the doorway to his office. Before he could say anything, Red said, "Simon, this is Deputy Director Cooper." He turned to Cooper and continued, "I was hoping you'd be here. This is Simon Wall. He wrote the encryption software that Aram has been trying to crack. He's here to help."

"Simon Wall," Cooper said. "We appreciate your assistance."

"Simon was held captive in Turkey by whoever organized last year's Dead Ring," Red continued. He turned back to Wall. "Tell them what you told me."

Wall looked at his feet. "Um... When I was locked up, in Turkey, the two guys that were kind of in charge, Corson and Yancy, used to talk about this guy they called the Turk. He seemed to be, like, the local organizer of this Dead Ring thing, or whatever they were doing there."

Cooper raised his eyebrows at Red with a look that said, *"A guy in Turkey known as the Turk" doesn't narrow things down at all.*

Red nodded and held up a finger, telling him to be patient.

"But there was another guy they talked about sometimes," Wall continued. "A guy they called the Cowboy. And I was wondering if maybe he's involved in what's going on now. Sometimes they called him 'the C-c-cowboy,' like with a stutter. They'd mimic him and laugh."

Red patted him on the shoulder. "Simon overheard some other bits and pieces, and he thinks the guy they were talking about is in the oil business, but not a driller, so maybe oil services, engineering, construction or the like. He's big but wants to get bigger. He's not a criminal by nature, but he wants to do business with criminals."

Wall nodded. "That was the sense I got. The way they were talking about him, it was like maybe he got outmaneuvered by some criminal gang or screwed over on a big deal, and he's doing whatever it is he's doing to prove he can be a tough guy, too. He wants to show he can hang with the big dogs."

Aram was typing frantically at his computer, but then he stopped. "So you wrote this encryption software. Can you help us break it, so we can hack into the uplink?"

Wall nodded somberly. "Yeah. I couldn't tell what those guys were up to, but I knew it wasn't good. My encryption is virtually unbreakable. But I put in a back door. And I can show you the key."

"Hold on a second, here. What's your security clearance?" Cooper asked.

Wall snorted. "Well, I had secret clearance a couple years ago. I don't know if that's good enough, but if you're not comfortable with me helping you people break the encryption software I wrote, then believe me, I can just walk. Frankly, I'm not crazy about getting involved in any of this stuff again."

Cooper put up his hands, soothing and a little defensive. "Calm down, son, I'm just saying we need to be careful here."

"You're right," Wall said, still vaguely indignant. "And I need to be careful, too. I don't know what you people are up to here. So you go ahead and make sure you're comfortable with my security clearance, and I want your assurance, in writing, that I won't be held legally liable if whatever it is I'm helping you do breaks any laws."

"I assure you, Mr. Wall, we are in the business of enforcing the law, not breaking it."

"Well, I've seen some well-intentioned representatives of this country's government cross some pretty definite lines, so excuse me if I'll take that assurance in writing."

Cooper stared at him for a moment. "Understood."

"And I'll tell you something else," Wall said. "You might think you're going to take these guys down, but with the money they've got they can pretty much buy their way out of anything. The only way to really hurt these guys is to get at their money."

Aram had been watching the exchange with his

mouth slightly open, but now he turned and looked at his computer screen as if something had grabbed his attention. "Huh," he said, "Dwight Tindley," as if he was surprised at how easy it was.

"I beg your pardon?" Cooper said.

"Dwight Tindley. Owner of an oil services company called Occitex. I think that could be our guy. He was 'Man of the Year' four years ago at a big fundraiser for a group called Big Talkers, which raises money to help kids with speech disorders. Two references mention him having a stutter."

He tapped a few keys and then sat back. "Two years ago, his company lost a huge contract in Azerbaijan. Occitex went public with allegations that Roskov Services, the company that won the contract, got it because of its ties to Russian mobsters, which were well known. Two days later they withdrew the allegations and issued a formal apology to the Azerbaijani government. Since then, Occitex has been expanding its presence in central Asia and at least three other companies have alleged the company has been doing so in conjunction with criminal gangs."

"Sounds like it could be our man. Excellent work, Aram," Cooper said. "And welcome aboard, Mr. Wall. Thanks for your help."

Wall nodded as he took a seat near Aram's workstation.

Red asked, "Excuse me, Aram? Was that Occitex as in O-C-C-I-T-E-X?"

Aram nodded. "Yes, that's right."

Red turned on his heel to leave, but Cooper called after him. "Reddington. A word before you leave."

Reddington followed Cooper into his office.

"Ressler and Navabi are on their way back from

Dallas," Cooper told him. "Edward Stannis is looking like a possibility for the Ringleader."

"Stannis?"

Cooper shared what Ressler and Navabi had learned in Dallas.

Red thought for a moment. "So Stannis liquidated his assets right before the first Dead Ring."

"Exactly. So I know you're concerned about Agent Keen's safety, as are we all. Having Wall on board is a huge help, and so is possibly identifying Tindley as the local organizer, and perhaps Stannis as the Ringleader. But right now, the situation is stable. Keen is not in immediate danger, and we are in a good position to execute the plan that we have carefully designed and take this whole thing down."

"What are you getting at?"

"I'm saying we can't have you tipping our hand. If you confront Tindley, or interact with him in any way, you could be putting Agent Keen in danger. I am putting Tindley under distant surveillance. We'll be looking into him, hard. Dorothy Stannis's sister, as well, in case either of the Stannises come to visit her while they're in the country. But we are doing it in a way that will not be detected. We have this under control, and you need to let us do our jobs, and let Agent Keen do hers. You need to sit tight, is that understood?"

Red flashed a smile that was tinged with acid. "Oh, I think we understand each other. And as long as you all do your job, I won't have to do anything, will I?"

Chapter 43

Keen had spent the rest of the day trying to get access to Yancy so she could kill him or seduce him, or somehow distract him enough that she could get the transmitter out of his shirt pocket. As he walked around the campground, she could see its vague outline through the thin, grimy fabric of his uniform shirt, as if he had forgotten it was there. She'd gotten close enough to smell him on several occasions, but never close enough to retrieve the TNT. And then it was lights out.

She spent the night tossing and turning in bed, wondering how she was going to get the transmitter back before the first round started at daybreak.

Yancy's cabin was visible from hers, and several times throughout the night she had gotten up and cracked her door to check, but there were two armed PMCs guarding it, awake and alert each time.

Best case scenario, he changed his shirt and she could sneak in and go through his laundry—a thought that made her gag—then get to the main square before anyone noticed she was missing.

As the sky began to lighten, Keen cracked her door

again, a tiny fraction, and set her chair so she could sit and watch Yancy's cabin. When the sky was almost light, his door opened and he stepped out. The two PMCs stood up straighter, then fell into step behind him. As he came closer, she saw to her disbelief that he was still wearing the same shirt. The thing was disgusting, and she wondered if he ever took it off.

She stared at it intently, and just for a moment, he twisted himself slightly and the predawn light picked up the edges of the transmitter, casting a faint but unmistakable shadow across his breast pocket.

Keen cursed and slumped back in her chair. She felt doomed. She also felt sore from the previous day's altercations and exhausted from stressing all night about what to do about the transmitter. Now it seemed that she was going to have to survive whatever it was they had in store, competing against these raging, murderous lunatics with virtually no sleep. She turned and looked longingly at her bunk, wondering if she had time to catch a minute of sleep.

Then the bugle sounded reveille and she cursed again.

Two minutes later she was dressed and out the door, filing down the rows of cabins with the other ringers toward the square. She was so tired she felt light-headed.

Corson and Yancy were waiting at the square, standing up front, already scowling at them.

A wall of low clouds was approaching from the south. The rising sun torched their undersides with pink and orange. As the rays cut sideways across the square, the sharp outline of the transmitter in Yancy's shirt pocket practically taunted her.

As everyone lined up, two black-painted school buses pulled up outside the gate. They had reinforced glass and Keen realized they were prisoner transports.

Yancy did a quick headcount and gave Corson a nod.

Corson said, "Get on the buses. We'll brief you on the way."

Keen angled toward the bus closer to where Yancy was standing. The driver was one of the private security types, with dark, reflective shades and no human expression.

She took a seat up front, hoping Yancy would get on and sit near her, and that she would somehow have a chance to get the transmitter. Maybe she could distract the driver, cause him to swerve, she could throw herself at Yancy and somehow lift the transmitter.

She let out a sigh as Boden and Dudayev got on and took the seat just behind her. They seemed like back-of-the-bus troublemakers, but so did pretty much everyone else, for that matter.

Then Okoye got on, as well. He started heading toward the back, but when he saw Boden and Dudayev sitting behind Keen, he sat across from them.

Okoye caught her eye and they exchanged a nod. He didn't look well, but she supposed she didn't either.

The bus quickly filled up, and Keen's heart sank as Corson got on with two armed PMCs and the door closed behind them. Yancy was on the other bus. At least she wouldn't have to smell him.

Corson stood over her, looking down. Staring. She couldn't tell if it was "I'm onto you" or "I hate you" or "I'm thinking lewd thoughts," but she just stared back at him, her best badass, psycho, what-the-hell-are-you-looking-at stare.

He continued to stare at her as they pulled through the gate.

A voice from the back of the bus called out, "Yo, man, where's my ride?"

An angry murmur arose as everyone in the bus looked out the windows to the left. Sure enough, all the vehicles that had been parked outside the gate were gone.

Corson smiled. "That's right, they've all been moved. Think of it as valet parking. Whoever wins will get their vehicle back. In fact, whoever wins can have their pick from all of them."

The ringers quietly sat back down as the implications sunk in, as if seeing their vehicles gone made it suddenly more real and they realized what they were risking by entering the Dead Ring.

Corson seemed to take pleasure in their reaction. "Now then, for the first official round of the Dead Ring, you will be knocking over a meth lab run by a biker gang called the Cossacks. Inside their lab there are eighteen one-kilo packages of crystal meth. Your job is to go in, take one package, and bring it back to the rendezvous point. There's eighteen packages, and I believe now there are twenty-eight of you."

He grinned. "So, to the ten of you who will be dying in the next fifty minutes or so, I'd like to say, 'Thanks for playing, better luck next time, and I'll see you in hell.'"

Chapter 44

Aram had stayed up late with Wall, decrypting the uplink feed he had recorded earlier. It was after three A.M. when they finally got it cracked. Wall had created the encryption and had put in the back door himself, but it was still impressive watching him break into it by memory, even if it took several hours to do it. Now that he had it all in place, it would hopefully be easier next time the signal was live.

Wall explained that using the back door was not the same as a full decryption. They were restricted to one channel of data in each direction, but it was more than enough to confirm what they were looking at. The footage was boring, yet surreal—these crazed killers dressed in white jumpsuits running across rows of tires and doing dashes and broad jumps.

And then right there was Agent Keen, running and jumping right along with them. He almost didn't recognize her at first. She had LE CHAT written across her front and back. Her hair was dark, but the biggest difference was her expression, her attitude. She looked hard and cold. He knew it was an act, but it was jarring to see.

He ran the video back and forth a couple of times. Somehow Director Cooper appeared at his side, watching, too.

Wall cleared his throat. "Is that your, um, colleague?"

"Yeah," said Aram, softly. Worried. "That's Agent Keen."

Cooper put a hand on Aram's shoulder. "She looks like she's doing fine," he said.

As the video continued to play, they saw two men in camo pants and uniform shirts telling the others what to do.

"Pause!" Cooper said sharply, leaning forward to look more closely.

Aram's hand hit the pause button before he even had time to think about it.

"Those two look like they're the ones in charge, don't they?" He pointed at the two men. They had sidearms but weren't carrying rifles.

Aram found a frame where their faces were clear, zoomed it in and enhanced it as much as he could.

Wall had turned pale. "That's them," he said quietly. "That's Corson on the right. He's in charge. Yancy, the one on the left, the filthy one. That's like, his henchman."

"Run them through facial recognition," Cooper said. "See if you come up with anything."

"Yes, sir," Aram said. "I'll see if I can capture the other contestants' faces, too."

"Good. Now I'm going to get some sleep. You should, too. Tomorrow could be a big day."

Shortly after, Wall pushed himself away from the workstation and pinched the bridge of his nose. "He's right. I need to crash, too," he said quietly. He seemed like he was still shaken at the sight of Corson and Yancy, Aram thought as they said goodnight.

Aram watched him retreat toward the classrooms with the cots, then got to work isolating as many of the faces as he could from the video. He sent twenty-three through facial recognition, but only got two hits, a former Army Ranger named Flynn and a South African war criminal named Boden.

According to the distance scale across the bottom of the screen, Keen's position was now fifty feet northwest of where it had been the previous night. In the darkness, Aram couldn't compare it to the CIRRUS video to confirm her location, but he figured it was probably just a calibration issue.

He set up a script that would alert them if Keen's tracking device moved more than twenty feet on the ground. Then he lay on a cot he'd set up next to his desk and tried to get some sleep.

After an hour of tossing and turning, he gave up on sleep and got up again.

Still just the two hits on the facial recognition.

He opened the file with the jigsaw fingerprints. He had become vaguely obsessed with them, wondering what surface they had been lifted from that left them so jumbled, wondering how they fit together. He had planned to work on them for only a few minutes, just to lull his mind by using a different part of his brain. But as he started tinkering around, the time got away from him.

He had already run two different configurations through the database, but they'd come back with errors. He ran two more and they came back as "no hits"—nothing usable but better than an error. He was still tinkering with them when he had to angle the screen away from the dim blue light coming in from the window.

He moved the screen three more times, yawning and thinking he really should get some sleep, before he turned and actually looked out the window. That's when he realized it was morning. He had stayed up the entire night.

And that's when the tracker alert sounded. Agent Keen was on the move.

Chapter 45

Thirty minutes after they left the campground, the bus turned onto a winding dirt road. Ten minutes after that, they rounded a small hill and drove slowly past two leather-clad biker types sprawled on the ground next to their bikes. They were both missing substantial portions of their heads and lying in patches of blood-soaked dust. Two gas station travel mugs were on the ground, as well, coffee staining the dirt around them as if they had bled out, too.

As the two buses pulled over side-by-side, Corson stood up and said, "Get out."

The clouds were lower and the sky darker as they got out of the bus. It felt like the sun had decided to skip the day entirely and sink back under the horizon. A breeze picked up, cool but ominous.

A quarter of a mile back, the RV she'd seen outside the campground was pulled over onto the side of the road in front of what looked like a troop transport. A quartet of armed PMCs stood next to them.

When Corson spoke, he kept his voice low, and the ringers gathered close and kept quiet so they could hear him. Yancy was right next to him, the transmitter still visible in his pocket, just a few feet away. Keen worked her way closer to him, squeezing between Yancy and a ringer named Flynn. The smell coming off of Yancy was enough to make her eyes water.

Flynn gave her a dirty look and pushed her back, but she pressed on, working her way closer to the transmitter. She was easily within reach of it, but she didn't have a plan and she didn't have an opening. She could have reached into his pocket and grabbed it, but not without exposing herself and scuttling the operation.

Flynn pushed her back again, causing her shoulder to bump against Yancy's.

It gave her an idea.

Without looking, she elbowed Flynn hard in the ribs. He shoved her back, hard, right into Yancy.

Keen raised her hands as if to break her fall, pressing each of them against Yancy's chest. Her fingertips grazed the TNT in his pocket. She could feel it.

Yancy scowled and said, "What the—?"

His shirt was oily with grime. His breath smelled of dead animals and old cigarettes.

She moved her hand toward the top of his shirt pocket, but before she could slip her fingers inside it, a boot that felt like a battering ram thundered into her side, under her ribs.

She hit the ground hard and rolled into a ball, clutching her side. She heard a wet *thunk* and Flynn landed a foot away from her, a trickle of blood coming down the side of his head.

Corson stood over them, his gun in his hand. "Save it for the game," he hissed. He looked at each of the others. "Anybody else?"

He waited several seconds, but the only sound was Flynn groaning and Keen trying to catch her breath.

Corson turned to Yancy and ordered, "Get them up."

Yancy grabbed Keen by her hair and jerked her upright.

She managed to get her feet under her, and even snatched at his shirt in an effort to grab the TNT, but he was gone, yanking Flynn to his feet as well. Then he was out of reach, scowling at them both as Corson resumed speaking.

The compound consisted of three double-wide trailers, he explained. They were in a "U"-shaped configuration, with living quarters on either side and the lab in the middle. The whole thing was surrounded on all sides by low hills, with a single winding road in and out, formerly guarded by the two dead bikers. It was up to the ringers how they went in and how they came out.

As he spoke the apparatus on the roof of the RV unfolded into a satellite uplink, like on a news van. The PMCs opened the storage compartment in the side of the vehicle and started lifting out boxes, four of them, that looked distressingly similar to the one containing the drone that had killed Borova. Keen felt a moment of mortal dread that was heightened when a drone rose out of one of the boxes and flew toward them. But as it circled them low in the air, she saw that it was armed only with a camera—no explosives.

Before she could register any relief, it occurred to her that the transmitter needed to be located within ten feet of a camera in order to work. Even if she was able to get hold of the transmitter, if the cameras were all mounted on quadcopters, that's what she'd need to attach it to.

As Corson continued speaking, Keen massaged her bruised side and looked around at the other ringers.

Boden and Dudayev were snickering and mumbling to each other.

Okoye's face was contorted with effort, as if he was having a hard time concentrating. The occasional twitch in his eye seemed to have gotten worse.

Everyone else, even the craziest of them, were all hanging on Corson's every word. They recognized what was at stake for them, and knew what would happen to them if they failed.

Keen had different priorities. She hadn't been thinking about the game. She was just trying to survive and get the transmitter back so she could execute the plan. But now she acknowledged to herself that wasn't going to happen. Not in time. The tac team was not going to ride in and shut things down. She had specifically told them to wait for her signal. A signal she now had no way of delivering.

She needed to survive this round, to get through the whole thing alive, just like the others. She tried to block everything else out and focus solely on Corson's words, and understand completely what the round consisted of, what was expected of them, how to get through it and not get killed.

Then the other three drones rose up into the air. On the one that was closest, she saw a small red light come on.

The cameras were recording.

The uplink feed was live.

Chapter 46

Cooper, Ressler, and Navabi had gathered around the computer so quickly, Aram knew they must have been up already and waiting for the alert. Wall ambled in, rubbing his face, and sat next to Aram in front of a black screen with green numbers scrolling up and a blinking cursor. "Any signal yet?"

Aram shook his head. "No."

"Where's our visual?" Cooper asked.

A second screen showed the blinking dot of Keen's tracking device, slowly moving to the east. The third screen was a flat field of gray.

"That's it," Aram replied, pointing to the gray screen. "That's what we're looking at. Meteorology said there's a layer of low clouds in advance of a cold front."

They watched the tracking dot moving more quickly across the screen. "She's in a vehicle," Aram reported.

A momentary break in the clouds revealed two black buses on a long straight road across the prairie. "That's probably all of them," Cooper said. The tension in the room dissipated just a little as everyone let out a breath.

Wall turned to Aram and whispered, "Is that good?"

Aram shrugged. "It means that they're all going somewhere together. Probably to start the actual games. But it also means they're not taking Agent Keen off by herself, which could have meant they had blown her cover. That would have been very bad."

Cooper got on the phone with Greg Nichols and gave the order for the tac team to prepare for action.

Ressler and Navabi got ready, too. The tac team helicopter would pick them up on the way.

But the dot just kept moving across the screen. After ten minutes, someone made coffee.

Aram pulled up the photos of Corson and Yancy, and told everyone that Wall had identified them as the two guys operationally in charge. He also told Cooper that he hadn't gotten any hits on them through facial recognition, but pulled up the files on Flynn and Boden.

The group was scanning them for any relevant information when the tracking dot stopped.

Aram acquired the GPS coordinates and searched for any previous mention of that location or anything near it. "Search of those GPS coordinates comes up blank. They're in the middle of nowhere."

Numbers started scrolling up the left side of Aram's screen and Wall's fingers attacked his keyboard.

"We have uplink feed," Aram announced.

Cooper updated Nichols and the tac team while Navabi and Ressler resumed prepping.

A second column of numbers and letters began scrolling up the main screen. "We have downlink, too, sir," Aram said.

The signal was live in both directions.

Wall pushed himself away from the keyboard and held up his hands. "We're in."

Aram's screen suddenly crowded with eight more

columns of characters. "It will take us a while to decipher the top video channels, but it looks like we have six video feeds and one data channel going out. And one data channel coming in."

"That's it then, right?" Ressler said. "If it's a two-way signal, that means there's bets coming in, right?"

"Nothing from Keen?" Cooper asked.

Aram shook his head. "No, sir."

"How long has the feed been live?"

Aram checked the clock. "Two and a half minutes."

"At five the tac team is supposed to go in regardless, right?" Ressler said.

Cooper watched the screens.

The cloud cover was still complete, but the transmitter was moving again, slowly. On foot.

Cooper took a deep breath. "Agent Keen said to wait for her signal."

"What if there is no signal?" Ressler demanded. "We can't see a goddamn thing. We have no idea what's going on down there."

Aram cleared his throat. "Um, we could bring the CIRRUS drone down below the cloud cover."

"Without it being detected?"

Aram quickly tapped on his keyboard and checked some settings. After doing some quick math he shook his head. "No... We'd be too low."

"What's the time?" Navabi asked.

"Four minutes and forty-seven seconds."

They stood there for thirteen seconds, staring at the screens and silently counting to themselves. Wall seemed to shrink into himself under the stress as he looked at each of their faces, one to the next.

"Five minutes," said Ressler. "We have to go in."

Cooper took another breath and let it out. "We wait."

Chapter 47

As Corson finished his explanation, the four camera drones circled them slowly.

"I hope you understand what you are to do," he said with a smirk. "Or that enough of you do so we have sufficient players left for rounds two and three."

As he clapped his hands and rubbed them together, the drones flew higher. He looked at his watch and said, "Okay, we'll meet you back here when you're done. Or some of you at least. On my mark..."

Everyone stood there for a moment, and then he shouted, "Go!"

Boden took off first, running down the center of the winding road. Dudayev took off after him and a fraction of a second later, almost all of them followed. Okoye looked back at Keen questioningly as he brought up the rear. One of his eyes seemed slightly skew.

Keen fell in behind them at first, her side aching where Corson had kicked her. After a few steps, though, she turned and sprinted off to the left, laterally, around the low hills that surrounded the compound. The muscles in her side were on fire, but she ran flat out anyway, and after forty yards, she curved around to what she hoped was the rear of the compound. She charged up the side of the hill and slowed as she approached the top, staying low and getting a look at the place.

It was exactly as Corson described it—three double-wides in a U-shaped configuration. The center one had a smoke stack. Nothing was coming out of it, but now that she was closer, she could smell that distinctive ammonia stench of a meth lab. She hadn't quite gone all the way to the back. To her right was one of the side units and to her left was the rear one, the lab.

Twenty feet away from her, a camera with a small antenna sat on a short tripod, looking down on the compound. An identical one perched on another hill on the far side of the compound.

She didn't have the transmitter, but it was still encouraging to see ground-mounted cameras, that they weren't relying solely on drones.

A dozen motorcycles were lined up along the far side of the compound. A lone gang member was tinkering with one of them, an assault rifle propped up against it.

To the right of him was the dirt road, and approaching along it, swiftly and apparently in silence, was Boden. Dudayev was just behind him. With the rest of the group farther back.

Boden sprinted straight at the gang member. He was almost there before the guy turned around and pulled a knife from a boot sheath. Boden went in low and took it from him, slicing viciously upward with it. An arc of blood followed the knife and the biker grabbed his face as blood gushed out of it.

Boden thrust the knife into the guy's chest three times in rapid succession, and when the guy lowered his hands, Boden slashed across his throat.

Before anyone else had caught up with him, Boden was on the move. He seized the assault rifle and his legs pumped fast as he charged straight for the compound.

Just before he reached it, he turned, fiddled with the rifle for a moment and fired a spray of bullets into the ringers approaching from behind him.

Half a dozen of them went down, injured or dead.

Dudayev laughed.

Boden kept running. As soon as he disappeared behind the roofline, he was shooting again. In the dim morning light, Keen could see the windows of the double-wide to her right flickering with the muzzle flashes.

As the surviving ringers flooded the compound, Keen threw herself over the top of the hill and slid down the incline into the space behind the double-wides.

Through the first window she came to, she saw a gang member lying on the floor with a bubbling chest wound and a gun in his hand. She opened the window and pushed in the screen.

The guy on the floor gurgled and raised his gun as she climbed in, but then his hand dropped to the floor. He shook once and let out a long sigh.

His last breath.

Keen took the gun out of the dead man's hands and kept moving.

Chapter 48

Keen moved silently into the next room, but it hardly mattered. The sound of gunfire and screams from outside would have drowned out the worst she could do. The floor of the room was covered with sleeping bags and air mattresses. It was empty except for two bodies: the Kenyan woman, Ebuya, and a biker, both stabbed multiple times. At first she thought the biker was one of the Cossacks, but his patches were different. Then she recognized him as one of the other ringers.

She opened the door to a third room, the noise growing louder the closer she got to the lab. In front of her, one of the Cossacks was holding Masri, the one-eyed Iraqi woman, up against the wall. He had one hand locked around her throat and the other one grasping a hunting knife.

Masri's face was purple and her feet were four inches off the floor.

Keen almost yelled, "Freeze," a misstep that could have cost her life and the operation.

As she bit the words back, the Cossack drove his knife up under Masri's ribs, hard. To the hilt.

Her one eye bulged and she shuddered.

Keen thought the Cossack hadn't seen her, but he whipped the blade out of Masri's chest and turned, poised to throw it at her.

Without even thinking, she had already raised the gun.

Now she pulled the trigger, filling the small room with sound and light, obliterating the Cossack's throat. He dropped the knife, took a step backward, and fell to the floor, thrashing and gurgling, then dead.

She hurried through yet another door, and found herself in the gap between the two trailers. Plastic sheeting was draped haphazardly over the top, held up with some kind of makeshift tent-pole.

She opened the door to the lab module just wide enough for one eye and the barrel of the gun.

The room inside was a shambles. Tables were upended. The air was filled with eye-burning toxic fumes. The walls were spattered with blood, and the floor was littered with bodies.

In the middle of the room was a metal cabinet, the door open wide. Inside it were two packages of white powder. Only two. That was close.

She darted in and grabbed one, then hurried back to the door. As she was about to slip outside, the door on the far side of the lab opened up and Okoye entered. He staggered for a moment, his face twitching before he shook his head and it stopped. He went to the cabinet and picked up the last package.

As he did, he saw her, looked into her eyes.

Then Keen noticed someone else, another ringer, coming up behind him. She saw the trail of tear-shaped tattoos coming down from one of his cold, sociopath eyes and she recognized him: a gang-banger named

Ramirez. He came up behind Okoye and raised a vicious-looking knife, its blade already slick with blood.

Okoye flinched when he saw her gun leveled almost at his face. He ducked as Keen pulled the trigger and hit Ramirez in the chest, knocking him backward.

Okoye, surprised that he was still bullet-free, turned to see the dead man sprawled on the floor, then looked back at Keen. He tipped his head in thanks and she pointed toward the door she was exiting through.

"Come on," she said.

Chapter 49

Okoye nodded and followed her. As they stepped outside, Keen looked out through the narrow gap between the two units. The dirt was wet with red and littered with bodies.

Together, they charged up the hill, away from the compound, each clutching their kilos of meth.

To their left, Keen could see two ringers lying dead on the slope she had run down ten minutes earlier. To their right was the camera on the tripod, slowly panning in their direction.

As they crested the hill, they paused. One of the quadcopters circled around them, rotating as it sank lower, keeping them in its view.

For a moment, she wondered if it was government issue, and if, with no signal from her, this was the first wave of the tac team sweeping in to shut everything down and extract her. For a guilty moment, she hoped they would, even though she hadn't activated the transmitter. But she had told them not to. She trusted that they wouldn't. She clenched her jaw, trying to find a deeper reserve of inner strength.

She had told them not to come until she sent the

signal, and they weren't. Because they trusted her. Not just her judgment, but her strength and her ability to survive whatever was being thrown at her.

They had faith in her. She needed to have faith, too.

The drone rose to look at the carnage behind them.

The only movement below was one badly injured ringer limping toward the dirt road and the rendezvous point. One hand was clamped over a bleeding abdominal wound; the other one clutched a package just like theirs. Then two others appeared, running at him from different directions. One moved fast and low, the other was practically shambling, his right leg drenched in blood. The quicker one closed on the man with the package, drove a knife into his back and took the package, then simply kept running.

The man with the leg wound paused for a moment, as if he was deciding whether or not to give up, then he ran as best he could after the other one.

Keen and Okoye started running, too, down the other side of the hill and back to the rendezvous point. The clouds had grown even darker, and as they ran, a volley of fat raindrops pelted the ground around them, rolling into little balls of mud. But it stopped.

As they rounded the next hill, the buses came into view forty yards away, surrounded by a crowd of ringers, many of them bloodied.

Keen wondered what it said about her that she was saddened to see Boden and Dudayev among them. She kind of hoped they had been killed.

Corson and Yancy stood off to the side with half a dozen PMCs.

The other two camera drones circled high in the sky.

As Keen and Okoye approached the buses, the man with the bloody thigh emerged from the road leading from the compound, running unsteadily out into the open, between them and the rendezvous point. It was Flynn, the guy she had provoked into shoving her when she'd tried to take the transmitter from Yancy.

His eyes were wild, bright blue in the middle of a face smeared with blood. When they looked at her, she saw recognition and hatred.

He looked at the packages in their hands. Then he charged at them.

The camera drones circled closer, buzzing like insects.

Keen raised the gun in her hand and shouted, "Get back."

Flynn veered away from her, toward Okoye, and she said it again. "Get back!"

Okoye braced his legs, prepared to fight.

She still didn't know what Okoye knew about her. He had helped her but she had helped him too, so they were even as far as that went. Still, they were allies of a sort—and that couldn't be a bad thing in a game like this.

Keen two-handed the gun in front of her, for control and emphasis. The man coming at them didn't slow down for a second. She didn't know how many bullets she had left, but even amid all that carnage, she didn't want to just kill him.

She took a chance and aimed at his legs. She pulled the trigger and he went down, tumbling into the dirt, clutching what had been his good leg. It glistened red just above the knee. He writhed and moaned, rolling around on the ground.

Keen grabbed Okoye by the elbow, and pulled him along. Flynn let out an animal scream and lunged at them both, but he fell short. It seemed like the last of whatever fight he had left in him. As they jogged toward the rendezvous point, he began to weep, in pain and frustration, maybe in fear.

Keen couldn't help wondering what had led him there, to that moment, to that situation. How many bad decisions and bad breaks had led Flynn to think the Dead Ring was his best option. She had to fight the urge to stop and help him—to save him. At that moment she wanted to do whatever she could to shut the whole nightmare down. But there was nothing she could do. Not then. Anything she tried would simply cost her life and the success of the operation.

So instead she kept jogging, her face a cold mask of indifference.

As she and Okoye joined the others, Yancy did a quick headcount and nodded at Corson. "That's eighteen."

Corson nodded toward the PMCs and then turned to address the eighteen ringers standing there clutching their packages of methamphetamine.

"Congratulations on surviving the first round of the Dead Ring," he said.

Four of the PMCs trotted off down the dirt road. Meanwhile Yancy walked over to Flynn. Two camera drones swooped out of the sky in unison then split, one following Yancy, the other following the quartet trotting down the road.

"Inside each of those packages is a key, which you will need for the next round, tomorrow," Corson said. "Go ahead and open your packages, dump out the contents and retrieve your key."

Keen looked around. A couple of the ringers were staring at the packages in their hands like they'd just been reunited with the true love of their lives.

"If you're partial to this stuff," Corson said, "now's

the time to take a taste, but you are not bringing it onto the bus."

Flynn pounded the earth with his fist, screaming a stream of obscenities. He seemed oblivious to Yancy now standing over him, as if despite his rage and anguish, he had completely accepted the inevitability of his fate. The camera drone slowly circled them, ten feet off the ground. Of course they were broadcasting it.

Yancy casually aimed his rifle at Flynn's head and pulled the trigger twice, silencing him.

The troop transport that had been parked next to the RV drove past them and toward the dirt road. The drone rose up into the air and followed. Yancy returned to his spot behind Corson.

Keen and Okoye exchanged a glance as the men around them tore open their packages, spilling the powder and white rocks onto the dirt at their feet. White clouds of toxic dust floated away on the breeze as they fished out their keys.

A handful hesitated, but only one actually took a taste, a wiry weasel of a man with a swastika tattoo on his neck. He put a small rock in his mouth, grimacing as he crunched it in his mouth and swallowed it down.

Keen tore open her package and dumped the contents onto the ground. Okoye did the same so there were two cascades of white rocks and two small clouds of dust. She stepped away from it, making sure she didn't breathe any dust. Then she reached in with two fingers and picked up her key. It was small and chunky, like a padlock key, with a red plastic cover over the grip.

She wiped the white dust off of it with her fingers, then rubbed her fingers on the ground to get the meth off of them. Okoye did the same.

As she straightened up, the sound of automatic weapons echoed from the compound, two short bursts, then two more. Everyone stopped and looked down the dirt road.

The PMCs were mopping up, taking out any surviving losers, and probably any remaining bikers, too. Three separate balls of black smoke rose up into the sky, trailing wisps that thickened into thin black columns that twisted around each other until they were one.

As the ringers got back on the buses, one of the PMCs jogged over to the spot where they had been standing and poured a can of gasoline onto the meth-covered ground.

The transport came back up the dirt road with the four PMCs hanging on the back. Keen realized it was taking out the bodies. Maybe the others realized it, too, because they all watched it go by, solemn but grateful they weren't on it. Also knowing that in all likelihood they would be within the next few days.

Chapter 50

It had been a glorious round. A dozen dead bikers and almost as many dead ringers. A last-ditch effort by a gravely wounded contestant to take out two others, desperately clinging onto life and a chance to win the Dead Ring by stealing their winning ticket. It didn't get much better than that.

And yet it did. Watching Yancy walking over and taking out the last loser. Perfection.

And then the Cowboy had to ruin it.

"Oh my god," he said. "Is that crystal meth?" He looked back and forth between the bright screens in front of him and the dark shadows behind him, no longer afraid of who he saw there, or not afraid enough. "Seriously, what is that... Eighteen? Is that eighteen k-kilos of meth? That's half a million dollars, at least."

The Cowboy scanned the room, looking from face to face, waiting for someone to confirm what he was saying, to agree with him, or acknowledge him even. But he was greeted with silence, and the tap-tap-tapping of the keypad.

"Come on," he said. "I mean, I'm no drug d-dealer,

but this whole thing is costing me millions. Are you telling me none of you are at all interested in recouping s-some of that?" He looked at the screen again, at the ringers dumping their meth onto the ground, then at the PMC bringing the gasoline can over. "Oh, no... no... Don't tell me you're going to... No!"

The guards and technicians paused, listening to the voice in their earpieces, and the Cowboy rolled his eyes.

"Oh, Jesus Christ. Are you k-kidding me?" he said. "Do you really think I don't know you're all connected over those headsets?" He squinted into the shadows. "Look, if you've got something to say to me, just say it?"

He looked around, as if expecting an answer from the shadows, but instead, the guard to his left clamped a hand around his throat and pushed him against the wall, squeezing hard, and then harder still.

"You don't question the Dead Ring," said the guard, whispering into the Cowboy's ear. "You don't do anything that would put the Dead Ring in jeopardy, like drug trafficking or anything else." He clenched his hand tighter, causing the Cowboy's eyes to bulge and his face to turn purple. "And you never second-guess the Ringleader."

The guard paused for an instant, listening to the voice coming over his earpiece. Then he looked up again. "Do you understand?"

Unable to speak, the Cowboy managed to nod his assent, and the guard released him, letting him crumple to the floor.

Chapter 51

For ten minutes they had all been standing there, wordlessly watching the unchanged screens. The tracker signal was strong and clear, moving just enough that they could be reasonably sure Keen was not dead. The CIRRUS drone, circling high overhead, picked up nothing but clouds—darker when it flew lower, lighter when it rose higher up. Aram checked the settings every two or three minutes, fighting off panic by making sure they weren't missing anything due to technical errors or a bad setting. But everything was right. This was all there was to see.

The third screen was dark, and in it, Aram could see the reflection of Cooper, Ressler, and Navabi standing behind him.

Cooper and Navabi were like statues.

Ressler was climbing out of his skin, occasionally flashing glares at Cooper, or opening his mouth to say something, probably to protest their inactivity. But he didn't say a word.

"The uplink feed just ended," Wall reported.

"We have movement on the tracker," Aram said quietly, his voice croaky and dry. The tracking dot had moved about twenty feet, according to the scale on the screen.

A few seconds later, the dot began moving again, more quickly this time. "They're driving," he said.

The screen showing the video feed from the CIRRUS began to brighten. "The cloud cover is breaking up," he said.

Spots of faded dusty brown began to peek through the gray.

The CIRRUS was following the tracking dot, and as the clouds parted, the screen showed the two buses and a canvas-covered military truck. Well ahead of them was a large RV, so far away it might not have been affiliated in any way.

The clouds continued to break up and slide out of the way.

Cooper leaned forward. "What's that?" He pointed at a black smudge on the far left of the screen.

Aram overrode the CIRRUS controls, pointing the camera back toward the direction the vehicles were coming from.

"Oh no," Aram said.

The clouds continued to part and as the CIRRUS flew on, the angle revealed the U-shaped configuration of trailers, fully engulfed in flames. Black smoke billowed up into the clouds.

"That fire," Cooper said. "Where is that in relation to where Keen's tracker was stopped?"

Aram checked the recording. "Looks like it's the same place."

"How far are those vehicles now?"

Aram zoomed out the camera and did a quick calculation. "Three miles."

"Do a quick reconnaissance sweep of that fire and

then resume following the tracker."

Aram paused the autopilot and took manual control of the CIRRUS. He felt a pang of anxiety as it peeled away from its pursuit of the truck holding Keen. He felt like he was abandoning her.

On the screen, the horizon pitched to one side as he circled back until the column of smoke was right in front of them. In a few seconds he was headed right toward it. He veered off to the left, so as to not fly directly into it. As he looped around lower, they could see the ground littered with bodies. At least ten of them, plus twice that many serious-looking bloody spots.

"That's a biker gang," Ressler said, pointing at two of the bodies, lying in the dust next to a row of burning motorcycles. "Look at the patches. The Cossacks. I don't get it."

Cooper was breathing loudly, aggravated. "Get back to following that convoy."

Ressler stepped up next to Cooper. "Sir, there's obviously some kind of problem," he said. "We need to go in there and get Keen out."

Cooper looked at him, concerned but also mildly irritated. "Thank you for your input, Agent Ressler. Duly noted." He turned to Aram and Wall. "How long before you can decrypt the video feed, so we can see what the hell went on down there?"

Aram looked at Wall. That was his thing, really.

Wall's face went blank for a moment as he did some mental calculations.

"About two hours?" he said, uncertainly.

"Make it one," Cooper said. Then he turned and strode into his office.

Chapter 52

"This place is amazing," said Orest Juergins, practically trembling with excitement as he looked around. "I can't believe I didn't know it was even here."

Juergins was a boring man. In fact, truth be told, he was exactly the type of "not quite our type" that places like the one they were in contrived to exclude. He would probably never see it at night, never experience the withering disdain of the bartenders. As it was, he would have to content himself with the passive condescension of the waitress. And if Red ever came back this way, he'd have some explaining to do. But that was okay. He never planned on coming back this way.

With its rich wood paneling and leather-upholstered furniture, the place felt as heavy and grounded as any place on earth. But the floor-to-ceiling windows belied that impression, showing off the city far below and the flat land stretching out beyond it.

Red knew that part of the point of a place like this was for idle rich people to show how unimpressed they were. It was nothing special to them.

Juergins had spent five minutes with his nose

pressed up against the glass, trying to see if he could spot his house.

Red envied the man his giddy excitement. It was a feeling Red treasured and it was increasingly elusive. A nice view of the Dallas suburbs wasn't quite going to do it. The brown tea they called espresso there wasn't either.

"An amazing view," Juergins said as he returned to the table with his orange juice.

"It certainly is something," Red said, sipping. "Thanks for joining me. As I said on the phone, before I add Big Talkers to my list of preferred causes, I'd like to get more of a feel for the place."

"Absolutely," Juergins said. "As I'm sure you know from the brochures and our website—"

Red held up a hand. "Yes, I've read the brochures and the website." He lowered his voice, conspiratorially. "I need to get a better sense of the people with whom I will be associating myself. You don't want to put your name on the side of a building without knowing what's really going on inside, am I right?" Juergins' eyes went a little rounder at the suggestion that a donation of that size might be on the table. "Who are your other big donors? Who are you naming scholarship funds after? Who is on your board? Who are you making your man of the year?"

"Oh," Juergins said, his face flushing crimson. "Well, as it turns out, I was this year's man of the year."

"Congratulations."

"But I've been volunteering with the organization for twenty years."

"I'm sure it was very well deserved. Who won before you?"

"Well, that was Jerry Simmons. He's a bigwig at Southwest Capital. He's only been involved in the last few years, since his grandson was diagnosed with a phonemic disorder. But he's given more money than almost anyone else, since then."

"And he has no skeletons in the closet? No youthful indiscretions or grownup weaknesses I should know about?"

Juergins looked indignant. "Good heavens, no. He is a deacon in his church and a coach in the local softball league."

Red stifled a smile. That would have raised a red flag if he had been in the slightest bit interested in Jerry Simmons' potential liabilities.

He put down his drink. "Who was it before that?"

All the indignity on Orest Juergins' face vanished, replaced by a wince that appeared before he could stifle it.

"Oh, um... that would be Dwight Tindley. He's a big-shot oil services guy. Had a bit of a stutter when he was a kid, but I think now it's mostly just when he's under a lot of stress. He was a big supporter for close to ten years."

"Was?"

"I beg your pardon?"

"You said was, not has been. Is he no longer a supporter?"

Juergins cleared his throat. "Well, no, not the last few years. His company has been growing very aggressively, internationally even. It's not unusual for donors to cycle into and out of different causes."

Red sipped his espresso. "You seem nervous talking about him."

"No, not at all," Juergins said, his jowls flapping as he shook his head. "We have lots of donors who move on to other causes after a while. Some even come back after a few years. I remember Gordon Stueben, man of the year about fifteen years ago. He went off the radar for five years, then came back, ran for the board and gave us one of the biggest donations we ever—"

"I'd like to hear more about Tindley."

Juergins frowned, like a child who had just been caught at something he thought he'd gotten away with.

Red smiled, reassuringly. "Look, I am very difficult to shock, believe me. But I hate to be surprised later."

"Well," he said, lacing his fingers together and flexing them back and forth as he chose his words. He looked up with a tiny, tentative smile. "Just like you, we like to be very careful about who we affiliate ourselves with. And... and who we ask our other supporters to be affiliated with. Dwight Tindley hit a bad spell, business wise, several years ago. And that's fine—we all understand that. Goodness knows, we've all had ups and downs. But he kind of fell apart, drinking a lot and so forth. And that's not the worst thing in the world either, you know? Lots of people hit a rough patch then go on to do great things. But he kind of changed after that."

"Changed how?"

"He was an oil guy and he used to associate mostly with other oil guys. Not roughnecks, either, more like, you know, Houston executive types. But all of a sudden, he's hanging out with all these hard cases."

Red put on a pained expression, hiding his delight at finally getting somewhere with Juergins. "What kind of hard cases?"

Juergins' shoulders did a wiggly dance, like he was trying to shrug his way out from under something. "Military types, but not soldiers. More like private military. Mercenaries and the like."

Red shrugged, like that wasn't so bad.

"But that wasn't all. There were also some serious bad guys. I don't know if it was drugs or, like, weapons dealers. But it was something bad."

"Oh my."

"Yes. And the worst part was, Tindley didn't belong with them. You could tell just looking at them. It reminded me of high school. You know when the bad kids let that one good kid hang around with them so they could cheat off his paper? That kind of thing. But I think he wanted to be one of them. He wanted to be 'bad,' for whatever reason."

"So you cut ties with him?"

"Well... let's just say I didn't follow up when his checks stopped coming."

"I see."

Juergins' eyes were drawn to Dembe as he rose from a booth on the other side of the room, then they widened as he approached their table and handed Red the cell phone.

Red held up a finger as he looked at the display. Cooper. "Yes?" he said.

"There's been a development."

Chapter 53

The CIRRUS drone had followed the convoy back to the campground, and since then, the tracker dot had barely moved. Not motionless, but less than fifty yards according to the scale at the bottom of the screen, moving around on foot and well within the confines of the campground.

Ressler and Navabi had retreated to the sleeping quarters to catch up on some rest.

Wall had decrypted the incoming portion of the two-way satellite signal—the portion that included the incoming bets—but it consisted of seemingly random numbers, meaningless without whatever key had been previously agreed upon by the various parties. Now he was up to his elbows in decrypting the uplink feed.

Left with the mundane task of monitoring the motionless tracker dot, Aram returned to idly reconfiguring the jigsaw puzzle fingerprint from the Turkish control room. He had created four prior configurations and run them through the database, but none had generated any hits. He tweaked the most recent version, pulling two of the sections closer together, and saved that as version number five. He had just submitted it to the database when the exterior door swung open and Reddington walked in, trailed by the blinding afternoon sun.

Cooper emerged from his office as if he'd been expecting him.

"What happened?" Reddington demanded.

Cooper stepped aside and motioned Reddington into his office.

Aram tried halfheartedly not to listen, but their voices, though civil, quickly became raised, and the flimsy walls did little to muffle them.

Cooper calmly explained what had happened that morning: what they had seen, what they had done, and, more importantly, what they had not done.

"So Keen went through a full round of the Dead Ring, that's what you're saying," Reddington said when he was done. "The one thing you said wouldn't happen?"

"We don't know that's what happened. Our camera was obscured. But we intercepted the satellite uplink and we're decrypting it now."

Wall's typing was growing more rapid and more determined, but the conversation between Cooper and Reddington grew louder right along with it, almost as if they were talking over it.

"So the uplink was live in both directions?" Reddington said, his voice incredulous. "And you didn't go in after five minutes, like you had told me you would?"

"As per Agent Keen's request," Cooper replied, his voice sounding like it wanted to be louder still. "As I explained before. And as I also explained before, this is Agent Keen's job. And going in was her idea."

"And what about your job, Harold? Isn't part of that not putting your agents into unnecessary harm?"

Wall hit the enter key with a flourish, then turned to

share an awkward look with Aram.

The door to Cooper's office swung open, and Red stormed out.

Cooper came up behind him and lightly put his hand on Red's elbow. "Look, Red, I share your concerns," he said quietly. "But I can't put this operation at risk and endanger countless innocent lives just to get Agent Keen out of harm's way. We've seen what these people are capable of. We can't risk losing this opportunity to shut them down. And we can't do what we need to do until Keen activates the transmitter during the live feed."

Wall cleared his throat. "Um... there might be another way."

Cooper and Red both turned to look at him.

"What do you mean?" Cooper said.

"I wasn't listening to you or anything, but um, if we could get hold of the login info, like, from one of the bettors or viewers or whatever, one of the subscribers, we might be able to get our code inside their signal even without the transmitter." His computer dinged and he turned to look at it. "We've decrypted the first chunk of video."

Red pulled his arm away from Cooper's hand, and they both came over to the workstation.

"Play it," Cooper said.

"This is just the first five minutes and just one channel," Wall explained as he set up the video.

The screen came to life, looking out onto the empty desert. The camera lifted into the sky, slowly spinning as it did, gradually revealing more and more of the tableau: the buses and the people gathered around them, including Keen, the dirt road, the double-wides, an RV with a satellite antenna, and something like a military transport.

The video captured the first few minutes of the onslaught. It showed Keen, paused atop one of the surrounding hills and bent sideways as if stretching out a muscle cramp in her side. It ended just as she ran down toward the rear of the double-wides, into the fray.

Chapter 54

In the moment of quiet following Red's departure, the ding coming from Aram's computer sounded ten times as loud as the identical one that had come from Wall's machine just a few minutes earlier.

Reddington was gone, Cooper was back in his office, and Wall was deeply engrossed in the process of using his back-door vulnerability to decrypt the rest of the satellite feed they had recorded. Aram had been staring at the motionless tracker dot, trying to picture Agent Keen, visualizing her being unharmed and ready to activate the transmitter as soon as the uplink resumed, hopefully soon.

He jumped at the sound, and was surprised that Wall didn't even flinch.

Aram clicked on the notification and read it several times.

He'd finally gotten a hit on the fingerprint, but it didn't make any sense. According to the database, the fingerprint belonged to Michael Hoagland.

According to Reddington's story about Hoagland and G78, Michael Hoagland had been killed in Peru.

Reddington was clearly upset, and Aram was

reluctant to call him so soon after his tumultuous exit, but he had to make sure he had the story right before he went any further.

He also didn't want Wall to hear his conversation. The room formed a slight "L" shape, so he got up from his desk and crossed to the far side of the room, around the corner.

As always, Dembe answered, polite but in no way chatty.

"Hi, Dembe, it's Aram. Can I talk to Mr. Reddington? It's kind of important."

After a moment of silence, Reddington came on the phone, his voice infused with a forced pleasantry. "Hello, Aram."

"Hi, Mr. Reddington. I'm sorry to bother you, but I just wanted to confirm something. When you were telling us earlier about Hoagland Services and G78, didn't you say that Hoagland was killed along with his board of directors and top management team?"

"Yes, that's right. Why?"

"Well..." He felt funny telling Reddington before telling Director Cooper, but then again, Reddington was sharing information with him, and he'd feel funny holding out on him.

But before he could decide what to do, the main door swung open.

He expected it to be Ressler or Navabi, or perhaps both.

But it wasn't.

There were three of them, two men and a woman. With the sunlight streaming in around them, Aram couldn't get a good look at their faces, but he could see that they each had a badge in one hand and a gun in the other.

"CIA," said the one in the middle, the tallest by far. "Where's Director Cooper?"

Aram whispered into the phone, "It's the CIA."

"What?"

Wall stood up from his computer and looked around. "What?" he asked, disoriented, like he didn't know what was going on or where everybody else was.

"Three CIA agents just came in, with badges and guns," Aram whispered, embarrassed at the level of panic in his voice. "They're looking for Director Cooper."

One of the agents walked right up to Wall. "Where's Director Cooper?" The agent was black, with a shaved head and a neatly trimmed goatee.

"Have they identified themselves individually?" Reddington asked.

"No," Aram said. "They don't know I'm here."

"Okay, put the phone on speaker so I can hear what's going on, then put it down and respectfully ask them to identify themselves."

"What?... Why?"

"Just do it. I'll be there shortly."

Aram gulped loudly enough that he hoped Reddington hadn't heard it. Then he put the phone on speaker and stepped out from around the corner with his hands in the air.

The female agent swung her gun in his direction. "Who are you?"

Wall slumped down in his chair, like he was trying to shrink away to nothing.

"I'm Aram Mojtabai. I need you to identify yourselves."

"We're with the CIA," she said.

"I need to know your names."

Before she could reply, Cooper came out of his

office. "What is the meaning of this?" he demanded.

"Hello, Director Cooper," said the tall one. "CIA. We're here to take over."

"This is an FBI operation," Cooper said, "so you'd better put those goddamn guns away."

The tall one shook his head and smiled. "No can do." He had blond hair, tousled, like a prep school kid who didn't care and knew he didn't have to, but graying, like he had outgrown the tousled prep school look but didn't know another one. He had a slightly stooped posture, like he had been living with a little more height than his body knew how to handle. "We're asserting jurisdiction here. National security."

"What are your names?" Aram asked again.

The tall one laughed. "I'm Agent Ronald Percival," he said in a patronizing tone. "This is Agent Dwayne Thomas and Agent Lorissa Beckoff."

"I don't care who the hell you are," Cooper thundered. "You can't come in here and interfere with a domestic operation."

Percival walked over to Cooper, casually pointing his gun at Cooper's midsection. "I've got two words for you," he said. "National. Security."

Wall looked like he was trying to wink out of existence and reappear in a less stressful universe. Aram half wanted to ask him how he was attempting to do it, just in case he succeeded.

"I'm sorry, but I'm going to have to ask you to hand over your weapon," Percival said, not looking sorry at all. "Two fingers."

Cooper paused, like he was thinking hard about it.

Thomas and Beckoff both aimed their guns at him. A few long seconds dragged by, then he slowly unsnapped his holster and pulled his gun out, pinched between his thumb and forefinger.

Percival raised his own gun so it was pointed directly at Cooper's forehead.

Cooper held out his gun, still between his thumb and forefinger, but as he did, he pivoted to the side, so that Percival was between him and the other two agents.

As Percival took Cooper's gun, his gun hand wavered and his eyes came off Cooper, just for an instant. But in that instant, everything changed.

Cooper's left hand came up, blindingly fast, and snatched Percival's gun. He had it turned around and pointed at Percival's head before the other man's fingers could come close to the trigger of Cooper's gun. At the same time Ressler and Navabi exploded through the door behind Thomas and Beckoff, hitting the floor rolling. The two CIA agents tried to turn, but not fast enough, and Ressler and Navabi were back on their feet, guns two-handed and solidly aimed while Thomas and Beckoff were still between targets.

"I've got two words for you," Cooper said, as he took his gun back from Percival. "And they're not 'National security.'"

Chapter 55

Red smiled as he walked into the task force's temporary field office. He could tell immediately that a whole lot of something had gone down. Wall was sitting at his desk, looking more shell shocked than when Red had first brought him in. Cooper was in his office with the door closed, his voice tense and terse with barely concealed anger and frustration. Obviously on the phone with Washington. As if that wasn't enough to make you turn to a life of international crime.

Aram appeared out of nowhere. "Mr. Reddington, thank God you're here," he said, his eyes filled with relief and gratitude, followed by confusion as he spotted the picnic basket tucked under Dembe's arm.

"You did good, Aram," Red told him, patting him on the shoulder as he and Dembe moved on toward the north wing of classrooms.

Ressler was standing guard outside one of the classrooms. He stiffened as Red and Dembe approached, as if anticipating some kind of trouble.

"Donald," Reddington said by way of greeting.

"Reddington," Ressler said, vaguely suspicious.

"Percival and his friends in there?"

"That's right."

"I'd like to talk to them."

"Cooper left strict orders, they are to remain inside this room."

"I just want to talk to them," he said, then, whispering, "I won't let them out."

Ressler eyed the picnic basket as well, but he sighed and stepped out of the way.

As he opened the door, Reddington whispered, "And if you could give us a few minutes of privacy, that would be terrific."

The room was empty except for a teacher's desk in the front and facing it, three student desks occupied by three bashful-looking spies, sitting awkwardly with their wrists zip-tied together and their ankles zip-tied to the desks.

"Good lord, Percival, it *is* you," Reddington said, laughing. "Amazing the places we run into each other, isn't it?"

Percival blanched gratifyingly. "Reddington?" he said. "Jesus, what are you doing here?" He actually tested his restraints.

The other two picked up on it right away, eyeing Dembe's picnic basket and looking suddenly alarmed.

Dembe put the basket on the teacher's desk and Red took out his knife. Percival again struggled against his restraints. Thomas's and Beckoff's eyes grew wider.

"Jesus, Reddington," Percival said, trying to inject some laughter into his voice even as his eyes stayed solemnly riveted to Red's knife. "Karachi was seven years ago. You can't still be holding a grudge about that."

Thomas and Beckoff both stared at him with an intensity that looked like it would have burned. But apparently not, because Percival seemed oblivious to anything other than Red's knife. His eyes were practically skewered on it.

"For Christ's sake, my orders came from the Secretary of State. You know how that works. You can't blame me for that."

Red laughed. "Percival," he said in a scolding tone, pointing the knife at him playfully. "You know that's not true. The Secretary of State had no idea you were there or what you were up to. I know this for a fact, because I asked him about it over a feast of Mongolian boondog at the embassy in Ulaanbaatar."

He turned to address the other two agents, Thomas and Beckoff. "Fascinating dish, boondog," he explained. "They debone a goat and fill it with red-hot rocks from the fire and basically cook it from the inside out. Truth be told, I found it more intriguing than delectable, but cooking goat can be tricky. Still, it was a fascinating chat with the secretary. He's a brilliant man—knowledgeable about an amazing array of topics. But what I found even more interesting were the things he didn't know about." Reddington smiled. "It turns out he knows nothing about the Mongolian copper export deals you brokered as part of your front corporation. Don't get me wrong, I fully appreciate that making tens of millions of dollars in export fees is a very solid cover for a working spy. And I can see how it might make a certain amount of sense to maintain those business relationships long after you've moved on to a different post and a different theater of operations, because you never know, right? Could come in handy some day. And I've never been a big fan of accurate financial disclosures, either. But then again, I'm not on the government payroll anymore. Of course, the fact that your partners in the deal are Chinese agents might make reporting it a little tricky, too. So I get it, why you decided for the good of all involved it makes sense to just stay quiet about it."

Percival looked suddenly ill—pale and sweaty with dark rings under his eyes. On the upside he no longer seemed quite so concerned about Red's knife.

The other two were staring at him with disappointment and disgust.

"You two didn't know either?" Red asked them. "Well, try not to be too judgmental. Thomas, I'm sure Percival knew that you were trading Malaysian police information to traffickers in Myanmar in exchange for intelligence about Islamists in Indonesia, and I'm sure that he understood that you continued to do so in exchange for money when there was no intel to be traded. I'm sure he understood that you were just keeping the lines of communication open, and that your daughter's private school isn't cheap. Or your boat."

Percival and Thomas looked appropriately defeated, their heads hung low. Now, Beckoff stared at them both with disgust.

"Agent Beckoff," Red said, turning to her. "Don't judge too harshly. You haven't been in the game quite as long as they have, or had the same opportunities for moral equivocation. But here's the thing: you are plugged into an old boy network. Boy and girl network, I guess. And after today, you are going to be faced with the dilemma of whether to ruin the careers of these two old boys, at the risk of ruining your own as well. Or to let things go, and move forward in your career knowing what you know about them, knowing they know you know, and knowing that they owe you big favors and are in a position to repay you."

She stared blankly up at him as his words sunk in. Percival and Thomas looked over at her with a strange and identical mixture of hatred and love, hope and despair.

"You might not know yet how you are going to choose," Red told her. "But I know. So I'm going to proceed." Brandishing his knife, he moved toward Percival with an abruptness that made them all flinch. "As much as I like reminiscing about old times, I'm much more concerned with the here and now."

With that he flicked out the knife and severed the plastic zip tie binding Percival's wrists. In a flash, he whipped the knife through the air and slit through Thomas's and Beckoff's wrist ties as well.

The move was unnecessarily grandiose, but theater counts in situations like this. He could easily have cut one of them, but that was a risk he was willing to accept.

The three of them looked down at their newly freed wrists in astonishment, and then up, with even greater astonishment, as Red opened the picnic basket and unpacked a picnic: red checkered cloth, fresh baguette, pate, *brie de champignon*, grapes, olives, and a 2009 Beaujolais.

"I figured you'd be hungry. And these school lunches can be just awful."

Chapter 56

Wall was a mess. Mumbling to himself, rocking back and forth. Aram didn't understand why at first, but when he tried to calm him down, Wall snapped at him.

"No one told me the CIA was going to be here. *The goddamned CIA!*"

"We didn't know," Aram said. "We weren't expecting them. But we've got the upper hand, and we're running this operation. We have jurisdiction over them."

Wall glared at him condescendingly. "No one has jurisdiction over them. They always end up running the show, and the people around them always end up getting hurt. That's how it works. And right now, I'm one of the people around them. So are you, if you haven't noticed."

Cooper was in his office, on the phone to Washington. He didn't sound like he was having fun.

Aram was trying to think of something reassuring to say to Wall, when he remembered that in all the excitement, he'd forgotten about the fingerprint. Hoagland. He needed to tell Cooper.

"Excuse me," he said. He glanced at the tracker monitor, which wasn't moving, then he got up and went over to Cooper's office. The closer he got, the louder and angrier Cooper's voice sounded. He knocked lightly on the door, but he didn't think Cooper could hear him over the sound of his own voice, and whoever was probably barking just as loudly on the other end of the phone.

He opened the door and stuck in his head.

Cooper was saying, "I don't give a goddamn about that, this is a sensitive operation and I have an agent embedded—"

He saw Aram and waved him away.

Aram held up a finger, but then Cooper started furiously snapping his fingers and pointing at the door with such vigor that Aram felt like he was being physically ejected from the room. Suddenly, he was out in the hallway, with his back against the door.

Reddington was with the CIA people, but Aram thought maybe he could talk to him. He walked around the corner and down the hallway to the classroom where they were being held. Ressler was standing outside the room with an assault rifle.

"Hey, Aram," he said.

"Hi, Agent Ressler. Is Mr. Reddington in there?"

Ressler snorted. "He sure is."

They could hear voices coming from inside the room, but it was impossible to tell from their tone what was going on. It sounded friendly enough.

"Can I go in and talk to him?"

Ressler sighed, for some reason annoyed at the question. "I think now is not the best time."

Aram nodded. "Okay. Do you know where Agent Navabi is?"

"Personal quarters. I think she's trying to catch a couple winks."

The implication was clear: So don't bother her. But

this was important, and Aram needed to tell someone. Somehow, he didn't think Ressler was the one.

Instead, he walked back through the command center and into the southeast wing, where the sleeping quarters were.

The hallway was darkened, but there was a light on in the third classroom down. Aram walked up to it and tapped lightly on the door.

"Agent Navabi?"

"Come on in," came her voice from the other side. Aram wondered what state of dress he would find her in. Luckily, she was fully clothed, wearing camo pants and a T-shirt, stretched out on one of the cots. She smiled when he walked in. "Hello, Aram."

"Hi, Agent Navabi."

"What's up?"

"I found something, and I need to tell someone, but Director Cooper is on the phone with Washington, and Mr. Reddington is talking with the CIA people."

Her eyebrow twitched at that last bit.

"What is it you've found?"

"I've been playing with different permutations of that distorted fingerprint you brought back from Turkey, and I finally got a hit."

"You did? Who is it?"

"Michael Hoagland. The former head of Hoagland Services."

"I thought he was supposed to be dead."

"He *is* supposed to be dead. But I think he's alive. I think he's the Ringleader."

Chapter 57

Navabi grabbed Aram by the wrist and dragged him back to Cooper's office. She didn't knock, she just opened the door and walked in, pulling him in with her.

Cooper looked up, annoyed, but he did a double take when he saw it was Navabi. Instead of waving them out he held up a finger.

"Well, you'd better straighten it out. Because I will not have CIA endangering this operation."

He put down his phone and exhaled loudly.

"Sir—" Navabi began, but Cooper cut her off.

"Did I see Reddington here?"

"Yes," Aram replied.

"Where is he?"

"He's in there talking to the CIA agents."

Cooper's eye twitched. "He what?" He launched himself out of his chair and stormed out of his office.

Navabi's eyes met Aram's for a moment, then they dashed off after him. By the time they caught up he was approaching Ressler.

"Is Reddington in there?" Cooper demanded.

"Yes, sir," Ressler replied, with a slight hesitation, like he was wondering if maybe he had screwed up.

Cooper moved past him and opened the door.

Inside, Reddington was sitting on the edge of the teacher's desk. Percival, Thomas and Beckoff were zip-tied to their desks at the ankle, but their hands were free. They were eating bread and cheese and pate. They were drinking wine. They were laughing.

"Harold," Reddington said with a smile. "So glad you could join us. I was just saying to Agent Percival here how sorry I was about your little misunderstanding, and how sure I was that we could all work together toward our common goal."

Cooper's rage was undermined by a trace of uncertainty.

"Reddington, a word outside please."

Navabi and Aram backed out into the hallway to stay out of Cooper's way.

"Director Cooper," Aram said, but Cooper held up a finger.

"Not now, Aram."

When Reddington came out and closed the door behind him, Cooper turned to him. "I don't like you talking to them in there without me," he said.

"I'm not sure you would have wanted to hear everything that was said in there."

"Washington is saying CIA has jurisdiction. If they're asserting national security then they can take over this operation."

Reddington smiled. "Well, you see there? That's not going to happen."

"What do you mean?"

"Because of our little talk. They are going to concede jurisdiction to us, in exchange for a very small concession."

"Which is?"

"When we put our Trojan horse into the video feed,

they want us to include one of theirs as well."

Cooper paused for a moment thinking about it. He turned to Aram. "Would that pose a problem?"

Aram took a step back, then shook his head. "It shouldn't."

"I guess that's okay," Cooper said, "as long as there's no technical problems."

"Good."

Cooper and Reddington both turned to go back into the classroom.

Navabi said, "Director Cooper? Aram has something important to tell you."

"Yes, Aram, what is it?" he snapped.

"I think I know who the Ringleader is."

Chapter 58

Keen's face was a mask of stone on the bus ride back to the campground. Boden and Dudayev both made comments trying to get a rise out of her, trying to upset her, but she kept her face blank and her eyes empty, and they eventually left her alone and even gave her some distance.

She didn't look at Okoye or speak to him.

Some of the other ringers were animated, celebrating their survival, but most of them, even some of the roughest, were quiet like her, nursing their injuries, both physical and psychic.

As they approached the campground, Corson stood at the front of the bus and told them the next round of the contest would begin at daybreak the following morning. They were to report to the main square. Even he seemed subdued.

When they got off the bus, Keen looked around for Yancy and spotted him already halfway back to his cabin, flanked by a pair of PMCs. She hurried after him as best she could despite the muscles tightening up in her side. She didn't dare run after him for fear of drawing any more suspicion onto herself, not after the incident with Flynn.

She was still twenty yards away from Yancy when he entered his cabin.

She slowed a step after that and headed to her own cabin. As she did, images from the morning came back to her. First, she saw Flynn pounding the earth with his fist, screaming unintelligibly, indifferent to Yancy and his rifle because he knew he was already dead, and that the bullet was just a technicality. She saw the man about to stab Okoye, the one she shot in the throat. She saw Boden aiming the assault rifle into the crowd of ringers and heard their screams as he fired into their midst.

The images came faster after that: the dead and the dying, the killers and the killing. All of it exploded out of her subconscious, bombarding the backs of her eyes and the inside of her skull. Each image screamed at her to be acknowledged and processed and dealt with in a way that she hadn't allowed herself to, because she couldn't. She needed to be hard and cold—a sociopath or psychopath, just like the rest of them. Only she wasn't, she was just pretending. It was a façade. A façade that was cracking, and she couldn't afford to let it. Not out there; not in front of anyone else. She needed to get inside.

She made it to her cabin and as she fumbled for her key, from the corner of her eye, she saw Okoye watching her.

She got the key into the lock and turned it, opened the door and slipped inside.

Slamming the door shut, she leaned against it with one arm wrapped around her bruised side. She closed her eyes and slid to the floor, processing the carnage she had witnessed that day.

After a few minutes, she got up, splashed some water on her face and tried to pull herself together. She took a deep breath and felt the icy calm descend over her.

Then she heard a soft tapping at her door.

She took another deep breath and summoned an even greater level of control, considering her next move. She had no idea who was out there or why. The doors did not have peepholes, and the cabin's three windows were on the back and the sides and they were bolted shut.

She took a deep breath and opened the door.

It was Okoye.

"What do you want?" she said flatly.

His eye was twitching again, worse than before. "We need to talk."

"Where?"

"That is up to you. Somewhere private."

She cast her eyes toward the cabin. "Do you think they're bugged?"

He shrugged.

"Let's take a walk."

He nodded.

They walked silently past the cabins, to the far side of the square. They leaned against the fence that surrounded the entire complex, and they looked back at the cabins.

The sun was high, baking them along with the earth under their feet. But they were alone out there.

Still, when they started to talk, they kept their voices down to avoid being heard, and their heads down so their lips couldn't be read.

"You are not Le Chat, whoever that is, but I will keep calling you that," Okoye said. It was a simple statement of fact. It didn't require a response, so she didn't give him one. "I don't think anyone else knows, but it's obvious to me you're not a contestant. You're an agent of some sort, Interpol, maybe, or FBI, whatever. infiltrating this game, trying to shut it down."

She remained silent for the time being, let him keep talking.

"My name is Jakob," he told her. He paused as his face was wracked with spasms, but he shook them off, and when they subsided, he continued. "My brother Daniel was a good man. Not like me. Both our parents died when we were young and we were orphaned together. Daniel took care of me when I was little. He got me into an orphanage, got me into a school. I didn't turn out so good, but he gave me every chance to do so. Seven years ago, Daniel and his wife were killed in a fire on a ferry in Senegal, leaving three boys behind." He shook his head. "I couldn't care for their children. I didn't know how. I'm not that kind of man. I am not my brother. I am a mercenary and I know how to kill. Luckily, I found a place I could take them, an orphanage run by Miss Badri. She took in my nephews and she gave them a life. Later, I learned Miss Badri's family had been on the ferry as well. They all died. She was left widowed and childless. Instead of giving in to despair, Miss Badri started an orphanage for the children who lost their parents in that fire. She saved my nephews' lives. But she didn't do it alone. Her husband worked for a man named Reddington." He looked at her. "Do you know him?"

"No," she said. "I don't."

He smiled. "No, probably not. He is a criminal. But he is a good man, as bad men go. Reddington and Mustafa Badri were friends, of a sort. After Mustafa's death, when Miss Badri started the orphanage,

Reddington sent her money to support her work. I learned about this when my nephews went there. When they were too old for the orphanage, they had no place to go, no school to move on to. Miss Badri saw this. She saw other children who also needed a school. So she started one: the Akaba School, for the older children who had left her orphanage."

He went quiet again, putting a hand over his eye as it convulsed in a spasm of twitches. When he looked back at her, his eye was almost normal. "I am a fighter, a killer. It is the thing I know how to do. But so is Mr. Reddington. I looked to his example, at the good he has done with his support for Miss Badri's orphanage. I decided I would give back as well. For the last five years I have been sending my money to the Akaba School, watching it save lives and produce fine young men and women who are already making the world better in small ways, and sometimes large ways." He took a deep breath and let it out. "I've done terrible things with my life—that's what I am good at. But with the Akaba School, I am doing something good as well."

"Why are you telling me all this?"

"I am dying."

"What?"

"I am dying. I have a tumor in my brain..." His eye began to twitch again and he put a hand over it. "I don't think it will be so long."

"I'm so sorry."

"I know this thing is evil, the Dead Ring. I know it more than anyone, but it was also my last chance to provide for the Akaba School, to leave something behind for them." He lowered his voice to the barest whisper. "I know you are trying to shut this thing down, and that is good. It was never likely that I would win the money, but as I am now, it's impossible. I will have no winnings to bequeath to the Akaba School. So instead I will help you, and do whatever I can to make sure the Dead Ring does not create any more orphans."

Chapter 59

"Sure, we want to shut this Dead Ring thing down," Percival said, having regained most of his insufferable self-assurance. Red was half inclined to mention his copper export scam again, just to remind him of the dynamic here, but he realized ultimately it would be counterproductive. "But mostly, we want the information we can get from the computers of the people betting on this thing, which you are going to hack into. And we also need to get information out of the Ringleader, once we get our hands on him. We want to bring him to justice, sure, but the information is important, too."

He sat back, smugly.

"We have an entire operation in place, and a considerable amount of intelligence gathered," Cooper said stiffly. "What do you bring to the table other than your druthers?"

Percival looked around the table, smiling with supreme arrogance, until he came to Red. Then his smile went away and he cleared his throat, looking down at his hands as he continued. "Well, apart from the obvious concessions as far as letting you retain jurisdiction and lead status on this operation, we have intelligence of our own." He smiled again, unable to stop himself. "We have reason to believe we have identified the Ringleader."

This time, Thomas and Beckoff also smiled.

"And who is that?" Red asked.

Percival let a dramatic pause accumulate. "Edward Stannis."

Cooper glanced at Red and at Aram, then back at Percival. "Why do you think so?"

"It's obvious if you look at it from the right viewpoint. The timing and manner of his disappearance. The fact that he maximized his holdings, then liquidated all of his assets before he disappeared, suggests he was up to something nefarious. Less than a year later, we start hearing rumors of what we would later learn was the Dead Ring. The fact that the only two people we've been able to identify in this operation, Corson and Yancy, both worked for him at G78, and left the company when he disappeared."

He spread his hands and sat back.

Cooper turned to Aram and nodded.

Aram cleared his throat. "We think it's Michael Hoagland."

Percival laughed. "Well, it could be. Except for the fact that Michael Hoagland died eight years ago."

"I thought they never found his body," Red said.

"They never found any of the bodies. They were blown to smithereens in Peru."

"We think Stannis was in on the attack," Cooper explained. "He was making a hostile bid for Hoagland's company, a bid Hoagland had rebuffed. He may have also been having an affair with Hoagland's wife, whom he married soon after Hoagland's disappearance."

"If he wanted the company so bad, why did he take out the entire leadership team?" Percival asked.

"Maybe he was really after their contracts," Red replied. "And their market share."

"I'll buy that," Percival said. "That's part of our scenario, too. But I don't see how you get from Stannis killing Hoagland to Hoagland being the Ringleader."

"We think Hoagland survived the attack," Cooper said. "And maybe Stannis and the widow didn't live happily ever after. Maybe Hoagland survived and saw Stannis taking over his business, stealing his wife, taking his entire life. And maybe he decided to take it all back."

"How?"

"Our thinking is that he gets hold of Dorothy, the woman who he sees as having betrayed him. Threatening her, he forces Stannis to do what he wants. Edward and Dorothy were last seen on April 5, as they were about to go on a short trip to their lake house. Everything they owned was liquidated over the next three days. And they were never seen again."

Percival smiled. "Well, that would all be very compelling except he didn't escape the attack. He's dead."

Cooper turned to Aram and nodded.

"We found his fingerprint," Aram said. "At the Dead Ring site in Turkey."

The room was quiet after that. Percival was no longer smug. Aram almost was, or as close to it as Red had ever seen.

"Well that's fascinating," Percival finally said. "I look forward to determining if that is actually the case. In the meantime, out of consideration to the amount of advance work your team has already done, and your willingness to accommodate our modest requirements, we will accede to your request to maintain lead status on this operation."

He turned to Beckoff, who put a metallic blue thumb drive on the table.

"Here is our program," Percival said. "It is encrypted and isolated. It will not interfere in any way with whatever code you are sending. Isn't that right, Agent Beckoff?"

Beckoff nodded.

Cooper turned to Aram and raised an eyebrow.

Aram shook his head. "I have no way of knowing, sir."

"Well, I can guarantee it. It is highly sensitive and heavily encrypted. You will not be able to open it, but I need you to give me your word that once the program has been sent, you will destroy any copies of it in your system."

Aram looked to Cooper, who said, "If this jeopardizes our investigation or our person on the inside, I will personally charge you with endangering our operation and the life of our agent."

Percival again assured him it was safe and then slid the thumb drive across the desk to Aram. Once Cooper had nodded his agreement, Aram reached out and picked it up.

With that, Cooper stood up and gave Red a nod of unenthusiastic gratitude. "Okay, let's get busy. We don't know when the next round is set to start, and we've got work to do before it does."

As Cooper pulled Aram aside, Red leaned toward Percival and said, "If any harm comes to Agent Keen because of your involvement in this operation, I'll hold you personally responsible. You don't want that to happen."

Cooper put his hand on Aram's shoulder and said,

"I want you to work with Wall to make sure you get that code into the uplink feed along with ours, okay?"

"Absolutely," Aram replied, and he hurried back to his workstation.

Percival seemed in a rush to get away from Red, almost crowding Cooper in his haste to leave the room.

Before he could, Aram reappeared in the doorway.

"It's Wall," he said. "He's gone."

Chapter 60

Reddington pulled Cooper aside, and said, "I take it Wall isn't crazy about our new friends here. Can't say I blame him. But I think if you guys show up with your guns out and bundle him into a black SUV, it might not strike the tone you're looking for. I brought him in. He trusts me. I'll go after him."

"We're relying on him now," Cooper said. "We need him. I want to be as respectful as possible, but one way or another we have got to get him back here ASAP. I'll give you a ten-minute head start to find him, and ten minutes from when you've found him. Then we're bringing him back using whatever means necessary."

Wall was on foot, and the only thing within walking distance was a tiny scrap of a town half a mile away. It was little more than an intersection, and even at that, most of the buildings were dilapidated and dark. The only signs of life were a bank, a gas station, and a luncheonette.

Dembe swung the car into the strip of parking spots in front of the luncheonette. He and Red got out.

Wall was one of five people inside the place. He was the one covered in sweat, with a laptop computer open in front of him. The one everyone else was staring at—

until Red and Dembe walked in.

Red smiled at the waitress behind the counter. "Two coffees, please."

Wall didn't look up as they approached, he just said, "The coffee sucks in this place."

The other customers looked down at their cups.

"And the cell reception sucks, too," he said, tapping at his computer. "I guess Wi-Fi would be out of the question."

He took a sip of his bad coffee as they sat down, then winced and glared at it.

The waitress brought two more cups.

Red said, "Thank you."

Wall looked at the two cups, then up at them, then shook his head and looked back at his screen. "Nobody said anything about the CI-goddamned-A."

"The task force is still running the show," Red told him quietly. "But in exchange, they have agreed to send a second program, supplied by the CIA. They insist it won't interfere in any way. Aram seems to believe them."

Wall looked dubious.

"We've learned the identity of the Ringleader," Red told him.

Wall looked up. "Who is it?"

"Michael Hoagland."

"He's dead."

"Apparently not."

Wall let out a strange, exasperated sound between a sigh and a snort. "And that's supposed to make me feel better? Look, if the CIA is involved, they're going to offer the Ringleader freedom in exchange for his cooperation, because whoever it is, he's going to have a lot of information. And if he's free, he's free to come after me. Now you're telling me the Ringleader is the ghost of the same psycho maniac boss that made my life miserable for three years?" He shook his head. "Nope. I'm done. I broke the encryption for you, and now I'm out of here."

"What I said before still holds true," Red told him. "If I was able to find you, the Ringleader can, too. That's even more true if it's Hoagland—someone who knows you. If you don't help us put him away, he's going to remain out there, free."

Wall's eyes were strained but clear. "So what do you think is going to happen? You think the FBI is going to arrest this guy and put him in jail? You think there will be a trial, and a jury of his peers will convict him and lock him up? That's not the way it works. You of all people should know that. These people have too much money for that. They buy lawyers and judges and powerful friends. They buy their way out of trouble."

"So you think you'll be more effective working with your friends at H3?"

"You'd be surprised what we've been able to accomplish on a shoestring."

Red paused, thinking for a moment. "Say you're right, and the CIA mucks everything up and the Ringleader and all the subscribers, whoever they are, all go free. Wouldn't you feel better knowing that you and your friends at H3 had hundreds of millions of dollars at your disposal instead of the people you're working to stop?"

Wall looked suspicious. "What are you getting at?"

"What if by helping us stop these killers, you could deal the Ringleader and his accomplices a devastating blow, use their own resources against them, and make sure H3 could continue operations for the next twenty years?"

"Go on."

"Percival gave Aram a thumb drive with software

that he's supposed to insert into the satellite feed along with Aram's program. They have insisted that Aram destroy any trace of it once he has sent it."

"What is it?"

"I have no idea," Red replied. "Not really my bailiwick. Aram said it's a Trojan horse encrypted using RIX. He couldn't open it, but he said he thought you might be able to."

"RIX?" Wall snorted. "In like five seconds."

"Do you mean literally five seconds, or are you exaggerating?"

Wall shrugged. "Okay, ten seconds. Why?"

"I don't know about these things, but if we're inserting two of these programs into the signal, and into the computers of everyone watching this wretched game, how much more difficult would it be to insert three?"

"Not difficult at all, you just have to... Wait, are you suggesting we add a third Trojan horse?"

"Again, not my specialty, here. But the thumb drive with the CIA's program is sitting on Aram's desk. It is a metallic blue. I can get you at least fifteen seconds alone with it."

Wall blew air through his lips. "And since Aram has to destroy the encrypted file that he himself has never accessed, there won't be any evidence." He looked at Red. "And you're saying this is not your specialty?" He laughed, but then the second thoughts showed up, etched across his face. "Technically, I could do it no problem. But legally..."

Red held up his hands. "Totally up to you. If you'd rather not, I understand." Then he turned deadly serious. "But you said the only way to take down these people in a meaningful way is to take their money. Seems to me, this could be your only chance to do just that."

Chapter 61

Reddington and Dembe returned with Wall less than an hour after they left. Aram tried to catch Wall's eye, see how he was doing, but he went to his desk without a word, head down, and almost reticent.

Dembe stood next to Wall, almost protectively.

Director Cooper came out of his office and saw Wall back at his desk. Before he could say anything, Reddington held up a finger to him and said, "Aram, a word," holding out his arm toward Director Cooper's office.

Aram nodded and got up, then followed Reddington into the office.

"He's scared," Reddington said, as soon as Cooper closed the door behind them. "Because of the CIA."

"Where was he?" Cooper asked.

"At the luncheonette in town. He wasn't going anywhere." Reddington turned to Aram. "Did he seem nervous or uneasy before Percival showed up?"

Aram thought about it for a moment. "A little. I think he was a little shocked to be here."

"What about afterward?" Cooper asked.

"Absolutely, oh yeah. He was freaking out."

"We're going to have to keep a closer eye on him," Cooper said.

"Just be discreet about it," Reddington said. "The last thing you want is to upset him again."

Cooper opened the door. "I need to speak with him. Alone."

Aram and Reddington left, and Cooper called Wall into his office. As Reddington and Wall passed each other, Aram thought he noticed them exchange a glance.

Reddington and Dembe headed for the door. Aram thought the room suddenly felt very empty. Percival and his people were in their room, working. Ressler and Navabi were in the sleeping quarters. Aram noticed the thumb drive Percival had given him sitting on the corner of his desk. He stared at it for a moment, trying to remember if that was where he had left it.

Then a message from Cooper popped up on his computer screen. A link.

Cooper strode out of his office and said, "Aram, can you put that up on the big screen?"

Within seconds, the room was full again.

Wall stepped out from behind Cooper, looking chastened but relieved, and went to his desk.

Reddington stopped halfway out the door and he and Dembe came back.

Ressler and Navabi entered from one direction and Percival, Thomas and Beckoff appeared from the other.

As Wall sat at his desk, Aram opened the link, a video file, and sent it to the screen.

Cooper announced loudly, "We just got crime scene footage from that fire this morning. Rather than investigating the scene with our people, I've been working through an intermediary with the Texas Rangers, to avoid revealing our involvement."

Ressler came in from the sleeping quarters and everyone gathered around to watch. Brief but devastating, the handheld video was narrated by one of the Rangers.

"This was a brutal attack, apparently by a rival gang," the Ranger said, panning across the smoldering remains of the trailers. Bodies littered the ground, all of them wearing motorcycle leathers with gang patches. Some had been shot, some had their throats slit. "We found twelve dead, all members of the Cossacks motorcycle gang, plus evidence of as many as ten others, although it appears that those bodies were removed by the attackers. Whoever it was, they were merciless, deadly, and overwhelmingly brutal."

Chapter 62

Keen was up well before dawn, wakened by the pain from her bruised side and half a dozen lesser injuries. She forced herself out of bed, drank two cups of coffee, ate three protein bars, and stretched, then put the key from yesterday's round in her pocket and went for a short run around the campground to loosen up her stiff muscles. Part of her was afraid she would run into Boden or Dudayev or some other violent psychopath. Part of her was hoping she would. But mostly she suspected no one else would be up, and she was right. The only souls she saw were the PMCs guarding Corson and Yancy as they slept. She ran once around the campground, barely half a mile. It felt strangely normal, almost liberating to be outside with no one else around, not having to pretend to be someone else. Just herself and her body and the cool predawn air.

She didn't know what her plan was. Hopefully, Yancy would finally change that disgusting shirt and she could somehow sneak into his cabin and get it. Otherwise, her only option was to try once more to come close enough to get the transmitter from him.

She knew it was virtually hopeless, but she also felt strangely optimistic.

The night before, she had been crushed by sorrow at the senseless death she had witnessed, horrified by the carnage, and devastated that humans were capable of such depravity. Today, Keen felt more focused on the fact that she had survived. So many people had died the day before, but one way or another, she had managed to not be one of them. The task at hand seemed all but impossible, but somehow she felt buoyed by an optimistic sense that she was up to the challenge.

The previous morning, Corson and Yancy had been waiting at the square when everyone else got there. Keen hoped that by arriving early, she might have a chance to get to Yancy before everyone else joined them.

But the bugle blared over the loudspeaker before there was any sign of him. For another moment, she was alone under the dull pink-gray sky. Then the other ringers started to appear, walking toward her. Corson and Yancy were among them, flanked by their entourage of contractors.

Yancy still hadn't changed his clothes, or apparently even bathed, as if his filth was supposed to be some kind of statement. From thirty feet away, Keen could see the transmitter still in his shirt pocket. She questioned herself, wondering if that could be possible, or if somehow her mind was drawing a picture of it there, transforming a piece of lint or a matchbook or fold of fabric. But she couldn't un-see it, couldn't convince herself that it wasn't the transmitter.

A shudder of trepidation passed through her body, but she shook it off, assumed the stone-cold demeanor of her Le Chat alter ego, and waited for the others to arrive. She maintained it flawlessly for all of five minutes, until she realized everyone else was there except for Okoye.

Then he appeared, shuffling toward the square. He stumbled as she watched. Boden and Dudayev pointed at him and laughed.

She tried not to betray any emotion as she stifled the urge to go help him.

"Line up," Yancy rasped, watching as Okoye regained his footing and quickened his pace. "If we have to leave without you, you're a dead man," he said, adding, "Probably a dead man anyway."

Okoye stood at the end of one of the lines and Corson nodded. Yancy did a quick count and announced, "Eighteen."

Corson nodded again.

Yancy said, "Everybody got their keys?"

A couple of them patted their pockets, but no one had forgotten their key.

They got on the buses, same as yesterday. Keen again tried to maneuver herself onto Yancy's bus, but somehow he again ended up on the other one.

This time the buses headed north from the campground. The sun was well up an hour later when a semi-demolished, multi-story factory building rose in the distance in the middle of nowhere.

Corson explained the terms of the game.

"This building is where the next round will take place. On the top floor there is a row of ten lockers. The keys you acquired in the previous round will open them, any of them. Inside each of them is a knife. By now you may have noticed that one strategy of surviving the Dead Ring is to make sure your competitors do not. That is okay. To survive this round, you must simply bring one of those knives back to the meeting point." He held up three fingers. "Three things to keep in mind, though. One, just because there are ten lockers and ten knives, doesn't mean there will be ten survivors. Two, the building is booby trapped, so it's not as easy as it looks. And three, it's also wired to implode five minutes after the first locker is opened. You need to get in, get your knife, and get out, before the whole thing comes down on top of you."

Chapter 63

At five A.M., Aram woke up and started working. By ten after, the lights were on and everyone else was working as well. Wall had put in hours the night before, and had decrypted half the video. They had watched the horrific footage of ruthless slaughter: contestants killing bikers, bikers killing contestants, contestants killing other contestants. The most violent of them seemed to be enjoying it, reveling in it even. As if maybe winning the thing wasn't the most important part of the Dead Ring. Some of them seemed to be enjoying the journey.

At six-fifteen, Keen's tracker dot started moving, slowly, as if she was on foot. Aram's alert dinged to let him know, but he was already watching as it moved toward the main square at the center of the campground. He announced it to the room and texted Reddington, who had asked to be notified.

The CIRRUS showed the tiny contestants moving toward the main square.

Cooper called Nichols to put the tac team on standby.

The CIA contingent assembled at the back of the

room, careful to stay out of the way as they observed what was going on.

Ressler and Navabi began suiting up, keeping one eye on the screens as they did. This would not be a drill.

Chapter 64

When Aram's text came in, Dembe handed the phone to Red, sitting in the back seat of the car. They were in a suburb of Dallas, parked on a circular, cobblestoned driveway behind a sixteen million dollar house that was on the market for nineteen-five. Red was grateful for the seller's irrational optimism, because it afforded them the perfect place from which to surveil Dwight Tindley's home, located on a slightly more humble street the next block over.

Tindley's wife Annabelle was already up. Red had watched her make coffee and let the dogs out into the spacious backyard.

Red didn't like being so far away from where Lizzie was, in case she needed his help more directly. But he had a gnawing sense that she already needed his help, and that's why he was there.

It was clear that the next round of the Dead Ring was to take place that day, and it was equally clear that, for whatever reason, there was a good chance Lizzie might find herself once more unable to activate the transmitter. Wall had said that any subscribers' login info would be a suitable substitute, and that's what Red was prepared to get.

If the next round started and, after five minutes, Lizzie still hadn't activated the transmitter, Red and Dembe would pay a visit to Mrs. Tindley, and do whatever it took to convince her husband to share his login.

Chapter 65

As the buses pulled up in front of the building, Keen could see that it was little more than a skeleton, four open floors, with a stairway in the front and one in the back. She couldn't tell for sure if it was partially demolished or if it had never been finished. Or both. The outer walls were missing from the front and back, exposing the inside of the building. She wondered if that was for the benefit of the camera drones.

It was surrounded by a rusted chain link fence, although they were so far from anything else, she couldn't imagine who it was intended to keep out. Maybe coyotes. On the ground between the building and the fence, there were piles of debris every thirty or forty feet.

Okoye stumbled getting off the bus, but managed to stay on his feet.

They assembled at the gate for a few last words from Corson about how only ten of them would survive, at most, and how anyone who tried to escape would be shot.

As if to underscore his words, one of the buses turned around and drove off. They would only need one for the journey back.

Looking behind her, Keen saw the RV and the transport truck parked a quarter of a mile away, as before. As Corson talked, the PMCs dragged out two boxes and released two camera drones. Turning back, she scanned the building in front of them, and immediately spotted two cameras on tripods and two more mounted on the building itself.

Corson said yet again that he would see them in hell, then, looking directly at Keen, he said, "Gentlemen, you may begin."

The pack moved forward as one, like the beginning of a foot race, but instead of clustering together, they moved apart. Even as they headed for the same place, almost everyone tried to keep a minimum distance from everyone else. There were a few exceptions, Boden and Dudayev among them, who were edging closer to the other ringers, reaching out to push them or slow them down. Dudayev intentionally slowed and tripped Okoye, sending him sprawling across a pile of rubble and rebar.

Keen had been hanging back to avoid that kind of harassment. She ran over to Okoye and helped him to his feet. He had a deep gash across his forearm.

"Are you going to be okay?" she said.

He seemed to be having trouble focusing on her. "Are any of us going to be okay?" Then he laughed and said, "Come on," and ran unsteadily after the others.

Once again, Keen didn't know if the tac team was going to come in hot after the first five minutes, but she reminded herself that getting the transmitter and activating it was her true goal, or at least her primary goal. She needed to find an opportunity to even try to make that happen.

The PMCs had fanned out and were circling the

outer perimeter, outside the fence. Yancy and Corson were approaching behind her, coming through the gate.

There might be an opportunity after all. But it wasn't going to be easy.

As Keen approached the building, the two camera drones circled overhead like angry insects. She paused, looking up at the exposed structure. Boden appeared, already on the third floor. He had one of the other ringers in a choke hold, with his arms twisted behind his back. He laughed as he threw the man off the side of the building, laughing even harder as his victim landed with a wet thud on a pile of jagged rubble.

Almost immediately afterward, another ringer running up the steps to the third floor vanished, replaced by a bright flash, a loud bang, and a red cascade of shredded meat that coated the steps and rained down on the ground below.

Yancy and two of the PMCs had started slowly circling the building in opposite directions inside the fence. Yancy laughed as he side-stepped some of the raining debris.

Keen's plan began to take shape, but she knew that in order for it to have a chance of succeeding, she would have to survive the round, or at least part of it. And that meant getting to the top of the building.

The outside of the building bristled with exposed rebar. She had already been thinking that scaling the outside of it might be the safest way to go. Now she was sure of it. She grabbed one of the iron bars protruding from the concrete, and started climbing. Her muscles protested at first, but as she pulled herself up to the second floor, she warmed up and got into a rhythm.

Chapter 66

Keen saw two more ringers obliterated as she ascended the outside of the building, further confirming her decision to avoid the interior as much as possible. But when she reached the top floor, she knew she had to go inside.

As she pulled herself up onto the fourth floor, a chunk of masonry landed on the concrete in front of her and bounced over her. She caught a momentary glimpse of Bodèn, standing next to a bank of lockers, hefting another rock in his hand. She ducked back over the edge as the missile sailed past her.

She took a deep breath and swung herself up onto the floor, but by then Boden was gone.

She sprinted past the lockers to the back of the building and looked over the edge. Yancy was just rounding a corner to the rear of the building. He looked up with a sick grin and blew her a kiss.

She hurried back to the middle of the floor and used her key to open the next locker and retrieve the carbon steel knife inside it. The key was now stuck in the lock. It wouldn't come out. All the open doors still had keys in them.

She turned to go back the way she had come, but Dudayev had just emerged from the front stairway. He smiled when he saw her. It wasn't a nice smile.

She had the advantage of a knife, but she didn't have time. Instead she ran away from him, toward the back of the building. She was still sure that scaling the outside would be the safer bet, but she didn't want Yancy to see her coming. Despite her better judgment, she took the stairs.

She was pretty sure the next level down was safe—judging from the charred and bloody walls, whatever trap had been set there was already sprung.

When she reached the level below that, she immediately spotted one booby trap and avoided it easily, but then she felt the faint tug of a tripwire on her toe. There was a second trap. She looked down and saw it, almost invisible, but it was too late.

Time seemed to freeze, and for a long fraction of an instant, she thought she was dead. She saw the impact grenade dropping from above. She didn't have time to think, she could only watch as her body spun and rolled, somehow not only getting her hand under the thing before it hit the ground, but catching it softly enough that it didn't annihilate her anyway.

She stayed on the floor for a moment, her nerves almost as shattered as if the grenade actually had gone off. But it hadn't. And in fact, she realized, it could come in handy. She got to her feet cradling it gently, took a deep breath, and hurried on.

She avoided both traps on her way to the ground floor, then ran and came up behind the camera aimed along the back of the building.

Part of her wanted to preserve the camera in case she did get her hands on the transmitter, but she knew she had less than five minutes until the building came down. There wouldn't be enough time for Aram to execute the plan.

She slid her knife into the back of the camera and pried out the battery pack.

She heard a footstep outside, and flattened herself against the side wall. Her plan had been to use the grenade to distract Yancy so she could sneak up behind him, but suddenly there he was, inches away. He stepped out in front of her, the smell wafting off him. Then he checked his watch, turned around and started heading back toward the front of the building.

They were almost out of time.

Using the wall at her back to push off, she spun around with as much force behind her knife as she could muster.

His eyes widened in surprise and horror. So did hers, as she saw the knife embedded in his chest less than an inch from where the transmitter sat in his pocket. Her horror deepened as she realized the knife was wedged between his ribs, that he wasn't going down, and that he was bringing his gun around to shoot her.

Still holding the impact grenade, she had to fight him one-handed. But she still had two feet. It felt almost wrong to plant such a vicious kick into the groin of a man who was essentially almost dead. But this was Yancy. It didn't feel *that* wrong.

His face contorted into a different combination of pain and horror, and he let out a lungful of foul-smelling air. This time he did go down. She pulled his gun away from him as he fell and tossed it aside, then put her boot on his chest and yanked out the knife.

As the blood bubbled up from his chest, she put the knife under her arm and retrieved the transmitter from his shirt pocket.

She almost staggered with relief at the sight of it, completely undamaged.

Yancy's eyes followed it as she took it from him. A kind of recognition formed in them, as if he understood that she had not only killed him, but that she was going to take the whole thing down. That she had gotten the best of him.

Keen wasn't sure how much time she had left, but she knew she had to warn off the tac team. While she was still out in the open, and there was no one around, she held out the transmitter and used the blade of the knife to cover it and uncover it, hoping that the same trick that worked last time would work again this time.

"H-A-V-E...T-N-T" she said. "W-A-I-T... 4... S-I-G-N-A-L... T-M-R"

She tucked the transmitter into her pocket, but as she took a few steps back into the building, toward the front, she heard Yancy groan and she stopped. He was still alive, still watching her. He was evidence.

If Corson discovered him before he died that could be the end of it.

She tossed the grenade in a low parabola that would end at Yancy's midsection. Then she ran through the building as fast as she could.

Chapter 67

This time, the CIRRUS drone followed Keen for close to an hour. The two buses were followed a quarter of a mile back by two other vehicles that looked like the RV and the transport from the day before. The field office had been vibrating with intensity, but as time dragged on the intensity died out.

When the buses finally pulled over in front of an isolated, half-demolished four-story concrete building, everyone in the room livened up.

The alert dinged a second time and as Aram announced, "The satellite uplink is live," the mood intensified even more.

Cooper marked the time, and immediately a display on one of the screens started counting down from five minutes. He got on the phone with Nichols and advised him to have the tac team prepare for deployment.

Wall was furiously typing, recording the feed and accessing the back door so he could start to decrypt it. He might have sensed Aram staring at him, because he glanced over and gave him an awkward smile. Maybe even a guilty smile. It was hard to tell.

Once again, there were six video channels and one

data channel out and one data channel coming in.

"We have two-way," Aram announced. Presumably, that meant bets were coming in. This was for real.

Wall turned in his seat and glanced at Percival and the others at the back of the room.

At four minutes to go, Aram could hear the tac team helicopter landing outside to pick up Ressler and Navabi.

Aram enlarged the video image as much as he could without rendering it unintelligible. He could make out Agent Keen, standing in a group with the rest of the contestants in front of the building. But the tracker dot had her located thirty feet away. He was wondering if it had somehow become miscalibrated when all the contestants on the screen, including the figure of Keen, began running toward the building.

The tracker dot moved in a different direction.

Outside, the helicopter sat with Ressler and Navabi on board, waiting for orders.

Aram zoomed in on where the tracker dot said Agent Keen should be, and saw a man in a uniform carrying a rifle, walking slowly around to the back of the building.

"Oh, no," he said, drawing a look from Wall as a chill ran through his body.

"What is it?" Wall asked, rolling his chair closer.

Aram pointed at the screen. "Keen doesn't have the TNT," he said, his voice suddenly hoarse. "Yancy does." He turned in his chair and called out, "Director Cooper! I think we have a situation here."

Cooper hurried out of his office. "What is it?"

The display said three minutes until the tac team would be going in, even without the transmitter.

Aram had to take manual control of the CIRRUS to get an angle on Yancy.

"According to the tracker, that's where Agent Keen should be, but she's not. It seems to be Yancy, one of the Ringleader's men."

They watched as Yancy continued to walk around the perimeter of the building.

"He's got the TNT," Cooper said. "That's why she didn't activate it before." He called Nichols, "The operation has been compromised. We need to go in ASAP."

As the helicopter lifted off outside, Cooper turned back to Aram, and asked, "Have you seen Agent Keen?"

"Yes. Just a few minutes ago. She seemed okay."

Cooper closed his eyes and relief washed over his face.

Yancy disappeared around the corner of the building, and Aram maneuvered the CIRRUS to bring him back into view. Just as the camera found him, Yancy stopped, looked at his watch, and abruptly turned around.

"There she is!" Aram cried out, pointing at the screen.

Agent Keen had jumped out of the rear of the building and struck Yancy hard, ripping his rifle out of his hands as he fell to the ground. A red blotch appeared on his chest and they watched Keen fumble at his body, clearly looking for something. Then the tracker dot started blinking on and off again.

"She's got it back! It's Morse code again," Aram announced, decoding it in real time, out loud to the group.

Aram turned to Cooper. "She says we need to wait until tomorrow."

Staring at the screen, Cooper hesitated for a brief second, then he got back on the phone to Nichols. "Abort the mission," he said. "Repeat: Abort the mission. Stand down until further notice."

Chapter 68

When the text came in from Aram that there was no sign of Keen activating the transmitter, Red directed Dembe to drive around the corner and park in front of Tindley's house. As soon as they pulled up, he got out and walked up to the front door.

The drive and the walk took one minute.

It took another twenty seconds for Mrs. Tindley to answer the door.

"Hello?" she said. She was duly suspicious, but Red looked respectable enough that she was willing to give him the benefit of the doubt.

The place didn't seem like the home of someone who would be involved in something like the Dead Ring. She didn't seem like the wife of someone who would be either.

"I'm terribly sorry," Red said. "Mortified, actually. I would never dream of bothering Mr. Tindley at home, but we've got a problem. A big, big problem. And he's not answering his cell phone. Is he here, by any chance?"

She snorted and shook her head, like that was typical of Dwight. "And you are?"

"Sorry," he put out his hand. "Sherman Phelps. I'm

kind of new with the company, which makes it extra awkward me coming here to Mr. Tindley's home and all."

"I'm afraid he's off on a hunting trip," she said, rolling her eyes as she said it.

Red screwed up his face. "Ugh. He really is, huh? I know that's where he said he was going, but I kind of hoped he was making that up. I thought he just needed some time away from work. And don't get me wrong, if anyone deserves time away, it's Mr. Tindley, am I right? A lot of bosses think they're so indispensable the place would fall apart without them, but with Mr. Tindley, it's really true. And so he goes away and, well, here we are?"

"What seems to be the problem?"

"The Kazakhs are at it again. They're saying the fee they agreed to includes us paying all internal corporate business taxes, which I know Mr. Tindley would never have agreed to. Never. It's only about twenty million one way or another, but they're threatening to back out of the whole deal if they don't get what they want, and that could be some real money. When we start talking 'B's' instead of 'M's' I know it's time to call Mr. Tindley. Even at home."

"Well, he told me not to call him unless it was an absolute emergency, but it sounds like this is one, huh?"

"Red lights are literally flashing."

"I'm surprised Clark didn't call or come by... Maybe I should call him."

"Clark is actually supposed to be on a hunting trip of his own, if you know what I mean."

She laughed and swatted at him, scandalized, but as if his reference was absolutely unambiguous. "Oh! Good for him, but wow, so soon after the operation."

"Well, you know Clark."

She laughed again. "Come on in, Sherman. Would you like a cup of coffee?"

"No, thank you," he said. "I've inconvenienced you more than enough."

She led him into the kitchen and as she picked up her phone, he eyed the knives on the magnetic rack over the sink. There was a filet knife third from the left that he would probably use if it came to it.

He looked at his watch. Four minutes since the uplink started. It was looking more and more like it would come to it.

Too bad. He kind of liked her.

She placed the call, then held the phone out to her side and said, "He told me to call once and hang up then call back if it was a real emergency."

She disconnected and had just hit redial when they both heard a tapping at the front door.

Mrs. Tindley gasped at the sight of Dembe, but Red said, "Don't worry. Just my driver."

"Your driver?"

Red walked to the front door, and Dembe held the phone up to the glass, revealing the latest text from Aram: KEEN BACK ON LINE AND IN CONTACT. SENT A MESSAGE. WE GO IN TOMORROW.

For a fraction of a second, Red considered going ahead with his plan anyway. But he decided it could put Keen at even greater risk. Tomorrow would have to do.

"What do you know," he called out as he walked back into the kitchen. "The Kazakhs have backed down. Crisis averted. No need to bother him."

He could hear Dwight Tindley's voice on the other end of the phone, angry and suspicious. "What is it? I t-told you not to c-call me today."

She smiled and shook her head at the sound of his voice. "I'm sorry, honey, I thought it was an emergency, but it's not."

The phone went dead without another word.

Chapter 69

Keen didn't watch the grenade go off. It wasn't about cool indifference or unwavering self-confidence. It was about only having minutes before the building came down, and running like hell out of there before it did.

The first level was littered with debris, including two dead bodies, one of them in pieces. But with no interior walls, she could see straight through to the outside. Hovering in the sunlight out front, right at eye level, was one of the camera drones. It sickened and infuriated her to think if she died, if the whole building came down on top of her, that her death would make great viewing for the sick bastards betting on the Dead Ring.

As she pumped her legs harder and faster, she heard someone come down the rear steps behind her, but she didn't pause, didn't look. She just kept running.

The sun was high overhead, lighting up just a sliver of the concrete floor, right at the edge. That's what she was running for—that sunlight. As she broke its plane she could feel the warmth of it, first on her nose, then her forehead. Her eyes filled with the glare of it.

Keen was halfway out from under the building

when she heard the rapid-fire percussive reports of the shaped charges going off behind her.

She didn't let up for an instant—she knew it was too soon, that she was too close for that. But there was a moment when everything else slowed down, as if the entire world was taking a deep breath, gathering its strength and fortitude for what was to come next.

She was almost entirely out from under the building, almost entirely out into the light, when the concrete and metal around her let out a brief, tortured groan. Then it all came down.

Rocks and grit pelted her back and shot past her, tumbling onto the dirt on either side of her legs. A chunk of concrete big enough to have instantly killed her sailed over her shoulder, inches from her head.

For a moment, she was overtaken by thick dust. But then it stopped and she didn't, still running until she was in the clear. She sprinted past the chain link fence. She stumbled on the rubble, lost her footing and fell, but rolled into it and came out of it in a three-point stance.

Corson smiled at her wryly.

Behind him were eight ringers, including Boden and Dudayev, and, miraculously, Okoye.

She turned and looked back at the roiling ball of dust behind her, the chunks of concrete still settling onto each other.

Nine of them had died back there, including whoever had come down the steps behind her as she was already running out. If she had turned to look back, to see who it was, there would have only been eight survivors.

It chilled Keen to think about it.

Okoye shuffled over and helped her away from the rubble.

"You okay?" he said, haltingly.

Keen nodded, then moved away from him, bent over and coughed out the grit in her mouth. The pain in her side flared, but she tried not to show it.

She still had the transmitter in one hand and the knife in the other. She leaned against the bus and in the best imitation of cliché toughness she could muster, she used the tip of the bloody knife to clean her fingernails.

She was pretty sure no one was buying it, but she didn't care. All she cared about at that moment was flicking the knife back and forth over the transmitter sending another message, just in case. A longer one: "H-A-V-E... T-N-T... L-A-S-T... R-N-D... T-M-R... W-A-I-T... 4... S-I-G-N-A-L"

Corson walked over and stood in front of her. "Got a hangnail?" he said, smirking as she finished.

"No," she said, putting the knife through her belt. "Not a scratch, actually."

He snorted and walked away from her.

She was surprised he wasn't more upset, and also that they were just standing around, but then she realized the dust was still settling. The PMCs were still coming in from the perimeter. They didn't yet realize that Yancy was missing.

After another minute or so, it seemed to dawn on Corson. He looked over one shoulder, then the other, confused. He looked at his watch. He laughed nervously then called over one of the PMCs and whispered in his ear. The PMC huddled with his comrades, then they all ran back out and swept the perimeter.

Keen looked away whenever Corson's eyes came anywhere near hers.

She was fascinated on some level, wondering how he would respond. Had he and Yancy been friends?

They seemed to have history, but she couldn't see either of them as capable of actual human affection. There was something in Corson's eyes, though, something that resembled pain.

His cell phone started ringing and he answered, looking back at the RV as he did. He muttered a few words, but mostly listened, his face hardening. He looked up and Keen looked away. She felt Corson's eyes rake across her and a moment later she looked back. His expression was fire and venom as he looked at the rest of the ringers.

They seemed oblivious and she tried her hardest to look the same.

A few seconds later, the PMCs returned with the lead shaking his head.

Corson said something into his phone before putting it away. He glanced at the rubble pile and shook his head. Keen was pretty sure he muttered, "Dumbass."

He stepped toward the group and quietly said, "Line up."

She wasn't sure anyone else heard him. They completely ignored him.

He took a step closer, and screamed at the top of his lungs, "*I SAID LINE UP!*"

They all jumped into formation, eying him warily and unsure what was wrong.

"The camera in the back went offline before it happened," he said. "We know it was not an accident."

He was scouring their faces with his eyes. They looked back, tough but bewildered. They had no idea what he was talking about. And Corson didn't care. He wasn't talking to them. He was talking to whoever killed Yancy. He was talking to Keen.

He laughed. "Yancy is still in there, apparently. He

did not make it out." He scratched his nose and laughed again, to himself. "It's not like Yancy to get himself killed. I can't think of the last time he let that happen."

The ringers looked at each other, like they were wondering if they were supposed to be laughing along with him. None dared. Keen was pretty sure that was wise.

"We're processing the footage from the drones. One of them should tell us what happened. It's possible that idiot Yancy got himself killed. But unlikely. Much more likely that one of you did it, and that is a clear violation of the rules. And a serious one." The muscles in Corson's temples were throbbing and he paused for a second before continuing. "Whoever is found responsible will be expelled from the Dead Ring. But if you are in this for the fame, the notoriety, you will get it. Because when we find out who did this, you will get a show of your very own. Just you." His voice was rising, louder and more ragged. "Twenty-four hours a day of torture, worse than anything even you sick reptiles could imagine. And if anybody here tries anything like that with me, we will track down your entire family, your second cousins and grand-nephews, your best friends from kindergarten, anyone you ever loved, or even said hi to. And as we roast them over a spit and skin them alive, I will tell them again and again that it is you who is responsible for their terrible pain, for the agony that will drive them out of their minds until they are begging to die so they can haunt you in hell!"

His chest was heaving by the time he was finished; his face dripping with sweat and his eyes filled with hatred and rage and something that she was stunned to recognize as fear.

The PMCs gathered on either side of him, their rifles raised and aimed at the ringers. Corson looked at them closely, as if trying one last time to intuit who had killed Yancy. Then he shook his head in frustration and snarled, "Get on the bus."

Chapter 70

The pleasure of watching the Dead Ring was a multifaceted thing, with different types of pleasure at different stages. But all of them were exquisite, and all of them due their rightful attention and enjoyment. Watching the actual rounds was the most intense, the most delicious, but the excitement of the lead-up was an integral part of it. So was the mellow afterburn that immediately followed, slowly coming down from the high, savoring it, basking in the flood of images and memories.

Even the damned Cowboy was learning not to interrupt it.

But once again the afterglow of watching the Dead Ring was ruined by the failures of associates and underlings.

The building had come down in an impressive explosion, but by far the best part of it was the narrow escape of the woman, Le Chat, and the even narrower failure of the man running behind her. The image of his face, his eyes opened so wide they looked like the skin around them would tear. The pure effort he was putting out, knowing it was absolutely everything he had, and knowing, in the end, that it was not going to be enough.

As the charges went off, he had somehow found a little more something from somewhere, but as the rubble started raining down, the grim truth was obvious in those terrified eyes. He didn't give up, not for a second. Not even when a chunk of concrete caught him behind the ear. He kept going. Barely visible in the hail of rubble and dust, his eyes dull from the injury, but his hands and feet scrambling to get out. Then another chunk hit him, and another. In an instant, he was a bloody, pulverized mess, but still pulling what was left of himself across the debris-strewn floor, until finally the building gave out and came down on top of him. There was a glimpse of red, and then nothing.

That's what he was savoring when he noticed something wrong down there.

He tapped at his keypad and one of the technicians put a hand to his earpiece and said, "I don't know, sir. It looks like Yancy is missing."

The Cowboy looked back and forth at them, trying to determine what was going on. To his credit, he remained silent.

The technician cycled through the camera feeds, until one of the screens showed Yancy, patrolling the outside of the building with his rifle. He had just come around to the rear of the building when he got a notice from his watch and he turned to go back, wearing that same stupid grin as always.

The camera shook, and then it went out.

"Someone might have killed the camera," the technician said. He cycled through the other cameras, the mounted ones and the drones, but none of them showed what had happened to Yancy.

The technician touched his earpiece, then got up and brought a phone to the back of the room.

"Where's Yancy?" the Ringleader hissed into the phone.

"We... we don't know, sir," Corson replied.

"You let those savages kill him?"

"We don't know, sir. He might have gotten himself killed."

"If you can't keep things under control, there is no point keeping you. Do you understand that?"

Corson went quiet as someone else spoke to him. He said, "Yes, sir," then he was gone.

The Ringleader breathed deeply, regaining his calm, trying to salvage a last wisp of the afterglow that he'd been denied.

Then a phone buzzed in the room and quickly stopped.

There were strict rules about phones in there.

The Cowboy said, "S-sorry." He looked like he meant it. "It's my wife. I told her it was just for emergencies."

The phone started buzzing again and Tindley picked it up. "What is it?" he whispered harshly into the phone. "I t-told you not to c-call me today."

As he listened to whoever was on the other end, in the back of the room, the Ringleader tapped at his keypad. One of the guards jammed the barrel of his rifle into the Cowboy's ribs and plucked the phone out of his hands. He ended the call then dropped the phone and crushed it under his boot.

The Ringleader emerged from the shadows. "No phones," he said. "You know that. Break another rule and we will crush you, instead."

Chapter 71

Corrello was helpful as always. He'd been glad to hear from Red, at first. Then Red had asked, "What do you know about Michael Hoagland and Edward Stannis?"

Corrello had gone quiet after that. So quiet that if not for the sound of his breathing over the phone, Red would have thought he was no longer there. Then Corrello said, "A lot. What do you want to know?"

"Well, to start with, are they alive?"

"I don't know for sure about that. No one has seen either of them in years. No one I trust not to be full of crap, at least. But I do know this. I worked with both of them. They were both crazy in their own way, but Hoagland was a different sort of crazy. Hoagland is supposed to be dead, and Stannis is supposed to be alive. But the story ain't always the true story, you know what I mean? I've heard some things."

"Like?"

"Well, for one, Stannis himself told me one time that he was in the room in Peru. He said it wasn't no narco terrorist attack or anything like that. He said the board of directors and senior management wanted him to be there when they told Hoagland he was out on his ass and they were selling the company to Stannis. But Stannis said he knew Hoagland was a nutjob, and he figured something might be up. Stannis was suspicious as hell, so when he goes in he hangs back by the door. Apparently, Hoagland must've somehow caught wind of the deal and didn't like it. Stannis said the vindictive nutjob pulled the pin on the grenade himself, says, 'This company lives by me and dies by me,' or some crap, and he tosses the grenade onto the table. Stannis said he managed to get outside before the thing went off. Watched the whole building come down. The place was crawling with Hoagland's men, and they put out the fire, but by the time they got back inside, it was like a barbecue, all these little pieces of cooked meat in there. His words, not mine. But he also said there was a big hole in the wall, shaped like the conference table, and the conference table was gone. He thinks Hoagland somehow managed to lift up the entire conference table, use it as a shield."

"Did he think Hoagland survived?"

"He didn't think so at the time. He said they found pieces of the conference table a quarter mile away down the side of the mountain, but they never confirmed finding Hoagland's body. He said he sometimes wondered if maybe Hoagland got out of there alive."

"What do you think?"

Corrello laughed, raspy and tired, betraying a wisdom that was usually hidden when he spoke. "I think I don't know, but Stannis and his wife— Hoagland's widow—disappeared a couple months later. Maybe they retired to some island somewhere, but that's not the kind of guy Stannis was."

"You think it was Hoagland?"

"I think seeing your rival steal your company and

your wife might be enough to bring a guy back from the dead. I think Hoagland was a vindictive nutjob with motive and a year to heal from whatever happened to him in Peru, if he survived."

"Why did Stannis go along with the whole narco terrorist attack story?"

"I don't know. Better for the brand, I guess," Corrello said. "So you're asking if I think Hoagland is alive. Does that mean you think he's behind this whole Dead Ring thing?"

"Perhaps. It would be hard to imagine him pulling it off, injured as he was, and without Hoagland Services at his disposal."

"He was a very determined guy. And I'll tell you this—Hoagland's men, the mercenaries that worked for him? They worshipped him. Like a god. Like it was some kind of cult. When Stannis came in, he gave them all raises and bonuses and stuff, but a lot of them left anyway. No one seems to know where they went."

"You think they found out Hoagland was alive and joined him wherever he was."

"I don't know. That could explain how he's been able to get away with it. Plus, the guy did a lot of dirty work for a lot of dirty people, all around the world. Back when he was alive, or, you know what I mean. He had his thumb on a lot of people in high places and a Rolodex full of sickos that might go in for this kind of thing. You going after him?"

"Perhaps."

"Well, in the interests of you still being around to keep giving me money, let me tell you this. If it is Hoagland, one thing he's shown is that if he thinks he's going down, he's taking as many people with him as he can."

Red got off the phone as Dembe pulled the car into one of the parking spots once set aside for the teachers at Cavelier Elementary School.

Inside, Cooper was talking to Aram and Wall. All three of them looked up as Red walked in.

Red met Cooper's eye as he walked straight into Cooper's office. Cooper followed him.

"So, I understand the last round of the Dead Ring is tomorrow?" Red asked, as Cooper came in and closed the door behind him.

"That's the information we got from Keen."

"So we have one last shot at this. What's your plan?"

Cooper glared at him for another moment, as if deciding how to proceed. To his credit he recognized that whatever the plan, it had a better chance of success with Red's input.

"We're four minutes out by helicopter. Since this is the final round and we won't have another chance, as soon as Agent Keen activates the TNT the tac team will take off. There's no reason to hold back, so we'll time it to arrive at exactly five minutes."

"I want to be notified when she is on the move, when and where they stop, when the transmission starts. I want to be kept in the loop."

"Fair enough."

"Once the tac team lands, then what happens?"

"Our teams will sweep in, clear the site, and extract Agent Keen. Percival and his team will locate the control room and pick up Hoagland."

Red laughed. "The CIA? I thought we agreed this was your operation, Harold. Aren't you concerned the CIA might be more interested in whatever intelligence Hoagland has to offer than in bringing him to justice?"

"What are you saying?"

Red lowered his voice, knowing Percival and the other two CIA agents were somewhere in the building. "I'm saying they're going to be more concerned with getting Hoagland out alive than getting Keen out alive."

Cooper shrugged. "I think that's overstating it, but regardless of whatever arrangement you think you made with Percival, this is the deal I had to agree to in order to keep the operation alive."

"Apparently Ed Stannis once claimed that he was in the conference room in Peru when Hoagland Services' entire board of directors and senior management was killed. He said it wasn't narco terrorists. It was Hoagland himself. He found out they were going to sack him and sell the company out from under him, so he took them all out instead. Almost took himself out in the process."

"So what's your point?"

"My point is that if Hoagland has the slightest inkling he's going down, he's going to set off whatever holy hell he can to take as many other people down with him."

Chapter 72

Riding back to the campground this time, the PMCs stood at the front and back of the bus, with their rifles trained on the ringers.

Corson seemed different. His face was pinched, not smirking.

No one said a word the entire trip, not even Boden and Dudayev.

Okoye looked out the window the whole time. His eyes looked blank and Keen worried he had gone catatonic, or worse. But when they approached the campground, he sat up straight and shook his head, blinking and yawning, as if he had been asleep with his eyes open.

When they finally got off the bus, a few ringers started walking toward the cabins, but they stopped when Corson said, "Line up."

He didn't say it loud, but the PMCs provided added emphasis, leveling their rifles at the crowd of ringers. Everyone assembled into lines, quicker, neater, and quieter than they ever had before. There were nine of them left. Three rows of three.

The PMCs now outnumbered the ringers. Keen wondered how many of them it took to make up for the loss of Yancy. Corson cleared his throat and moved so that he was squarely facing the nine remaining ringers. He seemed somehow discombobulated without Yancy, and Keen felt a slight, strange pang of guilt.

"It is not uncommon for ringers to get agitated before the final round," Corson began. Another PMC came up from the direction of the main cabin carrying a box. He began handing out futuristic-looking white bracelets in sealed plastic bags as Corson spoke.

"You have accomplished quite something by making it this far. And the end is in sight. But still the odds are very much against you. All but one of you will die before the next round is over."

When everyone had a bracelet, Corson ordered, "Put them on." The PMCs again provided emphasis, raising their rifles as he resumed his speech.

"That can be a stark realization. Because of that we must tighten the rules. Any infractions will be met with the harshest of consequences."

The ringers tore open the plastic and took out their bracelets. They looked like smart watches, except the displays were blank. Keen put hers on her wrist, fastening it loosely until one of the PMCs walked up to her and placed the barrel of his rifle under her chin.

"Tighter," he said.

He held the rifle there as she tightened the bracelet. When he decided it looked tight enough, he walked up and down the rows, checking the others' bracelets as well. Okoye seemed to be having trouble putting his on, but he managed to do so without any assistance.

"You are already facing death, so the consequences for violations must be much worse. Doubtless there are large bets on all of you at this point and we must protect those wagers." He smiled. "Trust me when I tell you, consequences will not be pleasant."

When the PMC was satisfied with everyone's bracelets, he gave Corson a sharp nod.

Corson nodded back at him and continued. "The bracelets you are now wearing contain a powerful high explosive. They have a minimum destructive range of five feet, which means that if you are under ten feet tall, your heart and brain will instantly be shredded upon detonation. Any attempt to remove your bracelet will trigger the explosive. Any attempt to flee this facility will trigger the explosive. Any attempt to break any rules or aggravate me in any way will trigger the explosive."

He stared at them for a moment, scanning their faces, one by one, as if trying one more time to determine who killed Yancy.

Finally he shook his head and said, "Go."

Keen slowly walked away, waiting for Okoye. They let the others move on without them.

"Are you okay?" Keen whispered to him as they walked.

"I thought you were going to bring this thing down?" he asked. "You are running out of time."

"I had a setback."

"Yes, you lost your transmitter thing. I hope you got it back when you killed Yancy."

She looked at him, trying to read his face.

"You did the world a favor," he said. "I just hope it doesn't complicate your plans."

Keen remained quiet.

As they approached the cabins, he continued. "You noticed the camper? The RV or whatever that has been following us?"

She nodded.

"That is where whoever is in charge is monitoring everything. That's where they connect to the satellite."

"I figured."

He paused for a moment as his eye went into spasm.

"I am not well at all," he said. "Even if it was possible that I could win this, I fear I will be gone in a matter of days."

"I'm sorry," she replied. "But remember, you don't have to win. You just have to survive. After we take this thing down, I'll make sure you get the best medical care available."

He smiled. "It is too late for that, if ever there was time. But don't worry, I won't be missing much." His smile went away. "I will help you however I can and maybe I can leave the world a better place, a place my nephews will miss more when they leave it than I will."

They said goodbye and she entered her cabin, saddened that no matter what she did, Jakob Okoye was still going to die.

Keen drank several bottles of water and ate a foil envelope of tofu doing a decent imitation of teriyaki chicken.

She slid the TNT out of her pocket and spent an hour studying it with her fingers, getting to know its contours, its lines, but all the while keeping it hidden in her hands in case her room was being monitored. When she was done, she put it in her bra. She figured it would be hidden, protected, and much more easily accessible than on her toe. Frankly, she wondered why they hadn't put it there in the first place. She smiled at the thought that it was probably because Aram was so shy. He'd had a difficult enough time with her feet.

The stress of the past few days seemed to suddenly

catch up with her, along with the aches and pains, the bruises and scrapes. It was compounded by the boredom of being stuck in the cabin. She lay gingerly back on her bed. As her eyes drifted closed, she thought she mustn't let herself sleep long. Otherwise, she'd be up all night.

She drifted off to sleep considering the very real possibility that she wasn't going to make it out. It bothered her that fake teriyaki chicken in a pouch could end up being her last meal. As her eyes closed, she thought how disappointed Red would be.

Chapter 73

It was seven-fifteen when the loudspeaker started blaring reveille. Keen shot upright on her bed, confused. Something wasn't quite right. Horizontal sunlight angled in through the window. She still felt exhausted, but apparently, somehow she had slept straight through till sunrise.

Then she realized it wasn't sunrise, it was sunset.

She splashed water on her face, checked that the transmitter was in place, then hurried outside.

Okoye was walking unsteadily by as she stepped out.

"Do you know what's going on?" he asked.

"No idea."

No one else was immediately visible, and for a second, she wondered if they had both somehow misinterpreted the reveille. But then she realized that most of the cabins around them were empty. Most of the others were already dead.

Okoye stumbled, but she caught his arm and stopped him falling over. She put her arm through his and helped him the rest of the way. He seemed steadier by the time they approached the main square, and reluctant to be seen being helped by a rival competitor. He pulled his arm away from hers as the other ringers came into sight, filling up from the rows of cabins on either side of them.

Corson was waiting for them, along with eight PMCs.

Night was rapidly falling, and as they ascended the slope to the square, Keen looked back toward the gate and saw the RV there, with its lights on. Somehow it looked even more sinister at night.

As she watched, an SUV pulled up beside it. She couldn't tell if it was the same one as before.

"Line up," Corson barked as they approached.

They did so, three by three, just like before. The entire group seemed subdued, even Boden and Dudayev, as if they were all reassessing things from this new vantage point so much closer to victory or death.

Corson walked up to Okoye. "You don't look well, Jakob. I doubt there is much in the way of wagers on you, but this event is supposed to be entertaining. You'd better not just keel over and die. Our viewers are expecting much more of a spectacle from your death."

He turned to Keen. "Le Chat," he said, in a way that made her wonder if maybe he suspected her true identity, or at least doubted her fake one. "If I was allowed to bet, I would have lost some money on you already. But I'd still be betting against you on this round."

The gate opened and the bus pulled in, its headlights bright in the growing darkness.

Corson stood by the door. Two PMCs got on first, then the ringers filed on board, followed by another two PMCs, guns raised, not taking any chances. Everyone was silent.

Okoye stumbled on the steps and Corson snorted and shook his head.

"This should be fun," he muttered.

Corson took his place at the front of the bus as it

pulled out of the campground. As they turned to head east, away from the dusk and into the night, he said, "Better get comfortable. It's going to be a long ride."

Chapter 74

The field office was quiet and tense. Part of it, Aram knew, was the adrenaline hangover from almost executing the plan and then holding back at the last moment. Leaving Agent Keen inside the Dead Ring for one more day didn't help, even if it was at her own request. That didn't sit well with anyone—especially not after Wall finished decoding the video.

Again they only had one channel to watch, and again, much of it was wide shots, taken from relatively far away. But there was plenty of violence, and every now and then they could see Agent Keen in the middle of it, usually trying to avoid it, but sometimes committing it.

There was also an awkwardness in the air, from being outnumbered by strangers in the field office. Navabi and Ressler were now embedded with the tac team to shed a few seconds off their response time. So Cooper and Aram were the only members of the task force on site. Percival, Thomas, and Beckoff pretty much stuck to themselves, but they still gave Aram the creeps. And Wall seemed like a decent enough guy, but he was odd, he was a stranger, and he seemed to have a lot of secrets.

Mostly, though, it was the grinding anticipation

of the next morning—the final round of the Dead Ring, the last chance to bring it down, arrest those responsible, and get Agent Keen to safety.

Wall had been refining his decryption techniques, studying the things he had done to exploit the back door and figuring out ways to do it faster.

Aram had watched the videos from the previous two rounds over and over. There was nothing more to be gained from watching them. There was nothing to do but wait.

It was seven P.M. and the sun had just dropped below the horizon. It was too early to sleep, but Aram's brain ached from the intensity of the previous few days. He was pondering how he was going to spend the rest of the evening.

Then he noticed the tracker dot slowly creeping across the screen. He zoomed in and confirmed it was moving from the cabin area to the main square. In the waning light, he zoomed in the video from the CIRRUS and confirmed as best he could that it was Keen, and that the two dots corresponded. She had the TNT on her.

"Sir," he called out. "We have movement."

In seconds Cooper was looking over his shoulder.

They watched as Keen lined up with the others in a tidy three-by-three square formation, bringing home the fact that there were only nine of them left. The bus—just one this time—drove through the gates and the contestants filed on board.

Cooper got out his phone and as soon as the bus turned and exited the campground, he called Nichols and put the tac team on standby.

Aram texted Reddington to let him know Agent Keen was on the move.

Percival and the others came in from the other room and Percival started making calls, as well.

Wall seemed to be watching Percival from the corner of his eye, tapping his fingers nervously on the table. He seemed especially keyed up. He wasn't just waiting for the satellite feed to start, so he could get to work decrypting it. He was waiting for Keen to activate the transmitter, so he could insert the two programs into the video feed.

They watched as the bus moved across the darkened prairie, followed a quarter of a mile back by the RV and, behind that, an SUV. The caravan stuck to the back roads, moving steadily across the darkened landscape, three sets of headlights in a sea of black.

Twenty minutes later, the distant thump of helicopter rotors approached.

"That's our ride," Percival announced. "Agent Beckoff will stay here to monitor the results of our package. Agent Thomas and I will be tagging along behind your team."

Cooper bristled. "If you interfere in any way—"

Percival smiled and put up his hands. "Don't worry. I'll have my people call your people and we'll set everything up."

It sounded like they were scheduling a lunch date.

Then they were gone. Wall seemed relieved. Aram was too. He didn't trust them. But in the wake of their departure, as the convoy continued across the plains, the energy in the room dissipated.

After an hour, Cooper called Nichols and had the tac team determine another launch site that would keep them within five minutes of the bus's new location. They relocated to a high school football stadium parking lot.

Aram texted Reddington an update.

After two hours, the tac team had relocated twice more, hopscotching across the West Texas plains to stay within a five-minute range of the bus.

Aram kept a running list of possible destinations, using a map overlay and satellite images. But it was a useless task when possible destinations could include a bridge or an abandoned building. As quickly as the possibilities were identified, they were discarded because they had already been passed by.

Finally, three hours after leaving the campground, the bus turned onto a dirt road. The RV and the SUV followed, then followed again when the bus left the road altogether a mile later.

"Sir, we might have something here," Aram said, texting Red the same.

Once again, Cooper had anticipated the moment and was standing right behind him. Wall returned from the personal quarters, yawning, and took his seat.

He had just turned back to look at the screen when it went completely black.

"Have we lost the CIRRUS camera?" Cooper asked.

"No," Aram replied. "They've turned off their lights."

Cooper said, "What's our list of possible destinations?"

Aram was already working on it, checking his list and simultaneously panning the CIRRUS camera across the horizon. Slowly, from left to right, a mass of lights lit up the night sky. At first he couldn't figure out what it was. It looked like a city, but there was no city out there.

As he zoomed in, he realized what he was looking at, and he whispered, "Oh, no."

Chapter 75

For three hours they'd been driving through the dark and desolate West Texas landscape. They passed a handful of small towns, but for most of the drive the only lights were the bus's headlights, stabbing into the darkness in front of them, and, on the occasional sharp bend, the headlights of the RV and the SUV a quarter of a mile behind them.

Then both sets of lights went out.

For a moment, all Keen could see was the faint lights of the bus's dashboard.

Then she noticed a glow on the horizon.

The driver put on a set of night vision goggles and a pair of tail lights swerved around them as the SUV passed them. A moment later, the bus surged forward. Over the next five minutes the glow on the horizon turned into lights that grew bigger and brighter as they approached.

Keen felt a cold sweat as she realized it was some sort of petroleum or chemical installation.

It was huge.

Her mind raced trying to think about how this round could possibly go down. There must be dozens, if not hundreds, of people working at a facility like that. And even out in the middle of nowhere, there were small towns scattered around.

The fallout from any kind of large-scale incident at a plant like that could be devastating.

Corson stood in the darkness as the bus slowly rumbled forward.

"Behind me is the Wolfcamp Petrochemical Plant," he said. "Part refinery, part processing plant, part chemical manufacturing facility. This is where you will be playing the final round of the Dead Ring. Any attempt to flee this facility will trigger the explosives in your bracelet, which, in case you have forgotten, will kill you instantly. There is a thirty-meter buffer around the outer gate. Do not exceed it. In the control room of the plant's primary operations center, there is a glass box on the wall with a red key for the plant's master shutoff. This is also the key for a metal box that has been placed just outside the main gate. Inside that metal box is a briefcase containing five million dollars in cash."

Boden and Dudayev high-fived each other, apparently undisturbed by the notion that at least one of them, and probably both, would be dead by the time that money was claimed.

"The object of the game is to retrieve the key and open the box. Once the box is open, you can safely remove the money, making you the winner. Any attempt to damage the box or open it without the key will detonate four pounds of C4 located inside it, obliterating the prize money and whoever was foolish enough to try to steal it. Upon completion of the task, the detonator in the winner's bracelet will be deactivated. The remaining bracelets will all be detonated, as will eight pounds of C4 wired to the main intake of the plant's primary chemical reactor. So, if it ends up that you are the winner, you might want to get as far away from here as you can, as quickly as you can." A smile appeared in the darkness. "The stakes are high, but you knew that when you signed up. So," he clapped his hands together. "Good luck to all of you. My sympathies to most of you. And congratulations to one of you."

Chapter 76

As Aram told Cooper where he thought the convoy was headed, he realized that as horrible as the first two rounds had been, they'd been tame compared to some of the previous Dead Rings. It looked like they were going to make up for that now.

Cooper called Nichols. "You need to get in the air, now. The buses seem to be headed for Wolfcamp Petrochemical Plant. If whatever they have in mind in there is anything like what they've done in the past, the results could be devastating."

On the screen, the CIRRUS showed the RV pull off the road, onto a trail that ascended a small bluff, overlooking the plant from half a mile away. The bus and the SUV remained on the road, headed straight toward the front gates, but the SUV pulled around the bus and sped ahead of it, stopping thirty yards outside the gate. Two men got out, ran around to the back, and pulled out a large metal box.

"What the hell is that?" Wall whispered.

"I have no idea," Aram replied, "but I'm sure it's not good."

The figures placed the box in front of the gate then

hurried back into the SUV and sped off the way they had come.

Cooper made a quick call, alerting the state emergency response teams to be on standby for possible terrorist activity. He tried to call the plant itself, but the call wouldn't go through.

On the screen, the bus came to a stop.

Aram zoomed in and said, "They're getting out."

Chapter 77

They got off the bus just outside the spill of light from the processing plant. Behind them, the plains stretched into the black, moonless night. In front of them, the buildings, tanks, and machinery blazed with artificial light that seemed brighter than daylight. Here and there, gas flares burned off waste products. The air was thick with the smell of petroleum and combustion and the loud white noise of countless machines whirring and buzzing and roaring and whining.

Keen could see a scattering of workers on catwalks here and there, a few of them stopping what they were doing to look out into the dark, probably asking themselves if they were really seeing something, or if it was a trick of the light.

Keen tried not to think of what would happen to them if she failed. Instead she took the moment to scan the grounds for a camera. She felt panic rising within her the longer she looked, until finally she spotted one, off to the side, thirty yards west of the gate itself. She tried to gauge its distance from the fence. It seemed to be about twenty-five yards, but with so much at stake, she questioned her ability to tell.

Corson stood in front, flanked by eight armed PMCs. He smiled, looking at each one of them, as if he was relishing the thought that eight of the nine would soon be dead.

"The game will begin on my mark," he said quietly.

A quartet of camera drones flew by overhead, a chorus of different tones from their different altitudes and speeds.

They all watched them fly by, and when Keen looked back at the ground-mounted camera, she noticed a tiny red light. It was recording.

Corson clapped his hands, drawing their attention. He rubbed them together, stepped aside and barked, "Now."

Chapter 78

"We have transmission," Aram announced, as soon as it appeared on his screen.

Half a second later, the computer chimed with the alert that he had programmed to notify them, but Cooper was already on the phone. Wall's fingers began slapping furiously against the keyboard—a blur of flawless accuracy and absolute confidence.

Aram allowed himself a brief moment to watch the scroll of gibberish floating up the screen, snatches of it making sense to him here and there, before it disappeared under the onslaught of Wall's fingers. A flicker of doubt passed through his mind, how much they were entrusting to this man they barely knew. It was followed by a flash of even greater doubt as he wondered what, if anything, Wall and Reddington had discussed in his absence.

But he took out his phone and sent a text to Reddington. "TRANSMISSION STARTED."

Aside from any doubts about Wall, Aram trusted Reddington, especially as far as Agent Keen was concerned. No one, not even Director Cooper, maybe not even Aram himself, was as committed to Agent Keen's safety.

* * *

As soon as Dembe gave the signal that the transmission had started, Red gave the thumbs up to the helicopter pilot and the blades started turning.

The chopper's cruising speed was two hundred and forty-three miles an hour. They had hopscotched after the convoy based on Aram's updates, never letting it get more than five minutes away by chopper. Now they were less than ten miles away, less than three minutes in the air.

They lifted off early to make sure there were no difficulties, and hovered fifty feet above the ground for two minutes, waiting so as to not arrive too soon. Then they went.

The pilot was Bud Jasper, one of Red's usuals. Ex-Army Airborne, he had absolute discretion, unflinching bravery, and a feather touch on the controls.

Other than Jasper it was just Red and Dembe.

A minute and a half into the flight, they caught sight of two other helicopters, skimming the prairie floor northwest of them, headed to the same location and maybe a minute behind them. One of them would be the FBI tactical team, the other Percival and his CIA.

Chapter 79

By now, the nine remaining players had some idea what to expect. The instant Corson said, "Now," the group dispersed like a rack of billiard balls hit by a break shot. Keen took off running laterally away from the gate, toward the camera on the tripod.

She took two steps then looked back over her shoulder, scanning the tableau from left to right.

Okoye was stumbling backwards, wisely and intentionally it seemed, getting himself out of harm's way. Dudayev ran straight for the gate along with several others. In a single motion, Boden grabbed the head of the man standing next to him and gave it a violent, wrenching twist. At the same time he lashed out with his leg and caught one of the other ringers in the throat. Before either of them hit the ground, he was off and running.

Before she turned back to look where she was going, Keen saw one of the PMCs aiming his gun at her, but then Corson put his hand on the rifle and gently pushed it down. His face twisted into a smile as he watched her, and at the same time, a camera drone swooped past her head, then fell into position above and behind her, pacing her as she ran.

Keen realized Corson was hoping she was making a run for it, hoping her bracelet would detonate and take her out in spectacular fashion.

Hunching her shoulder to hide what she was doing from the camera drone, she reached into her bra and took out the TNT as she ran. She bent it between her fingertips until she felt a soft but satisfying snap.

As she approached the camera, she slowed to a stop, as if having second thoughts about escaping. She bent slightly, pressing one hand against legitimately sore muscles in her side. The other hand she rested on the tripod as if to steady herself. She paused for a moment and faked a dry heave as she firmly affixed the now-activated TNT to the tripod.

She turned to look back at Corson. His smile faded with the realization that her death would be put off, at least for a few minutes. But he showed no sign of suspicion about what she had done or what she was up to. She turned away from him, and, with new resolve, ran toward the gate.

Chapter 80

Ressler and Navabi exchanged a glance across the crowded confines of the FBI's Black Hawk helicopter. Ressler looked almost nervous compared to the tactical agents on either side of him, but Navabi knew his agitation was due to his concern for Keen's safety.

For three hours they had all maintained the disciplined, Zen-like patience that was necessary to keep them from going crazy in the hours before battle, putting aside all the thoughts about what was at stake, who was in danger, and what they might face. But when word came that Keen had activated the TNT signal, they had scrambled—airborne in less than a minute, thanks to the pilot's efforts to keep the bird ready to go at a moment's notice.

Now, for the past two minutes, they had been hovering essentially in place, waiting for the CIA team to rendezvous with them. They also didn't want to arrive before the five minutes had passed. After three hours of patience, those two minutes had crawled by excruciatingly slowly.

Navabi knew Ressler was chomping at the bit to get going. He wanted to hit the ground, hit the people responsible, and make sure Keen was safe. Navabi felt the same way.

She hoped she showed it differently.

Finally, the interminable wait was over. The CIA helicopter appeared behind them and identified themselves over the radio.

With a slight lurch that felt wholly inadequate to the urgency of the moment, the helicopter surged forward.

Chapter 81

Keen could feel Corson watching her as she sprinted across the dusty ground toward the main gate. She didn't look at him, instead keeping her eyes straight ahead and her mind focused on the tasks at hand.

She had activated the TNT, so theoretically it should be transmitting, and, again theoretically, the cavalry would be there in five minutes to shut everything down and sweep up everyone involved in the Dead Ring. But things had gone wrong a few times already, and everything working out as planned this time felt far from a certainty.

She altered her course slightly to avoid the ominous metal box of cash, explosives, and sensitive triggering devices the PMCs had placed in front of the entrance.

The gate opened onto a short stretch of road, flanked by tall fencing that formed a brightly lit corridor, twenty yards long, funneling entrants to the plant past a gatehouse. Keen was running flat out when she passed it, trying to catch up with the others, who all had a substantial head start over her.

The guardhouse appeared to be empty, but the wall inside it was spattered with blood. Keen stopped and ran over. The guard was on the floor, dead. Her heart sank that the grim toll for this twisted game was already climbing again. She started to run on, but then she went around and entered the guardhouse, searched the dead guard and found his cell phone.

She pressed the home button and a message came up saying, "FINGERPRINT NOT RECOGNIZED." Looking down at the guard on the floor and his fingers splayed from his outstretched arms, she winced and said, "Sorry."

Chapter 82

Aram had estimated that it would take no more than five minutes after the TNT transmission started for them to know the plan had worked. As it turned out, a little over two minutes had passed before the window popped up on his computer confirming it—the Trojan horse had been successfully processed into the video feed, and the infected computers were already starting to ping results.

The logistics team had brought in a huge glass screen for this part of the process. It displayed a map of the world in soft gray, as if the glass had been frosted. When Aram announced they were in, all eyes in the room shifted to it. There was life or death action playing out on the smaller screens, but just for a moment, this was the center of attention.

As they watched, a point of light appeared on the map, just outside Washington DC. Immediately, another one appeared in Los Angeles, then London. A light appeared in Istanbul, Turkey, and Aram felt a momentary satisfaction, thinking it was probably the computer belonging to Agent Sadek's corrupt superior.

The dam seemed to break after that, and lights

began popping up in cities and remote locations across the planet—dozens of them, scores, hundreds—one for each of the now-infected computers reporting their IP address, physical location, and whatever else the Trojan horses were pulling from them.

Wall seemed uncomfortable with people standing behind him, looking over his shoulder. He unplugged his laptop and took it across the room. Moments later, Beckoff retreated to the work area she had set up in the opposite corner of the room.

Cooper gave Nichols the go-ahead, clearing the tac team to go in hot. Then he called Interpol, advising them to stand by for the torrent of data that they would then forward to the various appropriate law enforcement agencies around the world.

Aram texted Reddington, then smiled as he dove into the task of interpreting the data that was coming in from all the infected computers, tabulating the information and sending it along to Interpol. In the back of his mind, he thought about how a lot of bad people were about to have a really bad day.

Aram turned and glanced around the room behind him.

In one corner, Beckoff was huddled over her computer, eyes widened in astonishment and delight as she monitored the intelligence data streaming in from the CIA's Trojan horse.

In the opposite corner, Simon Wall stifled a giggle as he watched his own computer with an oddly similar expression.

But even in the fraction of a second as he took that in, Aram sensed something was not quite right on the map, and he turned his attention instantly back to it. The map was generously sprinkled with dots, all around the world, but his attention was focused on one of them in particular.

"Look at that," he said, turning to Cooper, who was still standing behind him. He zoomed in, then stood and pointed at one of the dots, almost on top of the location of the chemical plant. As the screen refreshed, the dot moved even closer.

"What is that?" Cooper asked.

Before Aram could answer, his cell phone buzzed. It was a number he didn't recognize.

"Hello?" he said, distant but polite, his attention still pinned to the dot on the screen.

"Aram! It's Keen!"

Aram shot to his feet. "Agent Keen!" The room went silent and he put her on speaker. "It worked, Agent Keen! The tac team is on its way!"

Cooper said, "Agent Keen—" but she cut him off.

"Sorry," she said, breathing hard as if she was running. "I don't have much time, so just listen." She told them about the bomb in the processing unit and asked Aram to look up the plant layout and tell her the location of the plant's primary chemical reactor. "They also have us wearing tracking bracelets. They're packed with explosives and set to go off if we try to leave, or try to remove them, or if the game is completed. I think they also have a remote control, so they can set them off at will. Can you hack into their system and deactivate them?"

His heart plummeted. Maybe if he had an hour, even forty-five minutes. But the game wouldn't last more than ten minutes, fifteen tops.

"Gotta go. Did you hear me?"

"I heard you..." he said, his voice hoarse and hollow in his ears.

"Good." Then she was gone. He felt overwhelmed by the likelihood that he would never speak to her again.

The room was silent, everyone staring at him.

"I... I don't think I can do that," he said, turning to Cooper. "Not in time. I mean, if I could get inside their system, I might be able to, but I have no idea where the bracelets are being controlled from. How to even access them."

Across the room, Wall stood up. "If they're radio controlled, I can get you inside."

Chapter 83

As the helicopter rocketed across the darkened desert, the scream of the engine and the percussive thrum of the rotors easily penetrated Red's noise-canceling headphones. He was filled with a cold and deadly determination, calmly considering each element of what he expected to find when they arrived, and what he planned to do.

Deep inside, he felt a smoldering rage at the world and everyone in it, including himself, for allowing Lizzie to be caught in her current situation. At the core of it was a tiny crystal of fear that she would not make it out, and that in large part it would be his fault. But he knew it was a fruitless line of thought just then. He needed to focus on what he planned to do to make sure the outcome was different.

He was engrossed in that thought process, barely registering the small town they flew over in a flash, when Dembe turned to him and started silently mouthing words.

Red had no idea what he was saying, and removing his headphones to hear better only served to let in the full assault of noise from the helicopter.

He pointed to his ears, shaking his head, and Dembe took off his own headset and passed it to him.

The headphones had remarkable noise canceling capabilities, and the outside noise once again faded away, but much less than his own had done. He realized some of the helicopter noise was coming through the speakers instead from the outside. Then Dembe held his hand up next to his head, mimicking a phone, and Red understood what was happening.

"Hello?" he shouted into the microphone, struggling to make himself heard over the noise that his own microphone was picking up.

"Mr. Reddington, it's Aram."

"What is it, Aram?"

Reddington listened, struggling to maintain his steely demeanor as Aram updated him about Lizzie's predicament, about the bracelets and the explosives rigged to the processing unit.

"I understand," Reddington said. He realized now that his part in all this had become much more than personal. Everything was now riding on it.

The lights of the plant appeared ahead of them, and in the foreground, barely visible without infrared, the matte black RV that served as the Dead Ring's mobile control center. Their actual destination.

It was parked on the side of the road that led to the plant. Two guards stood outside of it, both carried assault rifles and both faced the plant, watching. One of them flared in the infrared, then released a cloud of hot gas. He was smoking.

The plant itself was massive, and Red felt another fault line weakening his implacable façade. A plant that size would go up in spectacular fashion, taking with it hundreds of workers, and very likely much of the nearby town. One more thing he would think about after it was all over, one way or another. At the moment, he needed a clear head and steady hands.

He needed the same from his pilot. Bud Jasper was an artist with the joystick, who possessed an almost pathological lack of outward human emotion that gave him the steadiest hands in the business.

Jasper held up his right hand with five fingers extended. Dembe turned and nodded in confirmation.

As Jasper folded in his thumb, Red looked through the scope at the two figures standing outside the RV, taking in the details, rehearsing the muscle and eye movements.

Jasper was holding up three fingers now. The helicopter was still moving at over two hundred miles an hour, making it hard to keep the two men in the scope, but as the helicopter drew closer, the figures grew larger. Reacquiring them grew easier.

Two fingers. Red lined up the shot once again, went through the motions in his mind.

One finger.

Red took a deep breath and braced himself against the straps holding him in place. As Jasper pulled down his last finger, the helicopter came to a halt. Time seemed to stop as the helicopter hung for that moment, absolutely motionless in the air.

Red let out his breath as he lined up the shots and took them: one, then the other. As soon as the second man's knees started to buckle, the helicopter dropped into a mad descent, a seemingly suicidal dive that Red knew was coming, had, in fact, specifically requested, but which was unsettling nonetheless.

Red and Dembe released their straps and harnesses, holding on tight as the helicopter snapped to a halt once again, as if it had reached the end of its tether.

They were ten feet off the ground, twenty feet from the RV. The helicopter abruptly dropped to a height of two feet and Red and Dembe hit the ground running.

In one second, they were at the RV, one on either side of the door. They paused long enough to exchange a nod. Then they went in.

Chapter 84

They'd lost one of their own, even if it was just that disgusting Yancy. And the Cowboy had proven himself an annoying flea who sought to use the Dead Ring to improve his standing, rather than truly appreciating it for what it was. But it had still been an epic Dead Ring. And the fact that it was taking place within the United States of America proved the power of the Dead Ring, and the man who led it.

It had provided the spectacle that was, at the end of the day, his only remaining joy. And the best part was yet to come.

There were upwards of two hundred workers at the Wolfcamp Petrochemical Plant, plus another eight hundred in the nearby town of Martella, all of them sitting virtually on top of millions of gallons of highly flammable toxic chemicals.

The Cowboy seemed paralyzed by doubts and second thoughts, worrying it would be too big a spectacle, as if there was such a thing. Let him worry. And after all, if his goal in all this really was to gain a little credibility in the criminal world, he was going to need a lot of help. If anything was going to do it, this would.

The final round was always bittersweet. It was traditionally the most spectacular, and this one surely would be, but it was also the last one until the following year. It was also special because by this point you felt like you had gotten to know the handful of players left. You could really pay attention to each one and root for them or against them. Now it was personal.

There were always the favorites—in this case Boden and Dudayev—but there were also the dark horses, like the lovely Le Chat and the quite obviously dying, but miraculously not yet dead, Okoye.

The two of them, especially Le Chat, had drawn a respectable chunk of long-shot wagers. In fact, Le Chat was largely responsible for this Dead Ring having the highest take so far through two rounds.

The long shots never won, but it was always fascinating to see which unlikelies would make it to the third round.

Le Chat was a strange one, and as the final round got underway, she held true to form. Starting out with a lateral move that looked very much like she was going to be a runner after all. But at the last minute, just before her bracelet would have gone off and ended her unlikely run, she stopped at the camera and headed straight inside to confront her destiny. Good for her.

The others cut a swath of destruction through the plant, killing the guard at the front gate and anyone else who got in their way. The blood was just starting to spill, the glow was just starting to burn, and the Ringleader was just starting to settle in for the high point of the year when the technician said, "Sir, we seem to have a problem."

There was no need to ask him to explain. It was obvious he needed to explain, and he did. "The computer system is acting glitchy. I think... I think someone's trying to hack into our system."

From outside, they could hear the unmistakable beating of helicopter blades. That wasn't good.

It was never ideal to rush the Dead Ring, and there was a solemn pledge to allow the game to complete itself, to allow the winner to become the winner. But not if it meant arrest. And certainly not if it meant forgoing the sound and light show at the end of it all.

The Cowboy had been behaving himself, keeping quiet and enjoying the show. But it seemed he could no longer hold back. "What is it?" he said. "What is it?"

His money had paid for all of this, and he was, in a very real way, a partner. But he was an annoying partner at best. The urge to kill him was strong.

If he had to blow the whole thing early, if this year there had to be no winner, it might be better if there weren't any witnesses anyway. Or at least none that weren't on his payroll. Maybe he'd kill the Cowboy after all.

He considered blowing the whole thing right there and his hand moved toward the keypad. Then he heard a noise outside—two spitting sounds followed by two crumpling sounds. He had just enough time to wonder what it could be when the door to the mobile control room was kicked open and in an instant both guards and both technicians were dead on the floor.

Chapter 85

The phone had been keyed to the guard's left thumb, so that's what she took. She tried not to think about it as she wedged the thumb between the door to the guardhouse and the doorframe, or when she slammed her body against the door, lopping the digit off. She tried not to think about it as she cradled the thumb in the same hand that carried the phone. Add it to the long list of things she'd have to process later.

As she ran along the central road, past a couple of smaller outbuildings and into the middle of the facility, alarms started sounding, blasting through the noise of the plant's operations. A moment later, red lights started flashing, adding to the glare of the floodlights. Their presence was known—probably a good thing overall, but it could make her task more difficult.

She was surrounded by tanks, processing equipment, and a dense maze of pipes and conduits. A series of catwalks lined the tops of the structures, and yellow-clad workers were running back and forth along them. The ground was mostly the same dust, rocks, and occasional scrubby plants as the rest of the plains, but it was crisscrossed with concrete paths leading from each unit to each of the others.

She stopped at a place where three of the paths came together, trying to get her bearings and make sense of it. There was one building in the middle that had pipes and conduits leading out from it in every direction. It was taller than the others, and had windows throughout. At the top of it was an enclosed observation platform with even more windows, like an airport control tower.

She figured that was the operations center, the target of the game, but not what she was looking for right now.

To the left of it was another structure, with no windows at all, just a similar jumble of pipes. It seemed to be the biggest structure in the entire complex. She took off running toward it, gambling that it was the primary chemical reactor.

A pair of workers ran across the clearing in front of her, and another one ran the other way.

The phone buzzed in her hand. It was Aram.

Luckily she didn't need the dead man's thumb to answer it.

"Aram," she shouted over the racket as she ran. "What do you have for me?"

"I got the layout of the plant. I'm sending you a diagram right now, but there is a tall building in the middle, like a tower. That's the operations center. Just west of that is the primary chemical reactor."

"Okay, I'm headed to it now. I need to know where the main intake is. That's where the bomb is supposed to be."

"Okay," he said, almost to himself. "The main intake... the main intake... Okay, I found it. It looks like it comes into the unit at ground level on the west side.

There is an entrance right next to it there. Once inside, it goes straight up to the top level, and that's where it enters the initial processor. The closest stairway is thirty yards away, down a hallway on the north side of the intake. But there might be a ladder."

"Okay, thanks. Stand by." She was on the east side of the unit, meaning she had to run all the way around to the other side of it before she could even get into the building. One side of the unit was essentially a wall of piping that extended off at least a hundred yards. Looping around the operations center would probably be quicker.

She ran off toward it, hoping in the back of her mind that she didn't run into any of the other ringers.

The path headed straight for the main entrance to the operations center. The door had been torn off its hinges. The ground in front of it was littered with broken glass and the twisted doorframe. At least one of the ringers was already in there. Part of Keen thought about going in there, too, getting the key, and trying to head things off that way. But she knew most or all of the other ringers were probably already in there fighting it out. She would never reach the key before them. Her only hope of avoiding a catastrophe was to find the bomb on the chemical reactor's main intake, and remove it.

And she probably didn't have much time.

She ran past the entrance, pushing her legs to go even faster.

As she curved through the narrow gap between the two structures, a figure stepped out of the shadows just ahead of her and she jumped back, out of the way and ready to fight.

For a moment, she was relieved to see it was Okoye.

He smiled weakly as he shuffled toward her, but she could see he was much worse. His left eye, the one that had been twitching, was now drifting, unfocused as it looked up to the sky.

"Jakob!" she said. "Are you okay?"

He laughed faintly. "I will be fine soon, I think. Do you need my help?"

She thought for an instant. "Yes! My team should be here any moment, but in the meantime, I need to find that bomb in the chemical reactor and get rid of it. If someone gets the key and opens the box in the meantime, we all go up. If you can get the key and hide it or try to slow down whoever has it, that could make all the difference."

His good eye focused hard on her and he nodded with solemn resolve. He took a step toward the operations center entrance, but stopped and turned back. "It's been an honor to know you, Miss Le Chat."

"Keen," she said. "Special Agent Keen. And it has been an honor to know you, too, Jakob Okoye."

He turned and entered the doorway.

Keen turned away, too, and continued running the same way she had been before.

She didn't get far. Another figure emerged from the same shadows, and this time it wasn't Okoye. And he wasn't shuffling.

She considered trying to go around him, but she knew she didn't have the angle. As she made the mental calculation, the figure moved quickly out of the shadows, cutting her off completely.

It was Dudayev.

He came at her low and fast. His eyes were bright, flashing with animal excitement, like a predator. His hands were bloody up to the wrist.

Keen stifled a wave of fear and revulsion, imposing on herself a steely calm as she jammed the phone and the severed finger into her pocket and considered her best approach. She didn't need to take him down, she just needed to get past him. In order to do that, she needed to draw him out from the space between the two buildings.

She moved back, hoping he would keep coming after her, but he took a few steps and stopped, a flicker of doubt crossing his face, as if maybe he was wondering why she hadn't just gone into the door right behind her.

Then a truly evil grin spread over his face, a smear of blood across his teeth. If she wasn't headed into the operations center, maybe she had just come out of it. "You've already got the key," he said.

He closed on her again, with an even more murderous intensity.

Instead of denying it, Keen stepped away, spinning, and launched a kick to his chin that snapped his head back. He roared and tried to grab her, but as soon as she came down on her other foot, she bounced away, keeping her feet moving, staying out of reach as she tried to figure out what to do next.

If she could connect with another kick somehow, maybe she could get past him and outrun him. Maybe when he saw she wasn't headed back to the prize cabinet he'd rethink.

Dudayev laughed, reached behind him and pulled out a hunting knife. He closed on her fast and as she backed away her foot slipped in the dust. He lunged with the knife and as she moved out of the way, his left fist crashed into the side of her head. Keen felt her foot slide out from under her and she slammed against the ground.

Suddenly Dudayev was straddling her and the tip of his knife was pressed under her chin.

"Give me the key," he said, his breath foul in her nose, his eyes manic.

She flung a handful of dust into his face and tried to buck him off. It seemed to have no effect. He threw back his head and laughed, not even blinking at the grit that crusted his eyes.

Then he looked down at her, smiling, and said, "I guess I'll have to find it myself."

He drew back the knife like he was going to backhand it across her throat.

Involuntarily, Keen closed her eyes for an instant, waiting for the end.

She felt a soft breeze brush the skin of her neck, and she realized that somehow he had missed. As she opened her eyes, she saw him yanked off her and into the air.

Standing there, breathing heavily, was Okoye. He looked at her and said, "Go." Then he turned stiffly, and closed on Dudayev.

"He's got a knife!" Keen called out.

"I know," Okoye said without turning around.

Keen staggered as she got to her feet. She felt terrible leaving him behind, but if she didn't deal with that bomb, they would all die, along with many others.

"You fool!" Dudayev spat. "She's got the key!"

Then he sprang, ripping the knife in an upward arc that would have split Okoye open if he hadn't pivoted away. Instead, Okoye managed to grab Dudayev's knife hand and kick his feet out from under him.

Keen watched both men tumble to the ground. She knew that in his weakened state, Okoye would be no match for Dudayev. He wouldn't be able to hold him off for long.

She put her head down and ran, but just before she rounded the corner, she turned and looked back. They were on the ground with Dudayev on top. Each had one hand clamped onto the other's throat. Dudayev's knife was in his other hand, and Okoye gripped the other man's wrist, but Keen could see that he was clearly outmatched and losing his strength rapidly. The blade slowly pushed toward Okoye's eyes.

Okoye turned his head to look at her. "Remember the Akaba School," he rasped. Before Keen or Dudayev had an inkling what he was doing, he took his hand from Dudayev's throat and moved his wrist so that his bracelet was snagged on the tip of the knife. Then he flicked his arm off to the side.

The bracelet exploded the instant it was severed, echoed a microsecond later by Dudayev's. The explosions wreaked awful damage, sending out a red spray and shrapnel of bone and flesh.

"No!" Keen cried out, taking a step back towards them. But it was too late. Okoye was dead.

What remained of the two bodies collapsed together.

Keen stifled a sob, then she turned away from the sight and set her jaw in determination. She put aside any thoughts of Okoye's tragic death, his valiant sacrifice, and their brief friendship. She needed to use the time he had bought her to complete the task at hand, to prevent the countless other tragic deaths that would occur if she failed.

She lowered her head once more and ran as fast as she could.

Chapter 86

There were two guards, two technicians and two others in the mobile control center when Red and Dembe burst in.

They took out the guards first. Then the technicians drew weapons and they shot them too.

That left two others. One was standing by the two dead technicians. The other was sitting in the shadows in back of the control room.

Red picked up a gun dropped by one of the dead technicians.

Dwight Tindley was the one standing. He started raising his hands, his mouth forming the "D" sound that would inevitably have started the sentence, "Don't shoot," if it hadn't been pushed out of the way by the scream that erupted from his throat as Red shot him in the knee.

They didn't have time for unnecessary discussion.

As Tindley howled, Red turned to the seated figure, planning on opening with a similar gambit, but instead he paused. The man had no knees and no legs below them. He was missing an arm, and a good portion of his face. But the eyes were undamaged, physically at least.

They were bright and clear and vivid with insanity.

The chair was a wheelchair. The eyes were Michael Hoagland's.

Tindley was making an awful racket, but his screams faded to a loud, sobbing moan.

"Reddington?" Hoagland wheezed. His ruined face twisted even further into a bitter half smile. Maybe a full smile. It was hard to tell. "What are you doing here?"

Red half smiled back, so as to not show off. "It's been some time. Looking good there, Michael," he said, while scanning Hoagland for anything that could be a switch or a controller. The only thing within reach was the lighted control panel on the armrest of the wheelchair. "I'm here to tell you to shut everything down. It's over."

"I heard you were working with the FBI now. I never would have believed it."

"Our interests overlap. Now tell me how to access the system."

Hoagland made a shrugging motion and moved his hand toward the controls. As his fingers reached for the keypad, Red shot the cord connecting it to the battery pack and the lights on the control panel went dark.

Hoagland looked up at him in rage and disgust, and maybe legitimate disbelief. "You shot my wheelchair?! What kind of monster shoots a man's wheelchair?"

"Sorry, Michael," Red said. "I don't entirely trust you."

He nodded at Dembe, who pulled one of the dead technicians out of his chair and took his place in front of the computer.

"Now, tell us how to deactivate the bracelets and the bomb, and stop all this nonsense, and I'll get the wheelchair fixed for you. Good as new, I promise."

Tindley shifted on the floor, the movement causing

him to start screaming anew. Hoagland scowled at him. "Ugh," he said, disgusted. "Can you do something about that?"

Though the noise was indeed distracting, Red wouldn't have done anything about it if Tindley hadn't somehow produced a gun and started to raise it. But he did.

Red took the gun out of Tindley's hand and brought it down on his head, silencing him immediately.

"Thank you," Hoagland said with a sigh of relief.

In the relative quiet, Red could hear the other helicopters getting closer.

"Now, you're going to have to tell me how to deactivate the bracelets and the bomb."

Hoagland shook his head and laughed. "Reddington, I don't—"

Red shot him in the thigh and said, "I'm in a bit of a hurry."

Hoagland kept laughing but in a substantially different tone. He shook his head vigorously, then cursed Reddington through teeth clenched against the pain.

"You think I'm just going to tell you everything then let you arrest me? Sorry, Reddington. If I'm going out, I'm going out with a bang."

Red placed the barrel of the gun against Hoagland's other thigh, and said, "I assure you, if you don't tell me how to shut this down, it will be more like a long, drawn out whimper."

Chapter 87

Running toward the processing unit, Keen was assailed by thoughts and images of all the death she had witnessed in the past three days, but she knew she couldn't let it derail her right now. Too many lives were at stake, including her own, and those of the entire task force. They'd be arriving any moment, and if that bomb went off while they were on the ground, or even in the air nearby, they would all be killed.

She grimaced as she used the dead guard's thumb to unlock the phone and dialed Ressler's number.

"Keen!" he answered, his voice so soaked in worry and relief she could hear it through the sound of the chopper on his end and the cacophony of alarms going off all around her. "We're almost there!"

"Ressler," she said. "When you land, you've got to evacuate this place. Get all these workers out of here."

"Got it. Aram told us about the bomb, and they're working on deactivating the bracelets."

"There's a metal cabinet in front of the main gate. Don't let anyone touch it. There's a key in the operations center and if anyone uses that key to unlock the cabinet, everything goes up, the bracelets, the bomb, the whole plant."

"Got it. Where are you?"

"I'm headed toward the processing unit. I'm going to see if I can find the bomb."

As Keen rounded the corner of the building, she saw a dozen workers in yellow coveralls dashing out of the main entrance to the processing unit, scattering once they got outside, as if they didn't know where to run. She hoped there were service gates or some other way out. She had a feeling the front gate was going to get hot.

She sprinted to the entrance and caught the door before it closed. Next to it was a bundle of massive pipes that seemed to snake across the entire facility before penetrating the outer wall. The largest of them, six feet in diameter, had a label on it that said MAIN INTAKE—CAUTION: HIGHLY FLAMMABLE. Before she entered, she threw the door all the way open, and while it slowly began to close, she quickly checked all sides of the main intake pipe. There was no sign of a bomb. She again caught the door before it closed, and plunged inside the building.

As soon as she stepped inside, she was almost leveled by a large man in yellow coveralls running straight toward her.

"Get out of here!" he yelled. "Go on!" He was a big guy, with lots of beers behind him, but strong as well. His face was mostly beard and safety goggles. His name badge said FERGUSON.

"Hold on," she said, but he cut her off.

"You ain't allowed in here anyway, but we got to evacuate." With that he grabbed her wrist and started dragging her toward the door.

She swung him around and slammed him against the wall, twisting his arm behind his back. He struggled at first but she gave his arm a little more torque and he stopped.

"Look, Ferguson," she said. "I don't have time to explain, but I'm one of the good guys, and I'm trying to keep this whole place from blowing up. So you need to get out of here and leave me to it, okay?"

He nodded and she let him go.

He ran out the door without looking back, leaving a little smudge of blood where she had slammed his face against the wall. She felt bad, but she needed to make sure he got the point.

The intake pipe was clearly visible inside the unit. It continued horizontally for ten feet, before heading straight up. A narrow ladder ran alongside it, and at each floor, a catwalk branched off.

Keen looked up and around the pipe, even squeezing herself into the narrow space between it and the wall, but there was no sign of any device. The pipe started to rumble and vibrate, and for a moment, she thought maybe the bomb had gone off, then she realized the intake pipe was just in use, filled with a torrent of whatever flammable chemical it carried. Trying not to think of the seconds ticking by, or the likelihood that she was inches from a pressurized column of highly flammable chemicals rigged to explode at any moment, she grabbed the ladder and started to climb.

When she reached the second level, she stepped onto the catwalk and leaned out on either side, peering as far around the intake pipe as she could, again searching for anything that looked like a bomb. She didn't want to miss it, but she also didn't want to waste time looking where it wasn't. Five seconds later, she was back on the ladder, headed up to the next level, where she once again did her best to peer around either side of the massive pipe.

Again there was nothing.

At each level, she touched the phone to keep from getting locked out. At the fourth level, she was starting to worry that maybe she had missed it on one of the levels below, but then she spotted it, mounted just under the top level. The catwalk above it led deeper into the building, like all the others, but it also ran out through another door that seemed to lead outside. The bomb was affixed to the pipe just out of arm's reach from the catwalk: three bricks of plastic explosive, a coil of wires, and a detonator with a small display screen.

A mixture of relief and dread washed over her, as she realized that some part of her had irrationally hoped that the bomb wouldn't be there at all, and somehow she could just walk away, go home, and be safe. But it wasn't over. And if she didn't hustle, it was likely to end in a very bad way.

She barely winced as she unlocked the phone this time. She took a picture of the bomb and sent it to Aram, then called him. "What can you tell me about this?"

"We're looking at it right now," he said. "Can you see what's holding it in place?"

"It seems to be some sort of putty."

"Do you see any wires connecting it to the surface it's mounted to?"

"No, but I can only see one side of it."

"Okay, well, it would be great if we could see the other side of it. In the picture you sent, the screen says 00:00. Is that what it still says?"

"Yes. I'm thinking it's probably not on a timer, judging from Corson's explanation. It should be set to go via remote control."

"That's what I'm thinking, too."

"Okay, here's what we have to look out for. It could be triggered by vibrations..."

"I don't think so. The pipe is already vibrating pretty intensely from whatever is running through it."

"Okay, well it might be wired to the surface under it, and if the connection breaks, it'll blow. You're sure there's no way you can see the far side of it?"

Keen thought for a second, then said, "Hold on."

She took off her belt and buckled it around the top catwalk railing, then climbed onto the outer side of the railing. She wrapped the other end of the belt around one hand and climbed up onto the lower railing. Leaning out as far as the belt would let her, she held out the phone and took a picture of the far side of the bomb, trying not to look down or think of what would happen if the belt broke or her hand slipped and she plunged four floors to her death. Pulling herself back in, she put one leg back over the railing, so she was straddling it, and sent the picture to Aram.

She studied the photo and didn't see any sign of wires grounding it to the surface of the pipe. Aram confirmed it.

"Okay," he said. "That looks clean. Theoretically, the only thing we have to worry about is if it has some sort of level, something electronic or even a spirit level with a bubble in it that will detonate the explosive if the bubble moves too much."

"Well, that and the fact that at any second someone could bring the key to the prize box and detonate this thing and the bracelet around my wrist."

Cooper came on the line. "The tac team will be there in a few minutes to protect the prize box."

"Okay," she said. "Any progress with the bracelets?"

Aram came back on. "We're working on it," he said.

"We'll have them deactivated soon."

In Keen's mind, *soon* was meaningless. She could picture Boden or one of the other ringers, at that second, running down the concrete path, past the guardhouse with the dead guard, and through the gate to the prize box. She knew she needed to get that bomb out of there *now*.

"I'm going to see if I can remove the device," she said.

"Be careful," Cooper said. "And good luck."

Chapter 88

Keen leaned out from the railing again as far as the belt would let her, fully extending her body and wrapping her fingers around the bomb. It was larger than she had realized.

She applied gentle pressure, pulling it away from the pipe. It gave a little, telling her the adhesive was repositionable, or at least that it hadn't set. But it wouldn't come away. She pulled harder, but it was difficult, fully extended as she was with nothing to brace herself against.

Pulling even harder, Keen became increasingly concerned about the belt, about her feet slipping off the railing, about falling to her death and blowing up the chemical plant, and everyone in it.

Then it came free. Her fingers were locked onto it— there was no way she was going to simply drop it— but the weight was unexpected. Her arm sagged and without the bomb anchoring her in place, her body swung away from the pipe.

She clutched the bomb to her chest, trying to keep it level as she pulled herself back to the catwalk, swinging one leg over it, then the other, then climbing down onto the platform itself.

She had the bomb. It hadn't detonated. She was still alive.

Keen took a deep breath and let it out, then she glanced down at the bomb and cursed. Where the display had read zero, it was now at twenty-six seconds and counting down.

She looked at the phone, but the screen had gone black. She realized she no longer had the thumb. She must have dropped it while she was removing the bomb. She was alone. She had twenty-four seconds.

Climbing to the ground floor would take too long, and once outside, she'd have to run all the way around the building before she could even start to run for open space.

Instead she grabbed the ladder and started climbing up.

She had seen the catwalks crisscrossing the entire facility on every level, but mostly at the top. Workers had been running along them when the alarms had started. When Keen reached the top level, she grabbed the door and pulled it open, feeling momentary relief that it wasn't locked.

Stepping outside, she paused for an instant to get her bearings. The sky was a moonless black punctured by the gas flares. All around, red lights were flashing and the buildings and processors and reactors were lit up with bright yellow.

The alarms mercifully faded away. In the back of her mind she hoped it meant that the danger had passed, but the red lights kept flashing and she knew the alarms had probably just timed out.

In the relative quiet, Keen could hear helicopters in the distance, growing closer, but not close enough.

She had eighteen seconds.

She was too high up and too far back to see the fence or the gate. She could see the light reflecting off the ground and into the night sky, and there was one area that seemed brighter than the rest. She hoped maybe that was the floodlights at the front gate. One of the catwalks extended much further than the others, and it seemed to be aimed straight in that direction. She didn't have time for any more wondering or figuring. She had thirteen seconds. She needed to act.

She ran. The phone buzzed in her pocket, but there was no time for that. The end of the catwalk seemed impossibly far away, but as she ran toward it, the gate beyond came into view.

Under her, she could see plant workers flocking toward the gate, escaping whatever mayhem they had witnessed, and whatever they rightly feared might be coming their way. As she neared the end of the catwalk, she began to worry that she wouldn't be able to find a place to throw the device. She knew she had to—that much explosive could easily set off the rest of the facility, even from all the way up there. But she was horrified at the idea that she would have to throw it somewhere that it would kill innocent people.

She reached the end with six seconds to spare. Below her, people were running in almost every direction, straight toward the gate. She spotted one area that was empty, off to the side, but as she wound up to heave the bomb, she saw a lone figure in the darkness headed directly through it and toward the gate beyond. But the figure was not dressed in yellow.

It was one of the ringers.

It was Boden, running toward the prize box. That meant he had the key. If he reached the box with that key, she and every other ringer and a lot of other people would die.

Much of what she'd been trying to do was save all of the innocent lives hurt by the Dead Ring, though she hoped to save the not-so-innocent contestants, as well. But Boden was evil. The world would be a better place without him. There was nowhere else to throw the bomb anyway.

She heaved it as hard as she could, sending it arcing through the night sky in a wobbly spiral.

It hit the ground five feet behind Boden with a dull thud that she could hear even from where she was standing. Boden turned at the sound, looked at the bomb, then looked up at her, way above on the catwalk. Too far away to do anything to stop him. She worried for an instant that the impact had somehow broken the device. He flashed a taunting smile of gloating victory. Then he turned to keep running.

He took one step before the bomb went off.

Up on the catwalk, Keen saw the flash, then heard the bang and a microsecond later felt the concussion from the blast. Boden's broken body landed twenty feet from where he'd been standing, his limbs splayed in an unnatural configuration.

Keen sank to her knees and allowed herself a momentary sigh of relief. But her bracelet was still active and she needed to get the key from Boden's body. As long as it was out there, someone could open the box and get the money, killing her and the other ringers, if there were any still alive.

Keen hustled down the ladder leading from the end of the catwalk. By the time she reached the ground, the only sign of the workers was a handful of yellow smudges fading into the darkness as they ran out into the prairie.

She ran past the smoking crater where the bomb had gone off, over to Boden's ravaged body. The key was still clutched in his hand. She half expected him to come alive as she pried it loose, but he didn't.

As she straightened up, holding the key in front of her face to look at it, her bracelet spontaneously opened and fell to the ground.

She smiled and shook her head, then took out the phone and looked at it. It was still locked but she could see there was one missed call from Aram.

She was putting the phone back in her pocket when a voice she recognized called out, "Put down that key and step away from it or I'll blow this guy's head off."

Chapter 89

Bleeding from both thighs, Hoagland locked his one hand onto the dead control panel on his armrest, squeezing it hard as he glared at Reddington with eyes that dripped pure hatred.

"Sorry about that," Reddington said. "But like I said, I don't have much time."

"I'll never let you shut this down," Hoagland said, his mouth flecked with foam. "The Dead Ring is all I have left."

"Nonsense," Reddington said, pressing the gun against the bones in Hoagland's hand. "You've still got this hand. For now," he said ominously. "And you've still got your money. Or at least you did up until a few minutes ago."

A flicker of doubt passed through Hoagland's eyes. "What are you talking about?"

Outside, an explosion rocked the night, and Hoagland seemed to regain some of his wavering confidence.

They both paused for a moment, waiting for a secondary explosion, for an indication that the explosions were ripping through the plant. But nothing came after it.

Hoagland's confidence faltered again.

"They're draining your accounts as we speak," Red explained. "I don't know the technical details, but they hacked into your accounts, through your own system, I believe. Now they're taking all your money."

"Whatever. Take my money. I've got more than you know, and you'll never find it all. So then what?"

"They're draining your subscribers' accounts, too." Red laughed. "I bet they'll be angry about that."

"Who is they?"

"Does it really matter?"

"So what's your plan, to arrest me? I don't think so. I have too much value. I know too much, about America's friends, and her enemies, and her leaders. And you, too, Reddington." He cackled. "Don't forget that."

Red smiled. "Now, how could I forget that?"

"I'll make a deal, just like you did. I'll give them the bad guys I want to give them, they'll protect me from my enemies, and I'll live well, in my own way."

Red knew Hoagland had a point, which was why he knew he was going to kill him before Percival could get his hands on him. But he couldn't do it yet, not until Keen was safe.

Red heard the cell phone buzz in Dembe's pocket.

Dembe looked at it and passed it to Red.

A text from Aram. BOMB DISPOSED OF. BRACELETS DEACTIVATED. KEEN SAFE.

Red smiled and looked up at Hoagland. "Well, I guess we can't make you talk. And you're right. We can't arrest you."

Hoagland looked momentarily suspicious. "What are you going to do?"

"Well, I don't know," he said with a laugh. "But before I decide, I've got to ask. What was the deal between you and Ed Stannis?"

"What was the deal?" Hoagland laughed bitterly. "I'll tell you the deal. He was sleeping with my wife and stealing my company—him and those traitorous bastards on the board of directors. But I knew about both. So when they came to Peru to oust me, I took them out. All of them."

"But Stannis got away."

"Temporarily."

"And you didn't."

"I'm here, aren't I?"

"Well, most of you is. And then?"

"Then I healed, and I planned. And I took back what was mine. I took her and used her and made him liquidate everything according to my instructions. And when he was done, I took him, too." He laughed. "I guess he really did love her, shrew that she was. It was embarrassing how much he cried as I killed her in front of him. You'd think after a few weeks, he would have gotten used to it, but he screamed even more than she did. When she finally died, I let them stay together, for another year. A second honeymoon I called it, the two of them in that cell together. Just them and the rats. And when there was nothing left of her but bones, and nothing left of him but a gibbering idiot, I killed him, too. Even slower. And he screamed even more."

"And what about the Dead Ring?"

Hoagland smiled. "My proudest accomplishment. After Peru, I missed the thrill of combat. The Dead Ring helped me recapture it, and share it with some friends."

Outside, the helicopters were landing.

"Sounds like you've got backup coming," Hoagland said. "I guess our chat is almost over."

Red pulled up a chair across from him. "Let me tell

you why I'm really here. There was a man I used to work with, I daresay a friend. He was a good man, a family man, always on the righteous side of any fight. But somehow, we were friends nonetheless. Seven years ago, he and his boys were on a ferry in Senegal."

Hoagland smiled at the memory. "*La Mer Calme*."

"That's right. *La Mer Calme*. Some kind of terrible riot broke out on board, they said. The ferry caught fire and capsized. One hundred and twenty people died. I later found out, that was the first Dead Ring game."

Hoagland smiled at the memory. "It was spectacular."

"My friend and his sons were killed. His widow lost her entire family in one blow. All for the twisted entertainment of a circle of rich psychopaths, so jaded and decadent they can't find joy in the simple pleasures of life."

"What pleasure could be simpler than that? They say it is death that gives life meaning."

Red paused while Hoagland spoke, then continued. "His widow was a remarkable woman. Her name is Badri, and she didn't pine for vengeance. She mourned her family, of course. She was gutted by the pain but she saw all these children left orphaned by the tragedy. Just as she had lost her children, they had lost their parents. And she set up an orphanage. She took them all in. Took care of them, raised them and taught them. Can you imagine, losing your whole family like that and not wanting vengeance?"

Hoagland stayed silent and just stared at him.

Red casually moved his gun so it was aimed at Hoagland's hand and pulled the trigger. Hoagland shrieked despite himself, holding up his hand, now torn nearly in half.

"Me neither," said Red. "In fact, I think I bring it out in people. Case in point, our mutual friend Simon Wall. Do you remember him?"

Hoagland's eye twitched but he didn't say anything.

Red laughed. "Well, he remembers you. And he was ready to let it go, even after everything you did to him. He didn't want anything to do with you anymore. He said the same thing you did, that you knew too much, that you had too many friends and too much money. That's when I suggested he use what you had made him do against you. That's why right now he is hacked into your accounts and draining them. All of them. So he can use your money to help repair some of the terrible damage you've done to this world."

Hoagland had begun breathing harder and harder as Red spoke, his rage taking his mind off his pain. "I'll kill him!"

Red laughed. "That's exactly what Simon Wall said your reaction would be. I said you'd take it better, but he said no. And he was right. So there you go. But you were right about something, too." Then he raised his gun and shot Hoagland in the chest. "You're going out with a bang after all."

Hoagland's mouth quivered as he looked down at the hole in his chest. As he looked back up, Red shot him in the head.

Chapter 90

At first, all Keen saw was the guy from the processing unit, Ferguson, the guy she had slammed into the wall. For an instant she wondered how he fit into all this.

Then she saw Corson standing behind him, holding a gun to the man's head. She wondered briefly why Corson hadn't just pulled the gun on her. Then she saw the look in his eyes. Mixed in with the greed and the hatred was fear. It occurred to her that as far as he knew—as far as she knew—she was the lone remaining ringer. She was the winner of the Dead Ring, and he was scared of her.

But she also realized she didn't have any more tricks up her sleeve. The helicopters were finally coming in low, two of them. All she could think to do was try to stall and hope an idea came to her.

"The key is mine," she said. "I won it. I won the Dead Ring."

"The Dead Ring doesn't exist anymore," Corson said. "And that prize is my severance package. Now put down that key or I'll kill you both."

"You'll never get away with it," she said.

He smiled. "I appreciate your concern, but you let me worry about that."

As he spoke, the phone started buzzing in her hand and she saw that it was Ressler. She swiped to answer it and thumbed on the speaker phone.

"Shut up and listen to me," she said loudly. "I know you think that just because you're holding one of the workers hostage in front of the main gate and you're threatening to kill me, that you figure you can get away with this. I know you're thinking you can *just take your shot*."

Corson looked confused. "What are you talking about?"

"I know you want to *just take your shot*. Do you understand me?"

"Just drop the goddamned key before I kill you both!"

"I could just give you the key, but I don't think I can trust you," she said, glancing to the left as the helicopter approached through the night sky. "I can't trust that you're not going to kill the hostage anyway, and then kill me."

"I'm going to count to five," he said, his voice straining as the helicopters grew louder. "One..."

"Do you hear me, Ressler?"

"Two," Corson said. Then, looking around, "Wrestler?"

"I said: *Take. Your. Shot.*"

She saw the muzzle flash, then heard the crack of the rifle at the same instant that Corson's body jerked and he crumpled backward into the night.

The hostage stood motionless for a moment, then he turned, saw Corson's body on the ground, and ran off in the direction of his coworkers.

Keen went to Corson and picked up his gun. Kneeling next to him, she checked his pulse, confirming he was dead.

The helicopters came down outside the gate, hovering just above the ground. The tac team jumped out of the closer one—ten agents, including Ressler and Navabi.

As they swarmed through the gate toward her, four figures jumped from the second chopper and ran off into the darkness.

"Are you okay?" Ressler shouted as he ran up to her. Navabi put a hand on her shoulder and squeezed.

"I'm fine, I'm fine," she said. "Nice shooting, by the way. How about the Trojan horse? Did it work?"

"Like a charm," Navabi said. "Cooper said they're getting data from two hundred and thirty computers around the world. Interpol is already coordinating raids."

"Who's in the other chopper?"

Ressler screwed up his face. "CIA."

"CIA?"

"It's a long story."

She nodded. "Okay, later. We should sweep the facility. I don't know if there's any other ringers left. There shouldn't be any more bombs, but we should sweep for them, as well."

Ressler said, "You're not going anywhere until the medics check you out."

"We've got this," Navabi said.

Keen started to argue, but then it hit her like a wave, all she'd been through. Maybe it was the adrenaline leaving her body, but suddenly she was exhausted.

"We'll take care of it," Ressler said.

Keen nodded. This time, she decided, she'd let them.

Chapter 91

Reddington and Dembe stepped out of the mobile control center just as Percival and Thomas ran up, accompanied by two other agents. "Thank goodness you're here!" Reddington exclaimed, stepping over the bodies of the two men he'd shot from the helicopter.

"Reddington?" Percival said. "Goddamn it, what are you doing here?"

"Good lord, man, I thought you would have gotten here way before we did. Frankly, I thought we'd just be helping to mop up after you guys. What happened, did you get lost?"

"Where's Hoagland? Is he in there?"

"Well, yes, he is. Or most of him is. He's actually somewhat dead."

"*Dead?* What happened?"

"Good heavens, I have no idea. Very possibly some sort of bunker suicide thing, I don't know. There is one Dwight Tindley in there, I think he's still alive. He's no Michael Hoagland, that's for sure, but if you want to rendition him off to God-knows-where, I'm sure you could waterboard some useful intelligence out of him, or at least motivate him to come up with some very entertaining fiction."

Chapter 92

Ressler, Navabi, and the others hustled through the gate and swept across the facility, leaving a lull of quiet in their wake. A light breeze picked up, and Keen heard a faint but distinct creaking sound, like a door opening on hinges that could use a little oil. She looked past Corson's body, out through the gate, and saw the prize box, slightly open, the lid opening further on the breeze.

As she approached it, the wind kicked up again, stronger this time, and the lid swung all the way open.

She thought about Okoye and the Akaba School, how he had planned to donate his winnings so they could continue their work without worrying about money. He had been willing to risk his life for them but instead he had given what little life he had left for her.

On an impulse, she reached into the box and carefully removed the briefcase.

Behind where it had sat there was a massive brick of explosives wired to the sides of the box, and to a detonator, just like the other device.

As she backed away from it, she saw a black Humvee bouncing across the desert, approaching fast. She thought maybe it was CIA, but then she thought again.

It skidded to a stop, kicking up a spray of dust and gravel just outside the gate. Four men got out, each of them carrying an assault rifle.

The one in the front yelled at her in a thick French accent, "LeCroix!"

It was Corbeaux.

She almost laughed. She was so tired, so done, and so surprised by this turn of events. She looked around, but there was no backup in sight. Corbeaux and his men moved toward her, and she realized the situation really wasn't all that funny.

She still had Corson's gun, but she knew she'd never be able to take down all four of them before they killed her.

The only cover she had was the silver box that stood between her and them. She moved back, away from them, shifting to one side to keep the box between them.

"I'm not LeCroix," she said.

Corbeaux laughed. "Don't deny it, LeCroix. We know it is you. We saw you on the game." He laughed again. "Lucky you, I guess you won. But now I think your luck has run out."

The box was still between them, but the four men continued to move closer to her.

"LeCroix is dead," she said, saddened at the thought of it. Her words brought back images of the woman, bruised and broken in her hospital bed, dying from the injuries she suffered trying to escape this thug. She thought of LeCroix's tears and worry for David— justified as it turned out, because now he was dead, too. And she thought about LeCroix's family, and her fears of what would happen to them if Corbeaux learned her identity. He was calling her LeCroix, not Le Chat.

"LeCroix is dead," she said again, softly. Maybe to herself.

"Not yet," he said, with a smug smile. "But she will be dead soon enough."

"I keep telling you, I'm not LeCroix," Keen said. "But you know what?"

They paused where they were, eying her suspiciously, gathering closer to the silver box in case they needed it for cover.

"I kind of liked her," she said.

Keen dropped to the ground and fired once into the prize box.

The metal sides and the lid were instantly torn into razor-sharp shreds that spun off into the darkness, barely impeded by the French thugs they had passed through.

The fireball swelled out, engulfing Corbeaux and his men and then rolling up into the sky, briefly illuminating the carnage below and the desert around it before fading into a black smudge of smoke.

Chapter 93

Keen was exhausted and aching, covered in bruises and cuts, some deeper than others. She slept for most of the first flight. But for much of the second flight, after they touched down in Florida to refuel and restock for the remainder of the trip, she reflected on the outcome of the operation.

Aram's Trojan horse did exactly what it was supposed to. Interpol coordinated the arrests of one hundred and forty bettors on the Dead Ring—drug kingpins, human traffickers, dealers in illegal antiquities and endangered species—all sorts of the worst people out there. There would be more to come, and a lot of them were already trading information, which should lead to even more arrests.

The CIA was not one hundred percent happy. Percival had been livid about finding Hoagland dead before he got there, but mollified somewhat by the treasure trove of intel enthusiastically delivered up by Tindley. Percival also claimed that several of Hoagland's secret accounts were emptied during the last round of the Dead Ring, a claim that was given added weight when Interpol reported similar complaints from some of the bettors.

Percival accused the task force and Wall of having something to do with it, but he had no proof whatsoever. The fact that he had insisted the task force include the malware without knowing what was in it, and destroy it afterward caused speculation that the missing money had gone into the CIA's accounts, or Percival's.

Coincidentally, twenty-four hours after all this went down, an anonymous benefactor donated tens of millions of dollars each to a variety of human rights groups and relief agencies, including Doctors Without Borders, Amnesty International and a little-known group called Hackers Helping Humans.

After the plane landed the second time, Keen began to process all she'd been through the preceding week. Red and Dembe took care of the external things—the logistics of moving themselves and their cargo from the jet to the Land Rover. The internal things, they gave her the space to do on her own.

It took a while to get started. She'd had to block it all out in order to function and to survive. But once she began, it came to her in a rush.

The landscape they drove through was at times oddly similar to West Texas, then strikingly alien as they passed baobab trees and people in colorful traditional garb. Mostly what Keen saw as she looked out the window were the faces of the dead. She mourned all of them—even the ringers and those responsible for the game, the ones whose lives had left them damaged and evil. She mourned their lives as much as their deaths, especially the ones she herself had killed.

Even more, she mourned those like David Borova. Maybe he wasn't innocent, but he was definitely a victim. And like Marianne LeCroix, whose life she had briefly inhabited.

Most of all, however, she thought about Jakob Okoye.

As briefly as she'd known him, she considered him a true friend. And as flawed as he might have been in life, he had died heroically, unselfishly, and for a good cause. He had saved her life and many others. And now she and Red and Dembe were going to help make sure he would continue to save even more.

An hour after they left the airport, Dembe pulled the Land Rover off the dirt road and into a rutted driveway. A wooden sign read: AKABA SCHOOL.

The driveway curved in front of a simple, one-story mud brick building, with a wooden roof and a porch running along its entire width. In front there was a swing set, and in back an enclosed field where dozens of children played soccer.

As they got out of the Land Rover, a strikingly attractive woman in her late forties came out to greet them. She wore a colorful tunic and carried herself with a gentle authority that left no uncertainty that she was in charge.

She smiled proudly but her eyes were wet as she approached them.

"Miss Badri," Red said as they approached.

Badri put her hand over her mouth, as if to compose herself. "Mr. Reddington, Mr. Zuma, Agent Keen," she said, turning to each of them in turn.

Keen held up the briefcase with the prize money from the Dead Ring. "This is from Jakob Okoye. He wanted you to have it." There had been some controversy over whether the prize money had been obliterated in the explosion that took out Corbeaux, but there was no evidence to the contrary.

Badri took the briefcase, in a daze. Her eyes held a mixture of relief and sorrow. "He was a good man, but confused," she said softly. "I don't know if I can keep the winnings from such a terrible thing."

Keen put her hand over Badri's, keeping her fingers wrapped around the handle of the briefcase. "Jakob Okoye helped make sure those who participated in the Dead Ring answered for it. He made sure that what happened to your family, and to his, will never happen to another family again. Jakob Okoye didn't just win the Dead Ring, Miss Badri. He ended it."